Prais

"Consistently one of the best in the business. As good as any I've ever read. Dana King, to quote Don Kirkendall of Men Reading Books, is 'top-shelf entertainment.' *Ten-Seven* keeps that ball rolling."

—Charlie Stella

"Dana King's *Ten-Seven* is a propulsive mystery thriller that showcases his ear for dialogue, penchant for wry humor, and mastery of the police procedural, all while his finger is firmly on the pulse of America's Rust Belt."

—Eryk Pruitt, Anthony Award-nominated
author of *What We Reckon*

Praise for the Penns River Crime Novels

"King has created vividly drawn characters, a plot the late Elmore Leonard would appreciate, and dialogue that hits all the right notes. Let's hope *Grind Joint* is the first in a new series chronicling life and crime in the Alleghenies."

—Booklist

"Dana King's *Resurrection Mall* is a patchwork of desperation from a depressed river town written with genuine style and grit."

—Reed Farrell Coleman, *New York Times* bestselling
author of *What You Break*

TEN-SEVEN

ALSO BY DANA KING

The Penns River Novels
Worst Enemies
Grind Joint
Resurrection Mall

The Nick Forte Mysteries
A Small Sacrifice
The Stuff That Dreams Are Made Of
The Man in the Window
A Dangerous Lesson
Bad Samaritan

Stand Alone Novels
Wild Bill

DANA KING

TEN-SEVEN
A PENNS RIVER NOVEL

Down & Out Books
3959 Van Dyke Road, Suite 265
Lutz, FL 33558
DownAndOutBooks.com

Cover design by Eric Beetner

ISBN: 1-946502-65-0
ISBN-13: 978-1-946502-65-0

To Ted Suskewicz...

Don't be fooled by his namesake here.
A good man, a good father, a good husband,
a good friend, and a great cousin.
He is missed.

*Murder in the murderer is no such ruinous
thought as poets and romancers will have it;
it does not unsettle him, or fright
him from his ordinary notice of trifles;
it is an act quite easy to be contemplated.*
—Ralph Waldo Emerson

1

Vicki Leydig didn't gamble. Drank a little, and the Allegheny Casino had the cheapest booze in Penns River. When Mary Zelesko asked if she wanted to go to the casino—oh, and Doug Stirnweiss would be there—Vicki thought a few beers might not be a bad idea, summer coming on after a miserable winter.

She and Doug maybe on the brink of becoming a couple. Mary—a primary source on all Doug-related scoop—said he would've asked her for sure if they'd met a few months earlier, before his divorce became final. Two years since the formal separation, Doug as checked out of that relationship as he'd ever be, the final decree hit him like a death in the family. Which it was, Vicki thought, in a way. The death *of* a family. Two little kids Doug adored. She liked that about him, that it meant something, the recognized end of what had been the focus of his life.

Doug not much of a gambler, either. Told her once he'd made the obligatory trip to the casino when it opened, lost five dollars in a slot machine, didn't make another appearance until table games came in last spring. Liked blackjack because it was quick and didn't require a lot of concentration like poker or craps. Left him free to bust stones with the other players, like he was now, Vicki and Mary on stools near the table, drinking beer and watching and listening.

"What's that on your hand, man?" Doug talking to the guy at the next stool, early thirties, hair, beard, and waist all in need of a trim.

"Steelers logo."

"My ass. Let me see that thing." To the dealer: "Hit me."

Bust. The guy held out his hand. Doug took hold of it for a

better look. "That is the sorriest Steelers logo I have ever seen. What'd they soak you for?"

The guy passed the other hand over his cards, sticking on eighteen. "To be fair, they didn't have much to work with."

"What, your hand the wrong shape for tattoos or something?"

"There was another tattoo there already." Dealer hit on fifteen, drew a six. Bastard. "They were covering it up."

"What was the old one?"

"Girl's name." Bets were made.

"Really?" Doug pulled the hand for a closer look.

"Can I have that back?"

"I'm just looking."

"How bad's your eyesight?"

Doug released the hand, checked his cards. "I'm good."

They played a couple of hands. Doug tried to start a conversation with the dealer, a real sourpuss more interested in checking out Vicki and Mary than blackjack.

Doug won a hand, turned to the other player. "What was it?"

"What was what?"

"The girl's name."

"What girl?"

"The one with her name on your hand."

"You should know. She's your mother."

"Ohhhh. That's cold." Doug acted upset, putting it on, not mad for real. Stared at the hand. Squinted. "Can't be my mother. Her name's Samantha. No way that's big enough to use to be Samantha." Another close look. "Don't see how they could even make a Steelers logo out of Samantha. Gotta be your sister." The other player gave Doug a look. "Okay, okay, sorry. Cousin, maybe?"

Vicki wondered why the dealer didn't say something, keep their minds on the game. His interest focused on Mary fussing with the lace on her sneaker, taking advantage of her loose blouse for a look at the pair that had provoked many a wet dream among her students at Penns River High School.

Doug tried to double down on a soft eleven. The dealer not so engrossed in Mary's cleavage he forgot the Allegheny disallowed that small player's advantage. "Hard elevens only, sir."

"The Rivers lets you double down on any eleven."

"This isn't The Rivers."

"No shit." Doug said to the other player, "How come you didn't just have it lasered off? Your cousin's name."

Tatt man split a pair of eights. "Too expensive."

Doug nodded, like the mysteries of the world had been explained. "Attitude like that probably why you needed to have her name taken off."

They kept it up, back and forth, Doug scoring more verbal points than he lost. Most of an hour passed, Vicki half afraid a fight would start, not knowing why Doug kept pushing this guy. Knew Doug didn't have a mean bone in his body, this was how men talked to each other, but, damn. It seemed risky to her. Fun, too. Doug with no animosity in his voice, the other fella taking no obvious offense. Engrossed by their banter until her three-beer limit had been exceeded by at least two. Glad Mary drove them both until she saw the glaze in her friend's eyes and knew it would be Doug or a cab tonight, and asking Doug to give her a ride home because she was drunk a lot more forward than she'd wanted to present herself.

Tattoo Hand left at ten thirty and Doug lost interest with no one to talk to except the dealer, who didn't talk. Gathered his chips—tipped the prick a buck—swallowed the last of his drink. Turned to Vicki and Mary, said, "Ladies, I'm calling it a night."

"Do us a favor, Dougie," Mary said before Vicki had a chance.

"Sure. What do you need?"

"Give us a ride home. We both had a little too much to drink. Please."

"What about your cars?"

"I got it all figured out." Mary taught algebra and trig, every situation a solvable problem. "Take us in my car. Drop Vicki off, then take me home. It's only a few blocks for you to walk from there."

Doug had half a smile going. Vicki knew already he'd do it. "That leaves my car here. How am I supposed to get to work in the morning?"

"I'll come by and get you on my way to school. Won't take me five minutes to run you by here. You know I go in early enough."

Doug nodded toward Vicki. "What about her car?"

"She came with me." Mary not sloppy drunk, but Penns River police had developed a fetish about impaired drivers leaving the casino. "C'mon, Dougie. I'll pay for all your drinks next time we go out."

Doug laughed. "That's because you know I only drink one beer a night." He did, too. Vicki noticed it a few weeks ago. One beer, then iced tea or Arnold Palmers for the duration. Meant to ask him about it sometime.

Mary gave Doug a stagey up-from-under look. Batted her eyes like she was playing to the top row at Heinz Field. "Well, hell, Dougie. You know I did the math. It's what I do."

"All right. Vicki, you ready? Mary shouldn't get to make all the decisions here, even if the math does work out."

Vicki slung her purse over a shoulder. "Ready when you are."

They left through the Four-Leaf-Clover exit. Security man gave them a look, moved his eyes toward the Breathalyzer machine off to the side. Casino called a cab for anyone who blew more than point oh-eight, the police for anyone questionable who refused the test. Doug made eye contact with the guard, sober as a Mormon in the desert. Showed the keys. "They're with me."

The guard looked at Mary and Vicki and smiled. "Good night, ladies. Yinz have a nice evening."

They waggled their fingers at him, acting drunker than they were. If he wanted to think they were off to a hot threesome, let him. Doug walked between the two women, his arms linked with theirs. Mary guided them to her car, a month-old Malibu still waiting for its first scratch. Vicki pretty sure Mary more concerned about breaking the dent cherry than a traffic stop. Probably asked Doug to take her car so it wouldn't sit in the casino lot overnight.

Doug double-clicked the fob, opened both passenger doors. "Nice ride. You can afford this, maybe I should drink two beers when you pay me back. Live on the wild side."

"Dream on, Dougie. I can't afford this and pay to make you an alcoholic. We'd have to work something else out." Bumped him with her hip before she got in.

Everyone laughed. Mary and Doug grew up together, knew each other even before they started school. Sleeping with each other might as well be incest. Doug let the women get settled, closed the doors. Walked around front of the car while Mary leaned across to unlock his door. Giggled when she realized it was already open, adjusted the shoulder harness.

Doug opened the driver's door, tried to slide in. "Jesus Christ, is this how you make sure it don't get stole? No one bigger than you can get in." Reached under the seat from outside, pushed it all the way back.

Mary made an exaggerated face. "Take it easy there, Shaquille O'Neal. You ain't that tall."

"I'll pull it up when I get in. Easier to get settled pulling it up than pushing it back."

"No comment," Mary said and everyone laughed again.

Doug closed the door, made a production of getting comfortable. Took three tries to get the shoulder harness where he wanted it. Adjusted mirrors. Adjusted them again. Mary slapped his arm and he said, "Oh, no. No way am I getting the first ding on this thing. I'd carry it on my back if I thought I could lift it."

Mary called him a smartass, but stopped slapping him.

Everything as he wanted it, Doug about to crank the ignition when a knuckle rapped on his window. Vicki looked over, saw the question on Doug's face, not who had knocked. A hand gestured to wind down the glass. Doug pressed the button, the window slid down. The man said, "This your car?"

"No." Doug jerked a thumb toward Mary. "Hers." Vicki saw the stranger's hand come up and didn't even have time to scream before he shot Doug in the face.

2

"Name's Doug Stirnweiss. White male, early thirties. Sitting in his car and some asshole shot him."

Officer Sean Sisler and Detective Ben Dougherty—"Doc" to all but immediate family—the only people inside the crime scene tape. Two other officers kept the gathering crowd back. Crime scene tech on the way.

"He gonna make it?" Doc said.

"I don't see how. Half his face is shot off. I saw them taking him out, looked like it caught him in the neck on its way by. There's blood everywhere in there."

No exaggeration. Blood on the upholstery, seatbelt, steering wheel, dashboard, console. Christ, there was blood on the outside of the driver's door, below the window. Doc pointed. "Must've hit an artery. He's a goner if they can't get him to Allegheny General downtown."

Sisler had done two tours in Afghanistan, shook his head. "Not with all the blood he's lost. They'll be lucky to get him across the river to Allegheny Valley."

Doc rubbed his chin, thinking. Small, economically depressed towns like Penns River weren't supposed to get whodunits. Why not a nice clean domestic gone wrong, with the killer sitting in the living room, waiting. "I didn't mean to kill him, just get him to stop hitting me/the kids/the dog." Hell, Doc would've settled for a "Yeah, I killed the bitch and I'd do it again." Quintuple shotgun murders last winter and now this. Doc hated the idea of killers walking his streets, no one knowing who they were, wondering who might be next on the Pittsburgh news, after the first commercial but before the weather.

"Anyone call Neuschwander?" Rick Neuschwander another Penns River detective, doubled as the evidence tech.

"He's on the way."

"Witnesses?"

"Two woman passengers. They're in my unit."

"They hurt?"

"Scared shitless, is all."

"Well, I guess so. I better find out what they saw while it's fresh in their minds." Took three steps that direction, turned back to Sisler. "Where's Rollison? I expected to see him raising hell when I got here." Daniel Rollison, head of casino security.

"Gone home for the night. They called him, but he lives in Shaler Township or Fox Chapel. Somewhere down there. Be a few minutes before he gets here."

"He does *not* cross that tape. This is our crime scene. He wants a report, he can wait for me in his office."

"Copy that," Sisler said.

Two women sat in the passenger side of Sisler's cruiser, feet on the pavement. Both pale as newsprint. Doc stopped twenty feet short, gestured for the closest uniform. Handed her five dollars. "Do me a favor. Run in there and get a couple bottles of water for these two. I'll watch the perimeter." The young female officer took the bill, left at a brisk pace.

Back with the water not three minutes later and Doc said, "Hey, no offense sending you on an errand. I didn't pick on you because you're the FNG. I wanted a few minutes to think of how the hell I'm going to approach these two."

The woman early to mid-twenties, looked like the mother in a baby product ad. Handed Doc his dollar change. "FNG?"

The situation kept Doc from laughing out loud. "The new guy."

A second, then a nervous giggle. "No offense taken, Detective."

"How long you been here now...Burrows?" Damn, he shouldn't have had to read her name tag.

"Three weeks."

"I don't know what they teach at the Commonwealth's academy, but you can knock off the 'detective' shit right now. We're not that formal. Call me Doc."

"Katherine."

"What do you prefer? Katherine? Kathy?"

"Kathy's cool."

"Kathy it is, though it'll probably be Burrows in front of civilians. Listen, a guy's going to be here in a few minutes. Late fifties or so, thin, high forehead he tries to comb over. He'll act like he owns the joint, and he'll try to push you around to get inside the tape. Name's Rollison. He does not cross that tape under any circumstances. That's an order. He gives you any grief, call Sisler. He's handled him before."

"Will do."

Having postponed the inevitable as long as conscience allowed, Doc dismissed Katherine Burrows and walked to his witnesses.

"Ladies." Squatted in front of them, handed each a bottle of water. "You look like you could use these."

Both women attractive in a Penns River sort of way. Not models or trophy wives. Pretty girls who grew into women who worked regular jobs, had regular appointments at Hair Necessities on Leechburg Road, and bought their makeup at Walgreens. Neither wore much. Whatever had been around their eyes now washed across their cheeks, smeared like a high school football player's eyeblack. Both in their thirties, though the one in front with the Ivy League-caliber endowment looked ready for the next milestone.

Doc gave them time to wet their throats and make peace with the idea they were going to have to talk about what had happened. "Can I get your names, please?"

"Mary Zelesko."

"Vicki—Victoria—Leydig."

Doc wrote in his pad, said, "How do you know the—Mr. Stirnweiss?"

"He's a friend. Just a guy we know from hanging at Mogie's, you know?" Mary. "He has a group of friends, we have a group of friends, and some of our group knows some of his group and we kind of started running into each other when we were out, you know?"

Doc made a note. "Ms. Leydig? Same with you?" The younger woman nodded, more shaken than her friend. Doc had the impression she'd hoped to do more than just run into Doug Stirnweiss.

"Were you in the car when it happened?" Nods. "You all came to the casino together?"

Two head shakes. Mary said, "I drove Vicki. Doug was already here. Me and her had too much to drink"—both sober as Carrie Nation now—"and I asked Doug to give us a ride home 'cause he never has more than one drink when he goes out. I think he had a problem when he's younger and likes to test himself. You know, I can have one drink and that's all?"

"So this is his car?"

"Uh-uh. Mine. I just live a few blocks away from his place. He was gonna drop us off and I'd give him a ride back on the way to work in the morning."

"Okay. You come out of the casino and get in the car. Who's sitting where?"

"Doug and me in front, Vicki in back."

"Did you see anyone approach the car?"

"No. We were kinda jagging around, you know, teasing. I didn't notice anything till I heard him knock on the window."

"He knocked?"

"Yeah, like twice, I think." A pause. "Right. Two knocks. Then he made a signal like he wanted Doug to roll down the window, and then—"

Her face and eyes froze so hard Doc felt tempted to turn and look. No tears, not a sound, Mary Zelesko locked up tight as Scrooge's vault. Doc worried about shock or PTSD or whatever the hell it could be, tapped a knee to bring her back to the here and now. "Did you see the man? Are you sure it was a man?"

"Yeah." Mary's stare a thousand yards and growing. "He said something. It was a man's voice."

"What did he say?"

The stare remained undiminished. "He asked Doug if this was his car."

"Anything else?"

"Doug said no, said it was mine, and—and—"

Doc knew what came next, saw her start to unwind. "That's okay, I have everything I need for now. Drink some water." Tapped the bottle, moved her wrist up an inch or two until she raised it to her lips. Turned to the back seat. "Ms. Leydig, did you see anyone approaching the car?"

Commotion near the crime scene distracted everyone. Doc recognized Sisler's voice, then another he'd been expecting. "Excuse me a minute, ladies. I'll be right back."

Doc recognized Rick Neuschwander's ass hanging out of the Malibu. Neuschwander a Penns River detective, doubled as the crime scene team. Good at it, too; had a standing offer of a job in Pittsburgh. That would mean working shifts, not a requirement for the four-time father in Penns River, with exceptions for callouts to the latest act of random violence.

Far side of the car, Sisler and another man in the midst of a heated discussion in which neither party raised his voice. Daniel Rollison—head of casino security, former private investigator, suspected retired black ops agent—used disdainful tranquility to keep adversaries uncomfortable, and, make no mistake, whoever he spoke to was an adversary. Sisler served in Afghanistan as a sniper, made a point of being no more excitable than a cat lying in a shaft of sunlight. Doc didn't have to hear to know the topic. Stopped behind Sisler's left shoulder, said, "Mr. Rollison."

"I knew it had to be you, Dougherty. I want to see what's happening here. This is casino property and—"

"It's a crime scene. Doesn't matter if it's on casino property in the parking lot, your office, or on your dining room table at home. It's a crime scene, and you're a civilian." Doc knew Rollison would wait for him to finish. "I've heard the speech, about how the casino is the largest employer and taxpayer in Penns River and we have a unique arrangement for the continued flow of information between you and the department. I'll flow whatever information I have your way as soon as I get it straight. I suggest you wait in your office, because you will *not* trespass on this crime scene unless you want your information to flow to you between bars."

Doc's right shoulder behind Sisler's left from Rollison's perspective. No physical challenge implied. Rollison dipped his head once, said, "You know where it is."

"I'll get to you inside of an hour, nothing unexpected comes up."

Rollison walked away, face blank as drywall. "That was easier than I expected," Sisler said.

"He had his reasons. I'm sure I'll get to hear them."

Vicki Leydig and Mary Zelesko hadn't moved. Doc detoured toward Kathy Burrows. "The EMTs check these two out?"

"I really don't know. Enough to make sure they weren't hurt, I guess. They were kind of busy with the guy that got shot."

"Do me another favor and call for an ambulance. Low key, no siren or lights. Have them pull up on the outskirts of the crowd. These women look a little shocky. Having a doctor put them to bed overnight might not be the worst thing could happen to them."

Burrows nodded, keyed the mike on her shoulder. Doc sighed and returned to his witnesses. Flipped open his book, scanned the notes. "Ms. Leydig, did you see anyone approach the car?"

"No." Doc read her lips as much as he heard her say it.

"Tell me what you did see."

The delay so long Doc almost asked again. "I heard the knock and looked up. Alls I seen was like the guy's middle. You know, what would show up in the window."

"Was he tall or short?"

"I don't know. Like I said, I couldn't see all of him. Not his face or head at all. I don't know how tall he was."

"Do me a favor." Doc tapped her knees forward. "Scoot into the seat here like you were in Mary's car. I'll go around the other side and stand by the window. Tell me if I look shorter or taller than the man you saw."

"It was the other side. I was on the other side. He was over here." Pointed to the driver's window.

"That's okay. It'll be good enough." Directed her knees into the car, went around the back to stand next to the passenger window. "What do you think?"

Vicki looked over, then away. "I don't know. Close to the same maybe." Doc started for the rear of the car and she said, "He had a belt buckle."

Doc returned to his spot by the window. Whatever might prime her memory. "Do you remember anything about the buckle? A design? Words?"

She shook her head. "It was too dark and I wasn't really looking. It surprised me seeing someone there at all. It shined in the light, the only reason I noticed it."

"Anything else about him stick in your mind? Anything at all."

Doc saw her start to drift. "Just the shiny buckle and his hand come up. You know, like he had a piece of paper with an address on it and wanted to ask if we knew where it was. He said something to Doug and Doug said no and I saw his hand come up past the buckle and something else shiny and I looked...it was a gun."

Doc's voice soft, hoping she'd answer the question as if she'd continued on her own. "The gun was shiny?"

"Mmm-hmmm, shinier than the belt buckle. Had a round thing in the middle."

"Was the gun big or little?"

"Big. Oh, Jesus, I never saw a gun that big before...and... and..."

Doc hustled around to the other side, put his hands on her arms before hysteria set in. "It's okay, it's okay, I don't need to know anything else." Slid her legs out of the car, took her hands in his. "Shhh, that's all I need right now."

"No, it's his hand. The hand with the g-gun. It's coming up and I can see the long part pointing into the car and—and—" Tears sheeting down her cheeks, voice on the edge.

"Shhh, it's okay."

"It's his *hand*. The hand. On his hand. There's a-a—tattoo on his hand. It's the Steelers emblem, with the stars. *Oh my God!*" Vicki wailed and Doc wondered *Where's the fucking ambulance* and she said, "It's the guy from the blackjack table!"

"The dealer?"

"No, the guy from the blackjack table. With the ugly tattoo. Doug talked to him all night, made fun of it. He's the guy that shot him!"

3

"Whatever you need."

Doc stopped in his tracks, the door to Rollison's office not yet closed behind him. Replayed the past few minutes in his head to see what he'd missed. Finished with the witnesses. Touched base with Sisler, Burrows, and Neuschwander. Walked across the parking lot, any evidence more than fifteen feet away from the event trampled beyond recovery. Through the near-empty casino, where he decided everyone still gambling needed mandatory enrollment in Gamblers Anonymous. Knocked on Rollison's door, heard "come in." Entered to find a man who resembled Rollison in every way, down to the clothing he'd worn in the parking lot. This man said, "Whatever you need," opened his arms in a cooperative gesture, and Doc's mouth fell open so hard and fast he almost dislocated his jaw.

"Have a seat," the doppelganger said. Doc sat. Gave Rollison the first word, still recovering from the shock.

"You heard me. Whatever you need. I showed up ready to bust your shoes about what I was entitled to, but you were right, out there in the parking lot. So...what do you need?"

Doc still recuperating. "Video surveillance."

"Installed in the parking lot after those cars got stolen last winter. I looked at what we have while I waited, but it happened in a dead spot. You're welcome to it, but it's not going to help."

"A dead spot?"

Rollison took a second, first time Doc had ever seen him do it. "We agreed to add security cameras to the lot. Your chief's end was increased patrols. We put up about half as many as we said." Must have seen the look on Doc's face. "The camera on the light pole facing your crime scene is an empty casing."

Rollison's tasty dish of crow aided Doc's recovery. An altruistic spirit of cooperation outside his experience. He understood Rollison in damage-control mode. "You might be off the hook there. It's the inside cameras I'm most concerned with. One of our witnesses thinks she recognized the shooter from in here."

"Where and what time?"

"Blackjack table near that auxiliary bar by the buffet. Dealer's a…" flipped through his notes, "greasy little shit who spent the night trying to look down Mary's blouse."

Rollison said "Steve Onan" under his breath, made a note on a pad. "Follow me."

Down a hallway to the security center. Three men at terminals, split screens on thirty-two-inch monitors for each. Rollison stood over the shoulder of a twenty-something with no hair, pierced lip, and eyebrow. "Jared, I need to see Camera 11, starting at about ten o'clock." Jared typed and pointed and clicked. Two tables, players at both. "Squeeze left and zoom in."

"Squeeze?"

"You know what I mean."

Jared focused on the table at the left. Back of the dealer's head, two faces Doc didn't recognize, and it occurred to him he'd never seen Doug Stirnweiss. "Can I get a look at what's behind the players? Maybe zoom in and shift focus. I don't know what the guys look like, but I've seen the women who sat behind them."

"You know this isn't a live feed, right?" Jared doing all he could to confirm Doc's opinion of the stereotype. "All I have is what's there already."

"Get me as close and as clear as you can to what's behind. The women can give us a positive ID, but they're not up to it right now. I'm hoping to get lucky."

Jared tightened the focus. The zoom moved between the two gamblers, too low to see the faces of the women at the bar behind them.

"Wait, that's good."

"You can't see their faces," Jared said as if Doc couldn't figure it out on his own.

"I just talked to both of them in the parking lot. I recognize their slacks and shoes."

"Pull back so we can see the faces at the table," Rollison said.

"Their hands." Rollison shot Doc a look. "My suspect has a tatt on his right hand."

Rollison nodded. "Do it."

"Zoom that tight, I can only get one guy at a time," Jared said. "Maybe only one hand."

"Start with the guy on our right," Doc said. "The one on the left is closer to the women, and they're friends with the victim. Stirnweiss. I want to see the other guy."

"Right hand," Rollison said. Jared made a disgusted sound.

"There." Doc pointed to the screen.

"What is that?" Rollison.

"According to my witnesses, he says it's a Steelers logo."

"Right," Jared said.

"Get his face," Rollison said. Crosshairs appeared on the screen, drawing a box around the man's face. "No. Not there. Let it run a little. I want him looking as directly into the camera as we can get."

"Tell me when you're happy." Jared sounded like a sixteen-year-old girl whose mother said those shorts are too low at the top and too high at the bottom.

They watched the man's face in slow motion until Doc said, "I like that."

"Stop," Rollison said.

"Jesus." From Jared.

"Can you get me a still of his face from that?" Doc said.

"Yeah," Jared said before Rollison had a chance. Drew a square around the face, clicked. "That's it."

Rollison told him to let it run. "I want a profile, too."

Three minutes later they had a profile shot Doc could live

17

with. Rollison wanted better. "They're pretty grainy with that much zoom. Can you clean them up a little?"

An exaggerated sigh from Jared. "Yesssss."

"Email them to me as soon as they're ready." To Doc: "Let's go."

Not sure what Rollison had planned, Doc had no reason not to follow. Never having seen Rollison cooperate before, might as well ride the wave until he landed on more familiar ground.

Both men took seats in Rollison's office. "I'll email the files to you soon as I get them, or I can print up as many as you want. We might have a higher quality printer. No offense."

"Actually, a good printer is one thing we do have." Neuschwander spent two years wheedling the department into springing for a state-of-the-art job. Closed the deal when he proved how much the city would save not having to send hi-res jobs to Staples. "I appreciate the offer, though."

Rollison nodded, phone receiver in hand. "Send in Steve Onan...I don't care if he's getting a blow job from Hillary Clinton. I want his ass in here in ninety seconds." Hung up. "The dealer."

"Thanks." Doc looked around the room to be doing something other than talking to Rollison. Gave in, said, "I don't mean to seem unappreciative, but why are you doing this?"

"Doing what?"

"Helping me. Going above and beyond."

Rollison gave it thought. "Right now, we have the same job to do. A dick-measuring contest hurts us both. Next week you can go back to thinking I'm an amoral piece of shit, and I'll remember you're the same sanctimonious prick you've always been." Paused. "I had two phone calls from my boss and one from his boss while you were outside." His boss's boss being Daniel Hecker Himself. "Let's say it's in both our interests to work together and lock this up as quickly as possible." Someone knocked. "Yeah."

The door opened and a head half-covered with hair appeared.

"You wanted to see me?"

Rollison pointed an index finger to the empty chair. Spoke before the man Doc presumed to be Steve Onan could sit. "The shooting victim played blackjack at your table right before it happened."

"If you say so." Rollison raised an eyebrow. "Players come through there all night, Mr. Rollison. I couldn't say."

Rollison glanced toward Doc and back. "He was with two women, one of whose tits had more of your attention than the game."

Onan flushed. "Nobody got anything over on me, Mr. R. I swear to it."

"Do you remember the guy now?"

"Yeah."

"You know him?"

"I seen him before, is all. You know, not like I know his name, but I recognize him to see him."

"What about the other guy?" Doc said.

"What other guy?"

"The guy he was playing with."

"People come and go all night. Must've been half a dozen guys sat at that table while he was there, or right before. It's not like I keep track who's there and when."

"The guy who was there when he left, or left right before him," Doc said.

Rollison turned his computer monitor so Doc and Onan could see. "This guy, dumbass."

Onan took a good look. "He's been in before. Same as the other guy. I remember seeing him around. That's all."

"Know his name?"

"No." Doc asked if he'd ever sat at Onan's table before. "Once or twice, maybe."

"He talk to anyone? Anyone talk to him?"

"Sure, I guess. He ain't unfriendly. He also don't come in with a group of friends."

"How do you know?" Rollison said.

"Because every time I seen him he's alone. He comes in with friends, sooner or later I'd notice him with somebody."

"What about tonight?" Doc said. "He talk to the other guy? The one who came in with the women?"

"Yeah. The other guy was busting his balls about his shitty tattoo."

"The guy busting balls. He ever call this guy anything? Name? Nickname?"

Some thought. "Not that I remember."

"What about the other times you've seen him?" Rollison said. "Anyone ever call him by name?"

"Like I said, I never seen him with anyone else. Just whoever's sitting at the table."

Rollison looked to Doc. "Anything?"

Doc shook his head. Handed a card to Onan. "You remember something later, call me."

Onan took the card, said to Rollison, "I can go, then?"

Rollison waved him out. Waited for the door to close. "What's your email address? Jared did a nice job cleaning these up."

Doc handed him a card. "I'd appreciate it if you'd show those around to the help tomorrow. I can send someone back to do it, but I figure you'd rather keep the volume down."

"I'll do better than that. Not only will every employee get a picture, I'll make up flyers and post them around the casino. I don't know how many people to expect with this hanging over us, but we might get lucky."

Doc stood. "Thanks. I appreciate this. Really."

Rollison took a beat. "I know you do. Anything else you need?"

"There will be, but it looks like I know where to find you."

4

Doc balanced a chocolate-frosted doughnut on his coffee mug, tapped the doorframe with a knuckle on his way into the chief's office. Stan Napierkowski—"Stush" to everyone except his deputy—finished a glazed doughnut. A crème-filled awaited its destiny on his desk.

"Thanks for coming in early, Benny." Stush the sole non-relative who could call Doc "Benny." He'd known Tom and Ellen Dougherty for so long Doc called him "Uncle Stush" until leaving for the Army.

"This is a heater," Doc said. "We need to get on it."

"How do you want to work it?"

"Let me have Shimp."

Stush paused in his reach for the doughnut. "Not Grabek."

"We both know Willie's retired in place ever since his gall bladder exploded. He can do paperwork and local stuff. I need someone who'll bust ass on this."

"You think she's up to it? Hasn't been here much more than a month."

"You got a better way to find out?"

Stush chewed, almost back to his pre-heart-attack weight. "What time did you get home last night?"

"I got enough sleep. It's just...Rollison extended himself for me last night. Anything I needed. Said he'd already had two calls from Doocy and one from The Man himself. That means Hecker and his people will be on us like stink on shit by the time this closes."

"*Will* be?" Stush licked crème off a finger. "I got a call shaving, seven in the fucking morning. Rance Doocy wanting to

21

know if we'd made any progress and how long till an arrest."

"Jesus Christ. I knew it'd be bad, but this is ridiculous."

"Can't really blame them. This is their cash cow. You read the paper. The casino's the only thing keeping Hecker liquid right now."

"If you're trying to encourage me to close this in a hurry, telling me it'll benefit Hecker's the wrong way to do it."

Stush almost choked on a piece of doughnut. "You lay awake nights thinking of ways to stick it to him, don't you? It's okay to admit. I do it. You should hear some of the shit I tell Helen."

Doc finished his doughnut, washed it down. "You said the casino's Hecker's only liquid asset. The new amusement park's not doing well?"

"You didn't hear?"

"Just that he tried to buy Kennywood and they told him to pound salt, so he built his own. That was a couple years ago. Last I heard was it was ready to open."

Stush smiled. "Rushed it through in time for Memorial Day weekend, take some of Kennywood's business away just as the ethnic and town days were starting. Two days before they were—you sure you didn't hear this?"

"I went to the Outer Banks that week, remember?"

Stush nodded. "You still chasing after those sisters? What's their name? MacDonald?"

"First of all, I was never chasing after them. Second, they're both happily married now. The Outer Banks are nice. You and Helen should go sometime. I stop by, say hello, lay on the beach, and eat dinner at Sam and Omie's. So, no, I missed the excitement with Hecker's park."

"Two days before they're ready to open—the Thursday be-fore Memorial Day—one of the roller coasters flunks a safety inspection. Closed them all."

"So he's trying to compete with Kennywood—roller coaster heaven—with no coasters? I don't like roller coasters, and even

I know that's the place to go for them."

"It gets better. He built this big water park, and the primary ride there—big-assed thing with rafts that hold ten people—turned up with unsanitary water."

"Holy shit. I've been on rides like that. How dirty does the water have to be to shut one down?"

"So there he was, blew all that money on the park and the promotion, and he spends the big opening weekend with his dick in his hand."

"I had a nice vacation, but that would've been worth sticking around for."

"I'm sure he'll fuck something else up before too long, let you have some fun."

"How's someone that dumb get so rich?"

Stush wiped his fingers and mouth with a paper napkin. "What makes you say that?"

"Well, I hate to say it, but stupid people don't get rich."

"Ben Roethlisberger."

Doc snorted coffee into his sinuses, waited for the burning to subside. "I mean in business."

"Business takes in a wide range. Like athletes. Michael Jordan may be the greatest basketball player ever lived. Remember when he tried baseball?"

"He sucked."

"He sucked at *minor* league ball. Double-A team only kept him around because he bought the bus. Hecker made his money in real estate, cashed out just in time. Doesn't mean he knows dick about casinos or water parks." Stush wadded the napkin, tossed it in the wastebasket. "Look at that guy down Washington, owns the football team. Started his own company, made over a billion dollars in billboards and shit like that. Has to be the dumbest son of a bitch in the world when it comes to football. These guys think because they were smart enough to get rich, they know everything about everything. No one works for them has the balls to tell them different."

Doc let that soak in—thinking how many people took Stan Napierkowski for a rube—when Stush interrupted his reverie. "Where are we on the shooting? How's the victim?"

"I called before I came in. Doctor said if he can make it through another night he'll have a chance. I asked him how likely that was, and he said he can't say for sure why the guy didn't die last night."

"Jesus Christ."

"He lost too much blood. Sisler saw guys in Afghanistan, said he can't believe this poor bastard didn't bleed to death on the way to the hospital. He's not conscious, and I doubt we'll ever get to talk to him."

Stush clasped his hands, tapped thumbs against his belly. "Tell me the good news."

"We have a photograph of who we think is our prime suspect, and a couple of decent statements from the women who were in the car when it happened."

"What are we doing with them?"

"We'll paper every business in town, send flyers out within a fifty-mile radius. Rollison had a bunch of copies made to show around the casino. Our boy's been in there several times. Someone's bound to recognize him."

"You're not worried about driving him underground?"

Doc made an equivocal gesture. "I thought about it. Decided I'd rather have a name and take my chances."

"I'm not second-guessing. Just want to be sure between the two of us, we don't miss anything."

Doc knew. He also knew Stush's patience with being second-guessed himself had worn thin. Gave every sign of looking for an exit strategy, waiting for a quiet spell when he could retire on his own terms. Quiet spells fewer and farther between in Penns River these days.

"I know you're busy," Stush said. "Tell me if you have to go, but I wonder if I could pick your brain about the new hires a little."

"You mean the women?"

"We have any other new hires?"

Penns River's elevated media presence over the past few years had brought attention to more than the crime problem. An "activist," unable to gain adequate media attention in the already overpopulated realms of drug violence and poverty, took note of three black police officers in a force of thirty-eight and ran with it. This looked like a problem with a resolution that contained a photo op, which prompted media outlets that felt underexposed to take notice, hoping to burnish Pulitzer nominations with stories of the change their stalwart advocacy helped to bring about. Made it all the way to the federal government before someone acknowledged what Penns River's solicitor had been pointing out since Day One: Penns River's eight percent black population meant three African-Americans on a force of thirty-eight did not constitute a gross underrepresentation. Overcoming a non-existent problem would not count as a victory for the activist, the interested media, or the Associate Attorney General who'd planned to use his success as a platform on which to run for Congress.

Graduates of obscure law schools don't get to be associate attorneys general by missing opportunities. Only eight percent of Penns River residents were black, but over half were women. The police force had four females: two dispatchers, the juvie coordinator, and one patrol officer. Women vote, too, and a consent decree was signed to add three female police officers— two patrols and a detective—in return for a federal law enforcement grant that covered their costs for five years, by which time Mayor Chet Hensarling hoped three other cops would leave; no fucking way could the town pay for three more cops on its own.

"I worked with Burrows at the crime scene last night," Doc said. "She's *real* young but seemed to handle it well. No opinion, but she looks promising. Shimp is at least at Neuschwander's level as an interviewer. We'll see if she can step up on this shooting."

"I got George Ulizio working with Burrows as her training officer. He says she's green, but coming along. What about the other one, looks a little like Marian Widmer from behind? Snyder."

Doc gave his boss the finger. Marian Widmer played Dr. Moriarty to Doc's Sherlock Holmes. Up to her well-constructed ass in two homicides, walking around free as Doc and Stush. "I really haven't had a chance to do more than say hello in the hallway. Check with Sisler. They must've answered a few calls together." Pondered whether to ask the next question. "You worried about them?"

"Not about them, specifically." Stush reached for his bowl of jelly beans, thought better of it. "Bringing in three new people like that, all at once. What's it been? Three weeks? Four? That's a lot of inexperience walking around."

"Shimp and Snyder aren't exactly virgins. They're younger than me, but they still have some time in. Burrows's the only one of the three still has that new cop smell." An idea crawled into view. "Burrows's with Ulizio, and Shimp will be working with me. You want a read on Snyder, have her ride with Sisler for a while. I'd take her just for the chance to ride patrol, but I'm kind of tied up."

Stush raised an eyebrow. "Think she'll go for that? She has more time in uniform than he does."

"Not here she doesn't. Dress it up a little so it doesn't sound like you doubt her work. Call it some kind of orientation program. Sisler knows the town and most of the secret handshakes by now."

"That's not a bad idea. Sisler's new enough he can still relate to the learning curve." Stush rubbed his lower lip, succumbed to the jelly beans' siren song. "Anyone ever tell you you have chief potential?"

Doc had no desire to get into this discussion again. Eye Chart Zywiciel, the patrol sergeant, knocked in the nick of time. "Doc? Some guy's here to see you. Says a buddy saw his picture's hanging in the casino."

5

No question in Doc's mind he sat across the table the man in the Allegheny Casino photos. He'd parked Robert Virdon in the interview room while rounding up Teresa Shimp; Rick Neuschwander set up the video equipment. Everything and everyone in place now. "Have a seat, Mr. Virdon. You sure I can't get you any coffee or a cold drink or something?"

"No, I'm good. Thanks for asking." Virdon looked around the room. Seemed anxious, not panicky.

"What brings you in this morning?" Doc said.

"I'm friends with a guy does deliveries for the casino. You know, napkins, toilet paper, urinal cakes. Stuff like that." Virdon kneaded his hands as he spoke. Made it hard to see the tattoo, not impossible. "He called me half an hour ago, said he seen my picture hanging all over the place. The flyer said youns was looking for me."

Rollison better than his word, posting the flyers this early. Doc made a mental note to watch for flying pigs when he left the building. "Do you know why we're looking for you?"

"My buddy didn't say. Or I didn't make it out. The reception was shitty."

"You see the news last night or this morning?"

"I don't watch TV news. It's got so bad you can't even depend on Fox for the straight scoop anymore."

"What do you do for a living?"

"I work at 84 Lumber across the river. I'm supposed to be there now, but I called my boss when I figured I should come here first." Shimp made a note.

"Why'd you figure that?"

27

"If the police are looking for you, it's better to come to them than have them asking around where you work."

"Ever have the police looking for you before?"

"No, and I gotta tell you, I'm kinda nervous, wondering why you're looking for me now. You are, right? My buddy didn't get that wrong, did he?"

"Can I see your right hand, please?"

"My right hand? Sure, I guess."

Virdon extended his hand across the table. Doc took it by the fingers, pretended to examine it. "How long have you had this tattoo?"

"Coupla years, I guess. What's this about, anyway? Am I in trouble?"

"Is that a Steelers logo?"

Virdon looked down, exhaled. "I know. It's shitty. I got divorced and figured it would be hard to get back into circulation with my ex's name tattooed on my hand."

"Why not have it lasered off?"

Virdon retrieved his hand. "You ever see what that costs? I have a buddy getting started in the business. He covered it up for practically nothing." Doc and Shimp exchanged looks. "Like I said, I know. Listen, I gotta tell you, I'm getting a case of the ass, sitting here not knowing what's going on."

"Sorry," Doc said. "I'm getting there. How'd you spend your evening last night?"

"Watched SportsCenter while I ate supper. Took a shower and went to the casino for a couple hours."

"You go with anyone?"

"No."

"See anyone there you know?"

"Well, yeah. I go a couple times a month, so I know some people to see them. Not like we're friends or anything."

"Know a guy named Carl Stirnweiss?"

Not a flicker of recognition. "Don't ring a bell."

Doc took a photograph of Stirnweiss from a manila folder, a

blow-up from DMV. Laid it on the table facing Virdon. "This guy."

Virdon steered the photo into a better viewing position. "Yeah. We played blackjack together a few times. He was in there with a couple of nice-looking girls last night."

Doc not sure what to think. Either their suspicions were one hundred eighty degrees wrong or Virdon was the coldest SOB he'd ever seen. Snuck a look at Shimp. If she'd reacted, it didn't show. "Tell us a little about Mr. Stirnweiss."

"Like what?"

"I don't know...how'd you meet him?"

Virdon thought. "Last month—no, the month before. Remember all the rain we had in April? I remember talking about it with him at the table."

"Blackjack table?"

Virdon nodded. "I think that's all he plays. I like to mix it up a little. Blackjack's best for when I'm feeling sociable. You can talk to people and not worry too much about distracting them. Not like anyone's counting cards in a dump like the AC."

"What kinds of things you talk about?"

"Could be anything. That first night we complained about the weather. How cold it was all winter, and now it's spring and it rains every fucking day." Shot a quick glance at Teresa Shimp. "Sorry."

She smiled. "It's okay. I've heard worse."

"No offense, Mr. Virdon," Doc said, "but did Mr. Stirnweiss ever give you any grief about that Steelers tattoo?"

"All the time. Hey." Virdon looked from Doc to Shimp and back. "He in some kind of trouble? He seems like a pretty good guy."

Doc half raised a hand in a "be patient" gesture. "He give you any trouble about it last night?"

"I wouldn't call it trouble. I mean, he was in rare form, busting 'em left and right, but it was the usual stuff."

"Such as?"

"You know." Virdon moved his hands as if he could massage the words out of the air. "You don't pay much attention when you're going back and forth like that. He'd ask about it and I'd tell him what I told you, it covers a girl's name. He asks the same goddamn laser question you did and I'd tell him what I told you, so he asks what the girl's name was." Virdon getting into the story, looking like he had it playing back in his mind. "I told him 'Samantha' or some other long name, see what he'd do. It went back and forth like that for a while."

"He make any comments about your mother or sister?"

"Yeah, like he always does. I would've stayed to give him the usual ration about his hair, but it was later than I thought and I went home."

"What about his hair?"

Virdon tapped the photo of Stirnweiss. Hair thinning on top, otherwise nothing noteworthy. "It looks pretty good there. It's longer now on the sides, and he fools with it on top when he plays cards so it's all over the place. At least he can get it cut or comb it." Pointed to his hand. "I'm stuck with this bitch."

"You go straight home after the casino?" Doc said.

"Yeah—no. I stopped at Wendy's there, across the street. Got a Frosty. Listen." Leaned on his elbows, hands open in Doc's direction. "I told you everything I did last night. Now, what the hell's going on? I got a right to know."

Doc considered easing into it, decided not to. "Someone shot Doug Stirnweiss leaving the casino last night. We have a witness who thinks it was you and will swear you and he argued in the casino less than twenty minutes before it happened."

"We weren't arguing! It was just busting balls. You know how guys talk when they're out." Turned like he might make his argument to Shimp, then back to Doc. "That's all it was, I swear to God. I left before him and went right home. After Wendy's."

"You willing to swear to that?"

"Get me a Bible."

"Take a lie detector test?"

"Absolutely. I'll even take one of those gunshot wax tests. You know, where you can tell if I fired a gun."

"That won't be necessary. A polygraph will be fine."

"Where do I have to go?"

"We'll deliver." Doc turned to Shimp, who shrugged and put away her notebook. "It might take a while for us to get the examiner. You want to call your work, tell him you'll be later than you thought?"

6

Doc called the examiner in Pittsburgh on his way back to the interview room when the PA speaker told him of a visitor at the same time Stush asked for a minute. He asked Shimp to wait with Virdon. "You've taken polygraphs. Everyone thinks they're no big deal until they're strapped into the machine. Let him know what to expect. Bullshit around, see what his interests are. Come up with a couple distracters the examiner can use. If he lets something slip, fine, but we're not trying to break him. That's what the test is for."

Shimp nodded, went on her way. Doc noted she never needed to be told anything twice, entered Stush's office.

Stush cut right to it. "Stirnweiss died about fifteen minutes ago. The hospital called while you were scheduling the examiner."

"He ever wake up? Make any kind of statement?"

Stush shook his head. "Doctor said he didn't know why he wasn't dead when they brought him in. What they told you before, about how if he made it through another night he had a chance? They couldn't believe he made it through last night. Figured if he lasted one more, he might be immortal."

"I'll call for the autopsy."

"Already done. You were busy, I had the phone in my hand, so I called Pittsburgh." Penns River in Neshannock County—pretty much *was* Neshannock County—had no medical examiner of its own. Farmed the work out to Allegheny. "They'll pick him up, said they might even get to him this afternoon."

"Slow day?"

"Must be. When's the examiner due?"

"Probably an hour, hour and a half."

"What's up with your suspect?"

"I sent Shimp in to relax him, tell him what to expect. I don't want anyone coming back later saying he blew the machine because he was nervous."

Out of Stush's office, down the hall, through the locked door to the waiting room. Doc's visitor a fireplug of a man starting down the road to fluffy. A double chin covered most of the knot in his tie. Doc identified himself, asked what he could do. The man handed him a business card, said, "I'm here to see Robert Virdon."

"And you...Mr. Crenshaw, are?"

"I'm Mr. Virdon's counsel."

"He didn't say anything about a lawyer. I'm not arguing—he's certainly entitled to one—I'm wondering why he didn't say anything before."

"Can I see him?"

"Sure. Wait here while I find a place you can talk. He's in an interview room now, with a two-way mirror. We'll put you someplace more private."

"You don't have a room for client consultations?"

"We do, but I don't know if anyone's using it."

"I'll come with you."

"Uh-uh. You have a right to a confidential meeting with your client, not to roam our halls. I won't be a minute."

Doc found the small consultation room unoccupied, put up the "In Use" sign. Walked into the interview room where Shimp and Virdon talked about decks. "Mr. Virdon, your lawyer's here. I found a room where you can speak privately."

"Huh? I don't have a lawyer."

"You didn't call a...Alvin Crenshaw?" Doc as confused as Virdon seemed to be.

"How could I call him? I been here with you all morning."

"You didn't call him before you came in?"

"No. I didn't figure I needed one."

"You want to talk to him?"

33

"Uh-uh. He sounds like some kind of ambulance chaser. See what he wants."

In the visitor's area, Doc said to Crenshaw, "Mr. Virdon says he never heard of you. Who retained you?"

"That's between Mr. Virdon and myself."

"Well, Mr. Virdon doesn't want anything to do with you until he knows who you are. He sent me back to find out."

"Are you denying me access to my client?"

"No, sir, I am not. All I'm trying to do is find out if you have a client in the building. Mr. Virdon says no."

"This can be easily settled, Detective. Let me explain to him why I'm here, and he'll know I'm legitimate."

Doc wondered if these things ever happened to Lennie Briscoe or Andy Sipowicz. "Counselor, I'm good with that but for one thing: if he didn't ask for you, doesn't want you, I don't know if there are legal ramifications for any potential prosecution down the road. I can go next door and get the city solicitor to give me an opinion. That might take a while. He's been known to re-search things to within an inch of their lives." Doc sensed a Constitution citing about to spring forth, said, "Give me some little thing to tell him that'll set his mind at ease. I mean, it's not like we won't know who hired you sooner or later."

Crenshaw glowered as if debating the likelihood he'd get to argue the matter before the Supreme Court. "Tell him his mother hired me. Alice Virdon."

"Why didn't you say so in the first place? I'll be right back."

Through the locked door, down the hall, into the interview room. "Is your mother's name Alice, Mr. Virdon?"

"Yeah. So?"

"This lawyer—Crenshaw—says he was hired by your mother. Alice Virdon."

"How'd she know I was here?"

"You didn't tell her?"

"I told you I came over soon as I heard you were looking for me. I didn't call anybody."

"Well, he's here and she appears to have paid for him. You want to talk to him, I'll take you right over."

"I wouldn't talk to Patty Hewes if my mother paid for her."

Doc damn sure Vic Mackey never put up with this kind of shit. "Who's Patty Hewes?"

"On that show? *Damages*? The actress with the man's name plays her?"

Doc watched network television about as often as PNC Park allowed dogs to watch Pirate games. Looked to Shimp for help. "Glenn Close."

Deep breath. "So you're saying you don't want your mother's help."

"That's right. I didn't shoot this guy at the casino last night, but if anyone ever shoots that bitch, I'm the one to look for."

Out of the interview room, down the hall, through the locked door. "He doesn't want to see you."

Crenshaw failed to hide his amazement and disdain. "You told him his mother sent me?"

"Yes, sir. I told him. Do you know who Patty Hewes is?"

"Glenn Close, on *Damages*. So?"

"She any good as a lawyer?"

"Yes. So?"

"Then you're in good company. Virdon says he wouldn't talk to her, either. Not if his mother sent her." The polygraph examiner came through the main entry door. Doc held up a finger for him to wait. "I'm sorry. I have to go."

Crenshaw so mad his wattle trembled. "You can't prevent me from seeing my client! He has rights!"

Doc's voice icy calm. "That's correct. He has the right to an attorney. You, however, do not have a right to a client. I know you've been on the clock since you got up from your desk to come over here. My advice is to explain the situation to Mrs. Virdon and move on." Turned toward the examiner, came back. "I'll call her later and will damn sure take it to the solicitor if I hear you tried to run up a bill on her. We're done here."

7

"You make a good living here, Daniel. *Some* work is expected."

Daniel Rollison had worked for a lot of men like Rance Doocy. Operated on a higher plane, the how of getting things done not his concern. A bloodless, empty suit who derived his considerable power from the man he worked for, expected all to tremble at his feet because *his* boss was Somebody. It had meaning in government, where the Somebody might hold the power of life or death. Rollison alternated between suppressed laughter and revulsion to see the same relationships in business, where all that mattered were marginal gains or losses. Doocy would still be wealthy, and Daniel Hecker would be unconscionably rich, no matter how the casino shooting sorted itself out. Rollison liked money as much as the next four guys combined; his distaste for what it did to some grew by the day.

"I'm working as closely with the police as I can, Rance." Rollison watched Doocy absorb his first name with the usual discomfort. Preferred his subordinates to refer to him as Mr. Doocy, couldn't bring himself to correct Rollison. "Even Dougherty seems happy."

"That's appreciated." The words the only things about Doocy that implied appreciation. "I also hear you've had disparaging things to say about how...conscientious we've been in upholding our deal with the city."

Rollison's lips formed the narrow line that passed for a smile. "It's always better to call yourself on a weakness instead of waiting for an adversary to use it against you."

"I understand. I also understand you threw us under the bus when you did it."

36

That morsel had to have come from Jack Harriger, chief-of-police-in-waiting. No one else would give Doocy the time of day. "There was no other way for them to take it: we aren't honoring the agreement. I thought being frank might make Dougherty more comfortable working with me. You know how he feels about Hecker and the casino."

"I do. It makes me wonder if we wouldn't be better served with someone else in charge of the investigation. Someone with more incentive to clear it."

"Who do you have in mind? Dougherty and Grabek are the cream of the crop here."

"Small town cops in over their heads. If the mayor were to ask the state police to intervene, or—maybe even better—if Mr. Hecker were to step up and volunteer his resources to hire a private firm to look into it. Turn this into a win for us."

"Stop right there. Dougherty and Grabek aren't as good as they like to think they are, but they're still damn good. Much better than this shitburg deserves. They broke that quintuple homicide last winter."

"After making a complete bollocks of the murder the year before, right here on the casino's doorstep."

"Dougherty and his psycho cousin did the casino a favor there, cleaning up a mess that bimbo in the D.A.'s office never would've sorted out. He's a hero to a lot of people in this town. Hecker throws his weight around, tries to push him aside, that's not going to go over well."

"That's another concern. Stan Napierkowski will have to retire soon. We do not want Dougherty to become chief by acclamation."

The problem with people who thought of themselves as players: everything was an angle. Rollison had played more angles than he could remember, never more than were necessary. "Don't overthink this. Chief of police is an appointment, not an election. The mayor gets to pick who he wants, and Chet Hensarling doesn't put milk in his coffee until he checks with you.

From what I hear, Dougherty doesn't want the job, anyway."

"It wouldn't be seemly for him to politic too openly for it."

"Then you might want to tell Jack Harriger to back off."

Doocy's face showed what he thought of being lectured by a subordinate, even in private. "Harriger is our most...convenient option."

"Then have him do some real police work. Napierkowski's been chief since anyone can remember, but he was a real cop once. Word is, a good one. Harriger pushes paper, and I have a reliable source who tells me his continued employment with the state police was not a foregone conclusion. It may even have encouraged him to look for this job."

"He's a paper-pusher here because Napierkowski won't let him do anything else."

"He was a paper-pusher the minute he walked in the door. I don't like Napierkowski much, but he's not as stupid as you seem to think. Harriger went gunning for his job and fucked it up. You can't blame Napierkowski for keeping him on a short leash after that."

"Then how do you propose Harriger become a more palatable candidate?" Doocy's demeanor made it clear whatever answer Rollison gave would be quaint.

"It may not be possible. There's a real chance you'll have to look for someone outside." Doocy received that as if Rollison had pointed out an open fly. "He might at least want to take some initiative that includes police work, instead of sniffing around city councilmen every waking minute."

Doocy rose. "Where does this leave us with the investigation?"

Rollison gestured to include his office. "Where we are. Anything the police ask for, they get, quick as I can give it to them. The more cooperative I am, the more likely they are to talk to me. I'll let you know if I need any outside help. Until then, I have a handle on it."

Doocy's body language implied no confidence in Rollison's definition of a handle. Reaching for the door when Rollison spoke.

"Rance? About those cameras. I told you when you came up with the inspiration to install empty shells it was a bad idea. Hecker's hauling money out of here in truckloads. The last thing we need is to look cheap."

"A generous percentage of those 'truckloads' of money comes back to you," Doocy said. "This is how you earn it."

"I'm only saying not to throw away dollars to save dimes. I know things about you and Hecker, too."

8

"Is your name Robert David Virdon?"

"Yes."

The examiner made a tick mark on the scrolling sheet of paper. "Do you work at 84 Lumber in Tarentum?"

"Yes."

"Now lie to me. Is your mother's name Alice?"

"No."

"Another lie, please. Do you enjoy..." looked at a note, "Pitt basketball?"

"No."

A tick and a brief note. "Are you ready to begin?"

"Yes."

"Were you at the Allegheny Casino last night, Wednesday, June eighth?"

"Yes."

"Did you play blackjack?"

"Yes."

"Did you win?"

"I won some and lost some. You know—"

"Yes or no answers, please. Let me rephrase: did you win more than you lost at the casino last night?"

"I'm not sure. I didn't—"

"Yes or no, please."

"I'm not sure. It was pretty much a break-even night."

"I'll rephrase: did you win any hands at blackjack last night?"

"Yes."

"Are the walls of this room painted black?"

"No."

"Did you speak to anyone at the casino last night?"

"Yes."

"Did you speak to Doug Stirnweiss last night at the casino?"

"I didn't know he was—yes."

"Did you argue with Doug Stirnweiss at the casino last night?"

"No."

"Did you graduate from Kiski Area High School?"

"No."

"Did you buy a Frosty at Wendy's to take home last night?"

"Yes."

"Did you go directly home from Wendy's last night?"

"Yes."

"Have you ever traveled to Australia?"

"No."

"Did you shoot Doug Stirnweiss in the parking lot of the Allegheny Casino last night?"

"No."

Pete Stackhouse placed his blood pressure cuff in its case. "If he didn't shoot Stirnweiss, he shot somebody else. Been a long time since I've seen anyone shit the bed like that."

Doc rubbed his face. Put his hands behind his head and sat with eyes closed. "No offense, Pete, but could the machine have been miscalibrated? From moving it here from downtown?"

Stackhouse shook his head. "I wondered about that myself, eager as this guy was to take the exam. The machine's right."

"Thanks. You sticking around to do the report?"

"I have another exam downtown in an hour. We squeezed this in as a favor for helping us with that hot car ring. I'll try to get it to you by the end of the day tomorrow, first thing Monday at the latest."

"Tell Donnie Spak I said hello." Doc nodded to Shimp. "Let's talk in the office."

Four sets of desks, chairs, files, and other accessories filled an office more accustomed to three of each, better suited for two. Rick Neuschwander at his desk, writing a report. Willie Grabek in court. Doc took two bottles of water from a dorm-style refrigerator, tossed one to Shimp, who caught it one-handed. Both sat and took short drinks, waited to hear what Doc had to say, he as interested as Shimp.

"What do you think?" Saw the look on her face. "Not to put the burden on you. I want your opinion."

"You heard him." She gestured toward the interview room where Stackhouse packed his equipment. "If Virdon didn't shoot Stirnweiss, he shot someone. Is Stackhouse reliable?"

"Very."

Shimp considered her comment. "I'm not sure what you want me to say."

"You mind playing Devil's advocate?" Doc's most recent partner, Willie Grabek, hated when someone tried to break down arguments. Considered it a challenge to what he knew to be his superior detective skills. Doc had no reservations playing either side, didn't know how Shimp felt about it yet. "I'm not arguing. Let's see if we can find weaknesses in each other's positions. Noosh, if you're not fully engaged there, feel free to join in."

Neuschwander shifted his chair to better see the other detectives. Treated like the pain in the ass tagalong little brother by Grabek, he lived for opportunities to be included in more than evidence collection and scut work.

Doc waited for Neuschwander to settle himself. "Teresa, you start."

Shimp paused, breathed, said, "An examiner you respect tells us Virdon lied when he said he didn't shoot Stirnweiss."

"Then why was he so eager to take the test?"

"He thought he could beat it."

"Why would he think that?"

Shimp sat back in her chair, her posture less certain. "People think all kinds of things, you know that."

Neuschwander said, "Maybe he saw something on TV or read a book. There's articles on the internet on how to beat polygraphs."

"Takes practice, though," Doc said. "Far as we know, Virdon had no reason to think he might have to beat one until last night, if he did the shooting."

"That's why he failed," Shimp said. "He thought he could pull it off and it was harder than he expected."

"Good point." Doc rocked back in the chair, steepled his fingers.

Deputy Chief Jack Harriger entered, proved why he sucked at gin rummy: he never knocked. "I heard Virdon failed the polygraph." Nods all around. "Why isn't he in a cell?"

"We're discussing that now," Doc said.

"Discussing? He failed the polygraph. Lock him up and call Sally Gwynn."

"Teresa and Rick were talking me into that when you interrupted us. There are a couple of things I want to have straight before I put him in the cage."

"Such as?"

Doc made a show of forbearance. "I've never seen anyone want to take the test as bad as he did. Wouldn't even talk to the lawyer his mother sent. He wanted to get in there, get it over with, and get back to work. It doesn't play like he's guilty. Teresa, tell him what you told me when I said that."

"I said maybe he thought he could beat it, but it was harder than he expected."

"There you are," Harriger said. "He got too cute. It's the killer who calls in about half of all homicides. They think it throws us off."

Doc loved lectures on the finer points of investigation by a man who'd written tickets and jammed up poachers while Doc spent nine years as an MP, five in criminal investigations, turned down a chance to instruct at Fort Leonard Wood if he'd re-enlisted. "Thanks, Jack. I don't think any of us knew that."

In a force where even dispatchers referred to the chief as "Stush," Harriger insisted everyone call him "Deputy."

"Then why isn't he in custody? Virdon."

"For one thing, you know how Sally is about evidence, and we don't have any."

"He failed the polygraph."

"Inadmissible. All that tells us is to keep looking down that path."

"A witness identified him."

"She identified the tattoo on his hand."

"I've seen it. That's a unique tattoo."

"Yeah, well, I'm going back tonight to check the light. She'd just seen Virdon busting balls with Stirnweiss. The tattoo's distinctive and it was fresh in her mind."

"Didn't she say things got heated between Virdon and the victim?"

"She says. Virdon says no, and I believe him. Teresa, what did you think?"

"I'm with Doc on this part. Sounded like two guys pulling each other's chains."

"What did the polygraph say about that?" Harriger said.

"All we have right now is a preliminary. Should have the whole thing late tomorrow."

"Until you know otherwise, you have a witness and a polygraph. That's enough to hold him."

"It's for sure enough for a search warrant," Doc said. "Though I'd prefer to ask his permission."

"It'll just mean he's already gotten rid of everything if he says yes."

"Maybe. That's a lot harder to do than people think, too, especially on short notice when the police might come through the door any second. If we're willing to consider he volunteered for the lie detector because he thought he could beat it and miscalculated, why wouldn't the same thing apply to getting rid of the evidence?"

Shimp and Neuschwander nodded as if hearing something that had not occurred to them. Harriger as unconvinced as always when entertaining someone else's idea. "It's risky."

"How? If he says no, we get the warrant. It's not like he can run home and red up before he calls us back and says he changed his mind, come on over." Doc didn't wait for an argument. "We don't have the gun. We don't have a true eyewitness." Stopped an interruption with his hand. "Neither woman saw his face during the shooting. The tatt helps, but we'll need more. We'll check at Wendy's, see if anyone remembers him. We'll look at the tapes from the parking lot cameras that *do* work, in case we can see his car leaving. What time and how frantic it looks. That's the other thing that bothers me."

"What?"

"Teresa, stop me if you disagree. We spent all morning and part of the afternoon now with this guy. He came in of his own volition, never gave any indication he knew something had happened to Stirnweiss. Everything I saw says he's either innocent or the coldest SOB I've ever met." Raised his eyebrows in Shimp's direction. She nodded.

"He could be a true sociopath," Harriger said.

"I thought about that, too, but his record's clean. One underage drinking charge fifteen years ago, three months' probation. He's worked steady at 84 across the river for sixteen years, pretty much since he got out of high school. No crimes of violence. No assault or battery charges. Nothing to do with weapons. No threats or stalking, drunk and disorderly. Nothing. If he's a stone sociopath, he took a hell of a long time to discover his hidden talent."

All eyes on Doc. Time passed and they moved to Harriger. "I want him arrested."

"I'll type up the affidavit for the search warrant," Doc said. "Teresa, take his picture to Wendy's. Find whoever worked last night and see if they can identify him."

Glanced at Harriger. "I know that won't prove he's innocent, but I have a hard time believing anyone could shoot a man in front of potential witnesses and drive across the street for ice cream as part of his escape."

Back to Shimp: "While you're up that way, stop in the casino and tell Rollison we need the video from every parking lot camera from the time Virdon left the blackjack table until at least an hour after the shooting. Even better, get the video from the casino exits for the same period. I want to see what Virdon looked like on his way out. We'll meet here when we're done. I should have the warrant by then."

9

"Wasn't that long ago we had everything under control here."

Mike Mannarino gave Stretch Dolewicz a chance to agree. Stretch didn't acknowledge the comment one way or the other. Moody like that lately.

Mike continued, "There wasn't much crime and there were *no* drugs being sold."

"Good thing, too," Buddy Elba said. "Made it easier to do the transfers for the Pittsburgh packages here, no one looking this far up the river. Pain in the ass now." Buddy, as usual, not picking up on Mike's mood. Mike well aware of the inherent hypocrisy of the Mannarino family's operations, his rationalizations more complex by the month.

"What are you doing about it?" Mike said. "Do you know who's selling here in town?"

Buddy looked surprised. "Up here? In PR? Jeez, Mike, I'm down the South Side all day. We got some things going there and out by the airport that could make some money. I ain't been paying a lot of attention to up here."

Two made guys left in Pittsburgh, now that Carlo Stellino dropped dead of a stroke in Lewisburg's exercise yard, sixty-three years old. Buddy ran everything south of the Monongahela and Ohio Rivers; Stretch—as close to being a Friend of Theirs as any Polack would ever be—handled north of the Ohio and the Allegheny. Between the rivers belonged to whoever cultivated the business, with Mike arbitrating disputes. Penns River clung to the bank of the Allegheny—"between the rivers" for territorial purposes—the lines, and interest, diffuse this far from The Point. No one would care about Penns River at all had Mike

47

not lived there.

"Start paying attention up here," Mike said. "Get a couple of guys to see what's what. You know I don't want that shit where my kids go to school."

"That's not as easy as it sounds, Skipper." Buddy took time, deciding how to play it, deciding things not his strong suit. "My guys, they don't fit in that well, if you know what I mean."

"Jesus Christ, Buddy. I used to think you pretended to be this stupid so the cops would leave you alone. You supply those jigs from Wilkinsburg to Weirton. Detail a couple to come up here and, you know, fit in. Whatever it takes. We can't clean it up, maybe we can come to some kind of arrangement."

"Yeah. Okay. Sure," Buddy said, not sounding sure at all.

"Stretch, when's the next truck coming in?"

"They're looking for something next week. I should know for sure tomorrow or the day after."

"Good." On one level, Mike about to shit when the boys in New York told him his shipments were going to come in rental trucks. They had a man on the inside. When someone rented a truck one-way to Pittsburgh or someplace close, a package was deposited, unknown to the driver. Stretch or Buddy would have it picked up after the truck was dropped off. A clever plan, damn near foolproof if you didn't mind not being precise with the delivery schedule. And assuming the inside man didn't get careless, or turn on you.

What bothered Mike was the shipments started coming to him this way less than six weeks after he'd told the local FBI field office that was how drugs got to Baltimore. His deal with the feds did not include continuing to act as the primary supplier for the Pittsburgh area. Went so far to cover himself he made whoever picked up each shipment take it to Cleveland or Buffalo before someone else's crew "delivered" it to Penns River. Devised elaborate stories so wise guys in the pass-through cities wouldn't get too wise, start wondering why Pittsburgh's drugs had to take a northern vacation before they were cut and sold.

"You two ready?" Steak night, this week at Susini's on East Carson Street.

"You mind if I beg off?" Stretch said. "My legs are killing me all week. Fucking knees." Stretch every inch of six-four, grew nine inches in eighteen months in high school. His knees never quite caught up, tended to hurt in proportion to how far the restaurant was from his house in Etna.

"Go on home. Buddy, you still game?"

"Fuck, yeah. I love how they put the cheese on their potatoes. I been waiting for that and a porterhouse all day." Buddy lived in Mount Lebanon; Susini's on the way home for him. His sciatica sometimes acted up when the restaurant *della settimana* was in the opposite direction. Whole fucking operation falling apart, guys couldn't even get together to eat.

10

No reason for Jack Harriger not to arrest Virdon himself. A sworn officer; Dougherty's superior. Thought about it after he chose not to make an issue of a subordinate issuing Shimp her orders. No point to it. Stush Napierkowski would back Dougherty in any pissing contest.

Harriger knew the game: feed him bullshit until he quit, at which time Napierkowski would retire, Dougherty promoted to chief. Harriger felt he'd earned at least the right of first refusal, if not through his police work, then by the amount of said shit he'd eaten since what Napierkowski referred to as "that Russian situation." Harriger no more responsible for that than the guy who pumped Ted Bundy's gas killed any of those girls; the stink refused to wash off. Napierkowski liked to play the happy rube, but the fat bastard held grudges, and Dougherty was a vindictive son of a bitch. They'd missed no opportunity to belittle or demean Harriger since.

He had no intention of letting their plan work. Closed his office door, called Daniel Rollison at the casino. "Dan, it's Jack Harriger. Thanks for posting those flyers so quick. Looks like we have our guy. Listen, I just sent a detective around to tie up some loose ends so our hotshot prosecutor doesn't have to bargain this down to a misdemeanor. She's going to need all the parking lot video from the time our boy left the blackjack table till well after the shooting. Also anything you have on the entry and exit cameras so we can see him leave. We're trying to nail down his timeline."

Rollison happy to help. How soon did Harriger need it? "She may be a while running down the other lead. If it's not ready when she comes by, anytime the next couple of days is fine... great. Thanks for all your help on this."

Having shown his mastery of the situation to the man who had the ear of the man who had the ear of The Man, Harriger called the mayor. "Chet? It's Jack. Listen, you know people at the paper, don't you? Can you get a story out?" Sure, Chet knew a guy. "This murder at the casino is going to close quicker than we thought...yeah, he died. A few hours ago. The guy that did it's sitting in the interrogation room right now...No, he's not under arrest. That's why I called. Dougherty's building another one of his logic mazes. I think he's looking for an excuse to let the guy go...I don't know why...Could be as simple as I told him I want the guy arrested and he's showing his ass...I know everyone says he's a good cop. I just think he wants to close this one in his own good time when it could go down today, is all...Tell your guy we have a good suspect, an arrest is imminent. Have him call me on my cell. Light a fire under Dougherty...Yeah, I agree...Well, you said I needed to step up... Okay. Thanks, Chet."

Having done all he could to solve the Stirnweiss murder for the time being, Harriger tackled his inbox. Court pay had to be reconciled, and Willie Grabek late again with his vouchers. His day was coming, too.

11

"I know it's only been a few weeks." Kathy Burrows's sole police experience prior to Penns River had been the Academy. "They could at least give us our own shower."

Choir practice for the three new cops. Hard to agree on a place, all of them new to Penns River. The lounge at the Clarion too noisy. The casino had the cheapest drinks, but was too visible. Maguire's—closest to the bypass, easiest to get home from—would do until someone found someplace better.

"I'll talk to Stush," Teresa said. A detective, most experienced, first among equals.

"I can't believe we're all supposed to call him that." Kathy so green she still slipped and let out the occasional "Yes, sir." Sipped her wine, said, "I mean, he's older than my father."

"I was worried about that when I interviewed," Nancy Snyder said. "Older guy, had us pretty much forced on him. Now that I know him a little, I think he looks at us kind of like his daughters, but not in a condescending way. Does that make sense?"

"Sure it does." Teresa swallowed beer. "I think it's because he looks at everyone there as his kids, one way or another. Maybe not the older guys like Zywiciel or Ulizio or Harriger, but pretty much everyone else."

"He *hates* Harriger," Nancy said.

"Everyone seems to hate Harriger," Kathy said. "Why is that?"

"Something to do with Ben Dougherty, I think. Teresa, you work with him more than anyone. Do you know?"

"First thing I know is not to call him Ben. He's Doc."

"The chief calls him Benny," Kathy said.

"He's the chief," Nancy said between sips of Bud Light.

"He's also an old family friend. I think Stush and the Doughertys go way back. There's some kind of special bond there."

"So you think Harriger did Dougherty some dirt and now Stush is getting back at him?" Nancy said. "That's not real professional."

"It's more than that. Something's there, but I don't know Doc well enough to ask about it. It's not really any of my business."

"True. But he hates Harriger, too."

"I was with them both today, deciding what to do about the casino suspect." Teresa ticked the lip of the beer glass with a fingernail. "It's not like Doc hates him. It's more like he...refuses to acknowledge him at all, if he can. When he does talk to him, it's very patronizing. I've never seen anything like it, from a subordinate to a superior."

"It's not like Dougherty acts like he's subordinate to anybody."

"What happened about that guy?" Kathy said. "I heard he failed the polygraph."

Teresa spoke into her glass. "Doc let him go."

"He let him go?"

"Uh-huh." Teresa exchanged looks with the others, gestured for another round. "It was weird. I think Doc made up his mind before the exam this guy—Virdon—was innocent. He blows the test and Doc still thinks he's clear, but asked Neuschwander and me to talk him out of it."

"So what happened?" Nancy said.

Teresa considered her answer. "I don't know. It looked like Doc was leaning toward arresting him until Harriger came in and told him to do it. Doc said he wasn't ready, then came up with a list of the things we *didn't* have on Virdon, even though we had the polygraph."

"Like?"

"A witness who saw his face at the shooting, for one thing."

"I thought you had a witness," Kathy said. "Didn't the one chick see a tattoo?"

Teresa let the waitress deliver the drinks. "Doc said the tattoo was fresh in her mind from in the casino earlier. The light wasn't great at the scene. Maybe she confused what she saw, and when."

"What else?" Nancy said.

"The suspect told us he stopped for a Frosty on the way home. I went to check it out and got there just as the kid who worked last night came on. He recognized Virdon right away, said he stops in once a week or so."

"Does seem kind of funny, that he'd stop for ice cream right after shooting someone."

"Yeah, I don't see it, either. Anyway, I stopped at the casino to ask about the videos from last night. Doc wanted to see if there was a record of Virdon's car leaving, exactly what time. Maybe even catch him walking out of the building."

Teresa didn't go on. Nancy poked her arm after ten seconds. "And?"

"Something else weird. The head of security there—Rollison— was ready for me. Knew I was coming. Handed me a disk before I even got into his office."

"So?"

"How did he know I was coming? And what I wanted?"

"Maybe Dougherty called him."

Teresa shook her head. "He could've called anytime and asked for it. He wanted me to do it in person."

"Why?"

"Said he wants Rollison to see more cops than just him, so we're all on the same page. No wedges." Raised her glass, took a swallow. "I don't get the feeling he really trusts Rollison. I think they have history, too"

"Does he get along with anybody?" Nancy said. "Dougherty."

"He was nice enough at the crime scene the other night," Kathy said. "I mean, he came in and took over, but he's the senior detective. That's what he should've done, right?"

Nods from the others. Nancy said, "Did you get the search warrant?"

Teresa swallowed. "Oh, yeah. The warrant." Set down her glass. "Didn't need one. Virdon signed off."

"And?"

"Nothing there, and no signs anything had been gotten rid of."

"That doesn't mean nothing was done."

"No, but it's not evidence, either."

"What did Dougherty do?"

"He let the guy go. Apologized for costing him a day of work. I thought Harriger was going to have a stroke."

"He let him go?" Nancy's mouth hung empty until words found their way out. "Just like that? Honest to God?"

"Told him to be available. Not to leave town. The usual stuff. Said he'd call 84 Lumber first thing in the morning to make sure the guy shows up, but waited until Harriger left before he told me."

"That's extreme," Nancy said. "Bad history is one thing. Letting suspects walk is too much."

"I think Doc really believes the guy didn't do it. Whatever history he and Harriger have shows up in how they treat each other. Not what he does on the job. He was on the fence about what to do when Harriger came in."

"And he went that way to spite him?"

"I think it's more like Harriger's arguments for arresting the guy reminded Doc of how much we were missing. Once the search came up dry, what did we have, really? No evidence. No solid statement. He pretty much had to let him go."

"How's your field training going?" Nancy said to Kathy.

"Okay, I guess. Except for that guy getting shot, it's been quiet. We stopped a couple of drunk drivers, wrote tickets. Took some accident and property theft reports. Is that really all that goes on here?"

"You haven't spent much time in the Flats or the Allegheny

Estates, have you?"

"Drove through a time or two a day is all. We had a call in the Flats last week. Nothing major."

"Give it time. I helped break up a fight at Fat Jimmy's Friday night. Sisler stuck his baton under a guy's chin and dragged him out."

"Fat Jimmy's. Jesus." Teresa shuddered. "I went to talk to a guy there last week and made the mistake of going into the restroom." Nancy and Kathy gave "don't stop now" faces. "I wouldn't touch anything in there with my hands, let alone my butt. I almost threw up, but I made myself hold it in because I was afraid I'd have to touch the sink."

Nancy sputtered into her drink. Kathy said, "It can't be that bad."

"I've never seen a gas station men's room as bad as that ladies' room. Swear to God. You know who has nice bathrooms? The Edgecliff. I almost suggested we go there, but that's where Dougherty drinks, and I don't want to run into anyone from work. These nights out are for us to vent."

"Have you checked out the facilities here?" Nancy said.

Teresa cast a glance that direction. "Not yet."

"You want one of us to go first?" Kathy said.

"Or come with you as backup?"

"Go ahead. Laugh." All three were, with or without permission. "We sit on those things with our bare skin. I see anything nasty on the floor of a restroom, I don't even want to think what might be on the toilet seat. Think of who's been in there, a place like Fat Jimmy's."

"Damn, Teresa, relax," Nancy said. "We're going to have to start calling you Detective Monk."

"I just like clean bathrooms, okay? Is that so bad?" Teresa looked at her watch. "I probably better get going."

"So you can use the bathroom at home?" Kathy said. "I'll bet you can do surgery off the floor in yours."

Nancy put up a hand. "I need to ask you something before

you go."

"You better make it fast, Nancy. She's jiggling her foot. She might have to go real bad."

Teresa flashed her the finger. Nancy said, "The Sarge wants me to ride with Sisler next week." Teresa asked why. "Something about spending time with another cop who knows the town better. Sisler hasn't been here a year, and I know I have more time in uniform than he does."

"Don't they think you're doing the job?"

"I don't know what to think." Nancy drank from an empty glass. "He said no, at least twice. You know, 'I don't want you to get the idea anyone thinks you aren't doing a good job.' So, of course, the first thing I wonder is, who doesn't think I'm doing a good job?"

"You think Stush told him to do it?"

"I can't believe he'd do it and not get Stush's approval."

"Good point." Teresa considered what she knew of the individuals involved. "Sisler's new, but he's been busy. He shot the guy who killed those five drug dealers last winter, you know."

"That was him?" Kathy said.

"Uh-huh. And I know any time Dougherty wants backup and Sisler's available, he asks for him. Give it a chance, Nancy. This might be exactly what Sarge said. I know they think a lot of Sisler. Maybe they're just goosing your learning curve."

"Maybe." Nancy had to make up her mind to continue. "It's more of an old boys' club here than I expected. I thought, a small town like this, the low-key atmosphere would make it easier to fit in. But all the key players go so far back together—Stush, Dougherty, Sergeant Zywiciel—I feel like I have to prove myself even more than I did in Allentown."

"You knew we were Equal Opportunity hires." Teresa let that sit a bit. "For what it's worth, Sisler seems to be more or less included in that group you mentioned, even as young as he is. They trust him. Maybe this is a way to tell you you're more accepted than you think."

"Maybe."

"I'm working with Dougherty on this homicide. He knows everybody and seems like a decent guy." Nancy gave a quizzical face. "Okay, he hates Harriger. And maybe the guy from the casino. Rollison. I still don't know that it affects his work. Let me see what I can pick up."

12

"How are those new woman cops working out?"

Doc and his father, Tom, drinking iced tea under an oak tree in Tom's yard. Doc remembered his parents bringing the oak and its two brothers home in the back of the family station wagon. Each tree more than thirty feet high now, a steady line of shade from the edge of the driveway to the shed where Tom kept his riding mower and outdoor tools.

"Hard to tell this soon. The rookie, Burrows, did okay handling the crime scene the other night. I'm working the case with Teresa Shimp. She seems to know what she's doing. The other one, Snyder, I don't really know."

"Hell of a thing, forcing three new ones on you all at once."

"They weren't forced on us. We interviewed them all and picked who we wanted."

"You know what I mean. That the city had to hire three cops at all. It wasn't like we needed the extra expense."

"Come on, Dad. You've been bitching about the crime for a couple of years now. More cops has to help, right? Besides, that federal grant covers their salaries and benefits and then some."

"And what happens when that money runs out?" Doc made a noncommittal gesture. "That's what I thought."

"It is what it is. So long as they're good cops."

"Let's hope." Tom tasted his tea. "You say you're working this murder with the new woman detective? What about that older guy? Grabek. Seems a case like this, you'd want someone with more experience."

"Experience cuts both ways." Not the first time they'd had this discussion. "Willie's seen it all, and what he hasn't seen he likes to make fit into what he has. Shimp's been around some herself. It's not like she walked right out of the academy and got a detective shield."

Tom showed surprise. "How old is she?"

"I don't know. Early thirties, maybe? She worked patrol somewhere in Ohio—Dayton, maybe—then got an investigator's job at Ohio State."

"Campus cop? That doesn't count for much."

Doc laughed. "That campus has almost twice as many people as this whole town, and as many detectives."

"You're shitting me. For a college?"

"Colleges have a lot of valuable stuff. Cars, computers, iPads, all kinds of shit like that. Kids drink too much and get into fights. They got thirty thousand young women walking around more or less unescorted. Hell, they have their own crime lab, which is more than we can say."

"How do you know so much about Ohio State's police and crime?"

"I looked it up after I read her resume."

"They have such a great department there, why'd she leave?"

"I guess she got tired of investigating the same old shit, and the kids were wearing her down. Said she wanted to work around real people again."

"She's so good, why didn't she get a job in Cincinnati or Cleveland, or wherever the school is. Columbus?"

"Christ, Dad, I don't know. You want me to call her up, get your ass down here so my old man can ask why you wanted to work in this shithole?" Doc lost patience with his father more often of late. Tom's increased argumentativeness explained part of it. Felt bad about snapping at the old man, noticed he didn't feel as bad, or as soon, as time went on. "Maybe she just wanted a lower pressure environment."

Tom waited what he must have thought was a suitable interval. "She married?"

Doc turned his head so Tom couldn't see his eyes squeeze

shut. "Nope. And I don't know if she has been. And since I know you're wondering why she isn't married and won't dare ask it, I have no idea if she's a lesbian."

"It's a reasonable question."

"You think I'm gay?"

"No." Tom waved away the idea like a cloud of gnats.

"Why not? I'm almost forty and I've never been married."

"I *know* you."

"Ahhhhh." *Where was Mom?* Doc would rather talk about cleaning than this.

"I thought the whole thing was about blacks."

Doc snapped back to the present. "You thought what was about blacks?"

"That federal lawsuit. Pay attention. I'm the one who's supposed to lose the thread."

"It was about blacks."

"So how'd we end up with three white women?"

Something flew into Doc's ear. Heard it coming, the pitch getting higher, got his hand up too late to do anything more than scoop out the remains. "You talk to a cop almost every day, between me and Stush. You know how investigations work. Once you start looking, peel back a layer of the onion, pull the loose string on a sweater, whatever, they go where they go. The feds looked around and saw we weren't as short of black cops as they'd been led to believe. We were short of women in what they called 'public facing enforcement positions.' So we had to hire women. I told Stush to mention Lester Goodfoot."

"What for?"

"Him and his wife's the only Indians that live here, which means half the Indians in town are cops. That should count for something."

That went over as well as most of Doc's more fanciful comments. "Whole goddamn world's a mess. Glad I won't be around to see how it turns out."

You've been saying that for ten years almost made its way

out before Doc forced it back. "Is Mom *still* washing dishes?"

"She could be running the sweeper, if she didn't do it this afternoon."

Doc swallowed half a glass of iced tea in a gulp. "You need a refill?" Tom showed him a glass almost as full as Doc's had been ten seconds before. "I'm going for some more. See what's holding Mom up."

The kitchen table doing the job when he found her, one hand pinning the newspaper to the surface. Doc went straight to the refrigerator for his tea, not to disturb her reading. Filled his glass and turned in time to see a tear hit the paper.

"Mom? What's wrong?"

Ellen's mouth moved as if she might speak, didn't. Pointed to where her other hand held the paper. Doc came around to see what had upset her. An obituary, he assumed. All he saw were ads. "Mom, what the hell? Aaron's is having a sale?"

"If you say so."

Doc all the way confused now. "What do you think it says?"

"I don't know what it says! *I can't read the fucking thing!*"

Ellen Dougherty as liberal with her cursing as any blue-collar Penns River woman, avoided the hard consonant obscenities. Doc had heard her say "fuck" once before. Maybe. He wouldn't have been more shocked if she'd slapped him.

"Come here." Steered her into the chair by the shoulders. Knelt, their heads almost level. "Why can't you read it? Can you see it okay?"

"I can see it," she said, fighting back sobs. "It's just I can't read it. I mean, I can't see it good enough to read it."

"When's the last time you had your eyes checked? Maybe you need a new prescription."

"It's more than that. When I try to look harder, to focus, there's nothing there at all."

"It's just black?"

"Listen to what I tell you. I didn't say it went black. It's—it's too fuzzy to see if anything's there."

"It like that all the time?"

"It's not so bad except when I'm reading or doing something up close. Even then, I can see if I look to the side a little, but it's hard. Soon as I can make something out, I can't help it, I want to look. Then it goes all fuzzy again."

"Jesus, Mom. Have you seen an ophthalmologist?"

"I don't know if the insurance will cover it."

"Did Dad ask?"

Ellen's head sank lower. "He doesn't know."

"Mom, we gotta tell him right now. This could be serious."

"Wait, Benny. At my age, all kinds of things come and go. This might be gone in a week."

"How long since you first noticed it?"

"Not too long."

"How long is that?" Trying to keep his voice calm.

"I don't know. It was around Easter when I tried to—"

"*Easter*! Jesus Christ, Mom. That was almost three months ago."

"I don't know if we can afford it."

Doc considered options. "Dad really doesn't know?" Ellen shook her head. "Well, he needs to. Sooner rather than later." More thought. "You want me to tell him?"

A whisper. "No."

Doc stood, knees creaking. "Okay. I doubt he'll know what to do any better than I do. Your insurance has one of those registered nurse phone lines, doesn't it? Where you can call for advice?"

"I think so."

"They'll know what to do. I have one with my insurance. They're great."

Ellen sat, disconsolate; a kid who'd disappointed her favorite parent. "I'm worried about what it's going to cost."

"You guys aren't poor." Ellen had grown up in Depression-like poverty, never shook the idea she'd moved past it. "Dad didn't get laid off when he was fifty-nine. He retired because he could afford it."

"He retired because he couldn't do the work anymore. Not with his arthritis."

"And they retired him with disability and paid to have his hands fixed. The insurance covered that. It'll cover this."

Ellen didn't answer. The silver lining yet to be invented she couldn't find a cloud for. Bad fortune only a matter of time, in her mind. Laid awake nights when Tom used a home equity loan to buy a car, worried they'd lose the house until Tom convinced her, worst came to worst, they could sell the car to pay off the loan.

"Mom? Mom." Firmer, to get her attention. "I have someplace I gotta be, so I'll leave it to you to tell Dad. I'll ask about it when I come for dinner on Sunday. You can't wait too long, let it get worse." She nodded. "I hear you and Dad are taking Drew's family to Williamsburg for a week in August." Doc's brother, a letter carrier in Penns River.

"The end of July." Ellen's spirits already perking, thinking of her granddaughters. Doc let the conversation drift that direction, plans she and Tom were already making for things the girls— ten and eight—would enjoy. Talk evolved from future plans to memories, telling stories they both knew so the other could take a turn laughing.

The screen door opened. Doc looked up to see Tom in the doorway, darkness behind him. "Oh, shit. Was I supposed to bring you some tea, Dad? I'm sorry. We got to bullshitting about the Williamsburg trip."

"Nah. The bugs were eating me alive. I came in while I still had blood left."

Doc finished his tea, the ice long melted. Said his good-byes, how he was running late. Stepped toward the door, went back to kiss the top of his mother's head, then left.

13

Jefferson West handed Doc a cold Beck's, a small plate of melted Colby cheese, a fork, and a napkin. Doc said, "You ever get bored in retirement, you'd make a hell of a HoJo waitress."

"Seems the least I can do, and, as you well know, I always—"

"Do the least you can."

West smiled with ivory teeth. "All kidding aside, I know how busy you are right now, with that casino business. I appreciate you making the time."

"You said it had to do with the boys." Doc wrapped cheese around the fork. "Never apologize for calling about them."

"It's about Wilver, mostly." West had served as foster parent for Wilver and David Faison after they witnessed a murder while squatting in the vacant next door to his townhouse, their mother in county for the shot across the bow euphemistically referred to as detox. He stayed close with both boys when she got out, made sure they got fed regardless of Mom's position relative to the wagon. "I tell you I got the OP set up again?"

West's "Observation Post" a chair next to a window in an upstairs bedroom, from where he could see Penns River's primary drug corner. Saw it well, with field glasses.

Doc's stomach sank. "And?"

"I see Wilver there every day."

"Is he doing the lookout gig again? Or is he selling?"

"I think it's worse than that."

Doc stopped a fork load of cheese halfway to his mouth, returned it to the plate. Released the fork. "You mean he's using?"

West cleared his throat. "I think he's in charge."

Doc retrieved the fork, brought it to his mouth. Stopped, put everything back and placed the plate on the coffee table. "What makes you think so?"

"He comes by two-three times a day, stays ten-fifteen minutes, then goes. I can't hear what they say, but when he talks, the rest appear to listen, and when he says to shut up, they do."

"Ever see him handle drugs or money?"

"No."

"Shit." Doc's thumb under his chin, index finger bent, resting against his lips. A posture he recognized as coming from his father, Tom's "serious" look. "You can see pretty good with the field glasses. He showing any money? Jewelry or clothes?"

"No bling." West sent Doc a look as if to say *I know how younger people talk*. Both men exhaled humor. "Clothes are newer, but not too much different. He has a car, though. Can't say for sure what it is."

"I can check that with DMV. Not likely he's using another identity or bought it in someone else's name. Eighteen-year-old boy with his own car isn't going to set off any alarms. Is it something flashy?"

"Uh-uh. I think it's a Honda or a Toyota. Not brand new, but not old, neither. Not the kind of car that draws attention."

"Kid's smart." Doc reached for his cheese again, what to do already forming in his head. "You talk to him lately?"

"Not for a couple of months. Three, maybe. Not too long after all that Resurrection Mall business." Resurrection Mall the location of last winter's quintuple homicide, since burned beyond recovery and about to be bulldozed.

"What about David?" The younger brother.

"Comes by every Wednesday. Set my watch by him. More, sometimes, but Wednesday for sure."

"What's Wednesday?"

"Hamburgers on the Foreman grill and curly fries like at Arby's. Warmer weather here, I take him to Dairy Queen for a Blizzard after."

"You have a curly fry machine?"

"It slices them curly. They fry up like any other potato."

"Would you be willing to lend it out for a day or two later in the summer? My mother will shit to be able to make curly fries for my nieces when they come in from Colorado." Held up a finger to forestall whatever West had to say. "I believe we can even arrange for some homemade ice cream to find its way here. So considerations flow both ways."

"I see. Make it all legal and shit."

"I am a cop, you know. Legal's big with me."

"Deal." West waited for Doc to have a mouthful of cheese, said, "What you want to do about Wilver?"

"You keep an eye on David." Doc flipped a strand from his chin into his mouth. "I'll take care of Wilver."

14

Wilver Faison had learned to appreciate irony, three weeks shy of his eighteenth birthday. Pookie Haynesworth explaining a personnel problem to him, how JaJuan Leonard always late for work and shit if he show up at all. A year ago this could have been Cootie Highsmith complaining about Wilver. Now Wilver made the decisions.

"Tell JaJuan, he want to be a lookout all his life, keep doing what he doing. He want to make some money, he need to show he serious. Get his mind in the game." Wilver saw Pookie debating another question. "What?"

"Well, it's just...JaJuan, he been my boy since like forever. Be hard for me to come down on him like that, know what I'm saying? Think you could talk to him?"

"You might need to do a little stepping up your own self, yo." Pookie's face fell. "You don't gots to lean on him or nothing." Wilver aware of the changes in his speech since he started hanging more with his crew and less with Jefferson West and not at all with school. His boys acting like he not black enough to run the crew till he settled into their patter. "Think about it, you doing him a favor. He want to be a player in the game, he need to step up. He don't want to step up—don't think he have it in him—then maybe the game not the place for him. Nothing wrong with that. What we do here not for everybody. Better he find out sooner than later."

Pookie said, "Yeah, he might not be hard enough for this here," and Wilver almost laughed in his face. Almost. Not many days passed Wilver didn't wonder if he had the heart for this, and Pookie deferred to him at every opportunity. How Wilver became the top of the Penns River drug pyramid, filling the vacuum after the entire management team got offed at Resurrection Mall last winter. Pookie kept things together until Wilver showed interest. He got things running so smooth and quick, crews didn't know any better wondered if this boy some kind of criminal prodigy, the people who did know better lying dead in the food court.

"You got anything else for me?" Wilver said. "I been running all day and I'd like to spend some quality time with Xbox before I go to bed."

Another delay from Pookie. "Yeah, one thing. I maybe should've brought it up before, but you been busy and I wanted to be sure."

"I'm still busy, but if you're sure, let's hear it. If not, roll."

The inevitable delay, then, "I think someone else be selling in town."

"You think, or you know?"

"I know."

"How you know?"

"I walked over and checked it out."

That impressed Wilver, Pookie taking the initiative. "What'd you see?"

"You know the apartments over on Main Street, parking in back by Sixth Avenue?"

"You mean by the Sheetz?"

"The Sheetz? No, man, that way the fuck by Seventh Street, on Constitution. *And* it ain't even no Sheetz no more. Valero took it over. This farther down...past Fourth Street, I think."

"Yeah, by the new Sheetz. Up the street from that thousand beers place."

Pookie drew maps in his head. "Yeah...I guess that is a Sheetz now. Up the block a little."

"They selling right in the lobby?"

"Naw, mostly on the Sixth Avenue corners. I talked to a couple a the fiends there I recognized. Told me this other crew's selling a better product, and they has it more often than we do."

"You talk to anyone selling it?"

"Tried." Wilver made it clear he expected more. "Walk up to him all friendly like, nigger told me, I wasn't buying, step the fuck off. So I did. Didn't see no reason to go provoking and shit till I had a chance to talk to you about it, see what you wanted."

Wilver considered options. "You say you recognized some of our customers?"

"Beanpole Vernon and that bitch he hang with. You know her, Yolanda or something."

Wilver knew them both. "This new crew costing us money, taking our customers away."

"You want me to take Smooth and Slick and give them fiends a beatdown, let them know they buy from us only?"

"Won't do no good. Dedicated fiend happy to take a beatdown for better dope. Cost of doing business, to him. It's the hoppers we need to deal with."

"What you mean, 'deal with?'"

"Beanpole Vernon told you this new crew got better dope and a better supply? Maybe we needs to work with him. Improve our situation."

"What, you mean don't buy from Ike the Barber no more? Ike ain't like that much, losing our business like that. Could roll on us, you know?"

"Yeah, well, this other guy got better drugs, maybe he got better protection, too. Shit Ike's been sending us been stepped on so many times it's got footprints. This a capitalist country. We got a right to make a better deal, if one's out there."

"Still, Ike ain't take kindly to something like that. No way we can stand up to him."

"Pookie, people calls him Ike the Barber for a reason. He a barber. Ever hear anyone call him like, Ike the Assassin, or Ike the Mass Murderer? No. You know why? 'Cause he a fucking barber. He cuts hair, not throats. You acting like he some kinda Keyser Soze evil genius motherfucker. You afraid of a fucking barber?"

"No, man, don't get the wrong idea. I ain't afraid, like in pissing my pants scared. It's just like...I'm cautious, know what I mean? We could get ourselves caught in between. What if this new shotcaller don't want to throw in with us? And then Ike hear we looking around for this capitalist shit you talking about? Then maybe we ends up with no place to go and can't stay where we at. Then what?"

Pookie had a point. One thing Wilver had learned in his brief time in the drug business: it was unstable by nature. New people came in, territory got rearranged, opportunities presented themselves. People who missed opportunities ended up out of business. Just out of the drug business, if they were lucky.

"You not wrong, Pookie. See what else you can find out. Don't give too much away. Talk to the fiends. They make it their business to know how things work. We find out some more, we have a better idea of what to do."

15

Sal Lucatorre said it off-hand, like mentioning a Yankees pitcher threw a shutout the night before. "I hear they grabbed one of the crews in Baltimore picking up their shipment."

Tino DeFelice shot a quick look at Jimmy Valente, turned back to Sal. "Not the whole crew. Just the two guys come to make the pickup."

"Either of you two cocksuckers plan on telling *me* anytime soon? Or do I have to keep getting my news from the knock-around guys brought the calzones?"

Someone looking to get knocked around, Tino learned who talked out of school. Sal the official head of what had been the Lucchese crime family, back in the day. Time was, Tommy "Three-Finger Brown" Lucchese ran the best organized crime operation in New York. He owned the Garment District, ran the Teamsters and trade associations, and took care of the rackets at Idlewild Airport. Lucchese was the anti-Gotti, never in the spotlight, always looked out for his people.

Now they had Sal. Got the job more because the captains thought him least likely to turn on them if he got jammed up. How bad things had become, rank-and-file worried if the boss would dime *them*. Sal's trustworthiness due less to loyalty than to a lack of vision combined with stubbornness: he'd figure he could beat any charge, until he woke up in Marion one morning, the window to make a deal nailed shut.

Sal had gout. Painful, yes. Treatable, also yes, not the way Sal chose to handle it. Go to a doctor, take some pills, cut back on the booze; this, too, would pass. Sal prided himself on never having been to a doctor since his mother used to take him.

Drank more when he hurt, which aggravated the gout, which drove Sal to painkillers on top of the booze. Now Tino felt his stomach tighten every time Sal showed any trace of a limp, knowing the boss might not be lucid by dinnertime.

Today not a good day, Sal's stocking feet on the footrest. "I thought this was supposed to be foolproof. No way the cops could find a shipment, since we don't even know ourselves exactly where they're going. Told me it was so secure, it was worth a little irregularity in delivery." Slammed a fist onto an end table. Liquor sloshed over the side of a highball glass. "Costs me money every time we do it, because the niggers worry will it get there on time, so we cut them a break."

"We're looking into it, Sal. Really. Might be as simple as someone on that end getting tailed. Could be any one of a lot of random shit, never happen again in a hundred years."

"You guaranteeing me a hundred years?"

"No, Sal, it's a figure of speech. Like saying the odds are a thousand to one."

"So you don't know when someone might fuck up again? For sure?"

"No. I can't say for sure."

"Then shut the fuck up, you stupid fuck. Costs me money every time you get one of your brilliant ideas. Jimmy, give me a Percocet."

Jimmy looked to Tino. "It's only been like two hours."

"He's a fucking doctor now?" Sal threw a small bowl of nuts at Jimmy. "You think he knows when I hurt? How much? My feet hurt, my ankles hurt, my knees hurt. I got a headache feels like my head's in a fucking vice. He can't even get a package delivered without the feds knowing all about it. Might as well call them himself."

"It wasn't feds, Sal," Tino said. "It was local. That's why we think someone on that end might've been tailed. Maybe even for something else. The cops just got lucky."

"Maybe I'll get lucky, too, and someone will give me a *fuck-*

ing pill!" Jimmy looked again to Tino, who made a resigned gesture. Jimmy gave Sal the pill. "Cocksuckers. Both of you. Get me a drink of water, too. I'm dying of thirst here."

Tino nodded and Jimmy brought a bottle of water from the refrigerator. Sal guzzled half, looked uncomfortable. Put his feet on the floor, leaned over at the waist, hand to his midsection. When it passed, he snuggled himself into the recliner, the bottle of water cradled between his thigh and the armrest. His eyes drooped.

Jimmy took Tino by the elbow, steered him to a corner of the room. Both of them watching Sal. Jimmy said, "I got something you need to know," so soft Tino almost missed it, standing next to him.

"Just for me?" Jimmy nodded. "Hold on. He'll be out in two minutes." They made small talk for five, then Tino said, "Okay. What did you want to tell me?"

"You know that task force they got? Feds, NYPD, state police. Some Jersey guys?"

"Yeah, I know it. They cram their heads up my ass a little farther every day."

"Well, you know we got a guy on the inside, right? The Jew? Rosen? Worked Manhattan North when Jimmy Two-Tone got busted? Helped us out there?" Jimmy Two-Tone got his name when someone noticed the distinctive coloration of his penis, coming out of the shower after a *shvitz.*

"What about him?"

"Rosen says they know how the drugs get to Baltimore."

"You mean it *was* feds?"

Jimmy glanced toward Sal. "He didn't say they knew about that one in particular. But...Rosen says they share information with Baltimore and DC. If someone tipped them to the rental trucks, they could be sitting on the locations for when the trucks come in."

"I thought they don't know where the truck gets turned in. The guy rents it can drop it anywhere."

"That's right, but there's only so many locations close enough to make sense. Even if they can't cover them all, they pick a few and hope they get lucky. Or they tail a crew if they know one's due. He doesn't know how they do it. Like I said, he don't know for sure if this had anything to do with what happened down there yesterday. Still..."

"Fuck me." Tino sneaked a peek at Sal sleeping in his chair. "We gotta change it up."

"How?" Both of them looking at Sal now, see if he woke up. "You mean find a whole new way to do it?"

"Probably, but not right away. We're gonna change, we need to come up with something better or we're just jerking off. Tell them...tell them to send the next load farther out. Remember the time we decided to drive to Louisville for the Derby? There's a town out there, where 70 and 81 cross."

"Yeah, Hagersburg. Or Hagersville. Something like that."

Tino snapped his fingers. "Hagerstown. Out that way if they have to. Farther, even. Someplace the cops won't think to look."

"Them spooks ain't gonna like that, driving so far."

"Ask them how they like not getting their shipments. The bust was on their end. They have to make adjustments, too." Another look at Sal, snoring now. How many problems would Tino solve by pinching that *mezza morta* cocksucker's nose shut, put everyone out of his misery? Start a war, what it would do. "Have a seat. He'll be out a couple hours, the cocktail he just took. You want a drink?"

Jimmy did, so Tino had him get two beers from Sal's refrigerator. They sat, touched bottles, took a drink. Tino said, "How you figure the feds got wise to the rental trucks?"

"We don't know that they did, Tino. That's what I been trying to tell you. This could all be a coincidence."

"*This* could. Not all."

"What do you mean, 'not all?'"

"Feds have been crawling over us like ants for, what? Six months now?"

"About that. Yeah."

"Why? Read the papers, talk to just about anyone, they still got their panties in a knot about that counterterrorism shit. Why move on us? We had nothing major going on. No bodies were being dropped. Why shift gears?"

"There was that guy they found over in Staten Island around then."

"We got nothing going on over there. If that was it, they'd be busting Rudy G's balls, not ours."

"Do we know they're not busting Rudy's balls?"

"You ever known him not to complain if the temperature around him went up even one degree?"

"Maybe he don't know."

"This is Rudy we're talking about." A sip of beer. "He's a whiner, but he knows his business."

Jimmy nodded. Tino said, "It's us. So what happened a little over six months ago? Maybe a year, even more. It takes the feds a while to turn that aircraft carrier." They drank and thought. "Anything?"

"No," Jimmy said. "No idea."

Tino thought how to say it, decided to blurt it out. "Mike Mannarino."

Jimmy's jaw dropped open. "No, not Mikey. He's solid."

"Maybe. What was it, a year and a half or so? We met him in the Poconos. He had Russian trouble. We didn't help him."

"He took care of that himself, never missed a payment." Jimmy pointed his bottle at Tino. "Does more business with us now than he did before."

"Go back to 'he took care of it himself.' Maybe he figures, we didn't step up, he don't need us anymore."

"Then why'd he up his dope order?"

Tino tapped his temple with a forefinger. "He's smart. Mikey. He was right that day, you know. Kicked up, all those years, and the one time he needed help, he didn't get it. We told him to cut the best deal he could." Tapped his head again. "So

Mikey, he figures, what's he paying for? What's his end? He settled the Russian problem himself, why's he need us at all? I was Mikey, the only thing keep me from coming our way is there's too many of us and not enough of him. Think about it. We told him to be that Russian's bitch. How would that make you feel?"

Jimmy's answer not as sure as before. "I guess I wouldn't like it. But, still...come after us? How? Like you said, there's too many. What's he got? Three made guys, counting him?"

"Two. Carlo Stellino died a couple months ago."

"That's not enough to do anything."

Tino tapped his temple again. Jimmy's eyes got big. "You think he's in with another outfit? Chicago wouldn't fuck with us over something like this. Even if they would, there's no sign. No one's hurt. No business is stolen."

Tino kept tapping and Jimmy kept watching until his eyes got even bigger and his mouth fell open half an inch. "Jesus Christ, Tino. Are you telling me Mike Mannarino flipped?"

Tino stopped tapping. "If he wanted even, who else has the juice and the manpower to hurt us?"

"I know, but—his bloodlines go way back. He's a Mannarino, for Chrissake."

"His *name's* Mannarino. He's not *a* Mannarino. There's no more Mannarino blood in him than you or me."

"I thought Kelly was his great-uncle or grandfather or something."

"He *told* you Kelly was his great-uncle. That's bullshit. Makes a nice story when he wants some instant cred."

"There's gotta be some connection. I mean, his name *is* Mannarino."

"Everyone in New York named Valente related to you?"

"Well, no, but Valente's kind of a common name. Pittsburgh's not that big a town."

"You know how many Mannarinos there are in Western Pennsylvania? Almost a hundred. And that's just the ones with their names in the phone book."

"You been looking into this."

"Fucking A I have. You ever hear of Occam's Razor?"

Jimmy confused for real now. "What the fuck's shaving got to do with this?"

"Occam's Razor is a scientific theory. This guy, Occam something, said any time you have to figure a thing out, start with the simplest explanation first."

"What's a razor got to do with that?"

"I don't know. It's some science or logic term. Doesn't matter. The point I'm making, Mike flipping is the simplest explanation for everything that's been going on. Unless you can think of something simpler."

Jimmy tried, couldn't do it. "Jeez, Tino, how likely is it Mike flipped? After all this time?"

"Fuck likely. Can you think of anything simpler?"

Jimmy tried three times to say something, talked himself out of all three before a word got spoken. "You really think it's Mike?"

Tino finished his beer, sat back in the chair. "No. Not really." Jimmy showed exasperation, hands open toward Tino. "But we gotta be sure."

"How?"

"That cop of ours. Rosen. He has access to the task force files, right?"

"Not to the CI files."

"Doesn't matter. Next time you talk to Mike, I want you to plant something with him. I don't know what yet. Something that won't hurt us, but any rat would feel like he has to pass along. Then you tell Rosen to keep an ear open for it. Make sure no one but Mike knows what it is, so if Rosen hears anything about it, at all, he'll know where it came from."

"And if he does?"

Tino shrugged. "It's not like we never dealt with a problem like that before."

16

Mike Mannarino's day went into the shitter the second he saw Ben Dougherty walk through the door of Bypass Motors. Mike's days tended to circle the bowl of late. With luck, they stayed near the rim. An appearance from Dougherty almost guaranteed a trip into the siphon.

"What do you want?" Mike said before Dougherty had a chance to knock on the half-open door.

"Mike, I'm entitled to a little more appreciation after all I've done for you." Dougherty's shit-eating grin showed his day was complete. He lived to piss on Mike's Wheaties.

"The one courtesy you've ever done me was to try to turn me into a snitch. I'm supposed to be grateful for that?"

"I was only looking out for your welfare." The grin still pasted on Dougherty's face. "And I did all I could to sneak you into the station when Harriger made me arrest you."

"So you say. What you did was drive me to hell and back giving me a sales pitch. Every TV camera in three states was still there when you took me in."

"It's the thought that counts." Dougherty looked around the office. "You seem stressed. You getting enough exercise? Let's take a little walk."

"You arresting me?"

Dougherty put on a hurt look. "Mike, please. You know I wouldn't jerk you around like that. I came to arrest you, I'd of told you already. I just want to talk, and it's a nice day. Let's get some fresh air."

"Fresh air."

"We can walk around the lot, let you survey the legal portion of your domain. Is this month's novelty car a Maserati?" Bypass Motors displayed one car each month no one in Penns River could afford if they sold their house and both kidneys. Mike touted them as draws, get people in to gawk, sell them something else. The fact they served as nice covers for occasional out-of-town visitors who might have no other reason to come to Penns River helped, if any branch of law enforcement got nosey enough to look.

Mike knew Dougherty would continue with what he considered entertaining banter until he got what he wanted. Slid shut the drawer of his desk and stood. "This is harassment, you know. You're in here two-three times a year pulling this bullshit."

"You sure you don't want to lock that? Criminals are everywhere."

Mike made a show of locking the drawer, then leaving the key in plain view on the desk. He did lock the office on the way out. Walking down the hall, Dougherty said, "That harassment talk hurts my feelings, you know. You're a leading member of the community. Bypass sponsors a Little League team, has ads in all the football programs, the high school yearbook, the fences down the softball complex, pays for the Memorial Day parade—sorry. You used to do that. I guess the casino takes care of that now." Snapped his fingers. "You still handle the Christmas decorations, though. I know how much you pay in property taxes. Strictly speaking, I'm your employee. I just want to make sure you're getting what you pay for."

"Here, employee." Mike stopped at the Maserati, opened the driver's door. "Slam this on your dick."

Dougherty sighed. "Sorry to disappoint you, but I'm Irish. Not enough to work with."

Outside, Mike said, "Okay, now we're walking in the fresh air. What do you want?"

"What do you know about heroin sales in the old downtown? Near where the tracks cross Fourth Avenue."

"You know I don't sell that shit, and I sure as hell wouldn't sell it here even if I did."

"No argument from me. But you hear things. What do you hear about what's going on down there?"

An alarm went off in Mike's head. *He knows.* "What are you talking about, 'what do I hear?' What kind of bullshit is that?"

"All right," Dougherty said. "Enough screwing around. I brought you out here in case the feds have your office wired, so we can speak freely. Both of us."

"You telling me my office is wired?"

"I'm telling you they've tried, and they'll try again. You've done a nice job keeping it clean, so a warrant's been hard to get. Far as I know. I want to talk to you off the record."

"About drugs." Still walking, engaged in a casual conversation to anyone who looked at them. "A cop wants to talk to me about drug sales, and it's off the record."

"Special circumstances." Dougherty went quiet. Mike denied him the victory of asking. Dougherty said, "As many things as I can find to dislike about you, I know you love your family. Your kids. In your way, you do a lot of good here. I know you've done what you could in the past to keep drug sales out of the River."

Mike let him talk. Dougherty was right, which didn't mean any form of admission wouldn't result in jail time.

"I know a black kid, lives down the Estates. Him and his brother's had a tough time. Mom's a junkie, Dad's in jail down south. Tennessee or somewhere. Good kid, basically, but I think he's going wrong. I want to catch him before he goes so far down the road his only options are a cell or a box."

"And you want what from me?"

"Level with me, just the two of us, out here on a pretty day. You want me to strip down to prove I'm not wearing a wire, I'll do it. Are you supplying to him?"

"He's selling here, in Penns River?"

"Yeah."

Mike stopped, took a tissue from his pocket, wiped bird shit from the trunk of a Pontiac. "What's this kid to you?"

"Remember the murder in that vacant a couple years ago? We liked a guy from Youngstown for it, but he turned up dead on the steps of Bachelors' Club before we could make the case."

"I read about it."

"This kid and his little brother were the witnesses. I kept them under wraps when I should have turned them into Family Services and it almost went bad. I owe them."

Mike made it his business to know about people who could hurt him. Dougherty could be—was—a self-righteous prick. By all impartial accounts, he had a genuine love for Penns River and a reputation for extreme loyalty to people he cared about. He lived to bust Mike's balls, yet on the few occasions he'd made assurances, he'd been as good as his word, even when it cost him. "I'll say this much: *if* I were selling drugs, it wouldn't be to anyone selling here."

"Are you sure you'd know? No offense, but things got disrupted when those Russians came to town and during that clusterfuck at Res Mall."

"What are you asking here? You want a favor? You want me to run this kid out of town for you? Every time you come out here you're swinging your dick, 'you can't touch me, I'm a cop,' until you want something. Then you're a bigger tease than a cheerleader talking to a fat kid with a nice car."

Dougherty stopped. Looked as if he might turn to face Mike, then continued walking, slower. "You want me to spell it out? If you're supplying someone who might be wholesaling to Wilver Faison, I want you to ask the wholesaler to cut him off. Don't hurt him. Just cut him off. Get him out of the business. Whatever else happens..." He trailed off. "I'm not asking you to clean up Penns River's drug trade. That's my job. I'm asking you to put one kid out of business."

"Assuming I know anything about, and have any control over, whoever gets him his stuff."

"If you don't, you don't. I'm taking a special interest in this kid. If you can help, I'd appreciate it."

At the farthest point of the lot, circling back. "What's my end?" Mike said.

Dougherty closed his eyes for a step, wagged his head. "I should've figured. There's no quid pro quo to be offered here. Do it or don't. Knowing how you feel about family, I thought you might want to."

"He's no family to me. He's some kid I never laid eyes on."

"Never mind. I shouldn't of brought it up." Dougherty quickened his pace.

"Slow down or you'll break that stick off in your ass." Dougherty waited for Mike to draw even. "I didn't say I wouldn't do it."

"I gotta kiss ass first? That it?"

"Not the way you mean. Let's say I can cut the kid off. What's he do for money?"

"Something other than selling drugs."

"Like? Roll junkies? Mug retirees? Not a lot of straight opportunities down around the Estates."

Several silent steps before Dougherty spoke. "You know how drug dealers end up. It's only a matter of time before someone from out of town decides to add Penns River to their empire. Then the kid either has to roll over or get put down."

"So he ends up a hopper instead of the boss. Not a lot else to do down there."

Mike recognized the expression that flickered across Dougherty's face. "Things go bad, a hopper might take a beating. Shot callers take bullets."

Mike had no counterargument. "If I can get the kid...disengaged. Then what? Not like you have to kiss my ass, but, you ask someone for a favor—a substantial favor—you don't come empty handed."

A few more steps. "I'd be willing to overlook some youthful indiscretions. Your oldest. Vincent. He's developing a reputation."

"Kids talk. A lot of it's jealousy, because of who I am."

"Some, sure. Maybe a lot. Still, I have it on good authority he likes to throw his weight around. The other kids don't call him on it—also because of who you are, I imagine—and he's been upping the ante. I hear he's a smart kid with a future outside the family business. He's gonna fuck it up, he's not careful."

"What are you saying?"

"A lot of things can be handled unofficially. Property damage, you can take care of. He gets out of line so someone calls us, I'll set you wise and let you deal with it off the books. No one can get hurt, though. And he better not put his hands anywhere on a girl who didn't volunteer. He's mine then."

"He puts his hands on a girl and I find out, you'll be the least of his worries." They walked speechless a minute. Twenty feet from the showroom door, Mike said, "I'll see what I can do."

17

Teresa Shimp not sure how to feel when she knocked on Vicki Leydig's door. Nice to know Dougherty trusted her to handle the re-interview of their prime witness solo. Also aware she had no body of work to fall back on if she botched the job. He'd put it to her as a favor, cover it for him so no one—even him—could think he'd talked Vicki out of anything, having staked his reputation on letting Virdon go. Recommended she go alone—not an order, she didn't work for him—Grabek would've tried to take over, and Neuschwander wasn't much good with interviews.

Now she sat in Vicki's living room, the two of them on opposite sides of a small coffee table. "Ms. Leydig, understand a second interview is routine. Sometimes even more than two. People think of things they didn't mention before, or remember them differently. We get new information and need to double back sometimes. Thank you in advance for your patience and cooperation."

"Where's the other detective? The one who talked to me that night?"

"Detective Dougherty is working on something else right now."

"Does he send you for a woman's perspective?"

"No, I don't think so." Teresa thought about it again, agreed with herself. "I happen to be the one who's working this case with him. Now, if we could go through what happened that night."

They went back and forth about Vicky and Mary Zelesko meeting up with Doug Stirnweiss at the casino. Watching him play blackjack. The conversation with Bob Virdon.

"Tell me what Doug and Virdon talked about."

"Mostly it was that horrible tattoo on the other guy's hand." Vicki hadn't referred to Virdon by name once. "Doug was really giving him a hard time and the guy starting talking back."

"Did either of them seem to be angry?"

"I don't know if angry's the word I'd use."

"Pick a word you like better. What's important is for me to get your impressions."

Vicki looked for the words over Teresa's left shoulder. "Pissed off, maybe? No, that's not right, either. At least not Doug. He didn't seem mad, more like he was egging the other guy on."

"What about the other guy? Virdon."

"He seemed more pissed off."

"Did he raise his voice?"

Thought, then, "Not really."

"Could you see his face?"

"Yes. Doug kind of had his back to us, but we could see the other guy real well."

"Did he look...pissed off? You know, red in the face? Maybe the veins in his neck standing out?"

"Well, he did..." Vicki took time. Teresa felt for her, trying hard to remember an evening all she wanted to do was forget. "It was the things he said. He didn't look all that mad, or... sound it, if you mean like raising his voice. But, my God, how could you say some of what he said and not be mad?"

"Did it bother Doug to be talked to like that?"

"One was as bad as the other, talking about mothers and sisters. I was worried they might start punching each other."

Teresa flipped back a few pages in her notes. "Did the dealer seem concerned about them?"

"He was too busy trying to look down Mary's blouse. They could've robbed him and he might not have noticed."

Teresa lacked detailed experience with casinos, still doubted a professional dealer would be that inattentive, even in a grind joint like the Allegheny. "So he never asked them to tone it down or anything?"

"I don't think so."

"Did anyone else from the casino pay any attention to them?"

"Not that I noticed."

Teresa flipped back farther, more to look like she was checking something than to do it. "How have you been since this happened? Are you sleeping all right? Normal appetite?"

"Not bad. I don't sleep great anyway. I guess I wake up easier than usual the last few nights. Like if a car door slams. I took a couple of those Z-Quils. That helped."

"Are you eating?"

"Not a lot, but it's not like I'm skipping meals. I don't eat as much in the warm weather, anyway. Why are you asking?"

"No real reason. I know this is hard—I can't imagine *how* hard—I'm a cop and I've never seen anyone actually get shot. I don't want to push you any more on this than I have to."

"I'm okay. There is one thing...no. It's not a big deal."

"What is it?"

Vicki needed a few seconds to talk herself into it. "I work in Vandergrift, so I take Leechburg Road up to the Rite-Aid and catch the bypass. Today I drove all the way back to Craigdell Road to get on the bypass down by the hockey rink. I don't even want to drive past the casino no more."

"I don't blame you. I think I forgot to thank you for coming home to talk to me."

"My boss told me to take the rest of the week off. He's a nice guy, says to take it easy, everyone will cover for me. They're real nice there."

"It sounds like it. Do you have any siblings?"

"Two sisters. Why?"

"No brothers."

"Just Kathy and Monica. Why does that matter?"

"It doesn't. I'm making conversation. Talking with a cop is

hard, and talking with a cop about something like this has to be ten times harder. I'm lightening the mood, is all." Note flipping. "Now the part we can't avoid. Did you see the shooter's face, either during, right before, or right after he shot Doug?"

"No. All's I seen was that tattoo and what I thought was a belt buckle."

"What you thought was a belt buckle?"

"Yeah. Turns out it must've been the whaddayacallit, the cylinder. On the gun, you know?"

Teresa made a note. "Could Doug see the shooter's face?"

"I think so. He looked up and didn't twist his head around like he couldn't see."

"Did he recognize the man who shot him?"

"He didn't seem to..." Vicki paled as her voice tapered away.

"I'm going to tell you something, and I want to be sure you understand I believe everything you've told me today. I'm not questioning or asking you to change a thing."

"What is it?" All the color had disappeared from Vicki's face.

"Did you know that Doug Stirnweiss and Bob Virdon had played blackjack together at the casino before? We verified it with casino employees and surveillance videos."

"Doug knew him?"

"According to the dealer, what you heard was how they usually got along. No offense meant either way. Men talk to each other like that sometimes."

"Then Doug should've recognized him. Later, in the car."

"Maybe. The light wasn't great."

"It wasn't that dark." Vicki stared straight ahead, watching events replay on a screen only she saw. "What was on his hand. Like a smudge, kind of how that tattoo looked. It was a...a scar, maybe."

"Are you sure?"

"It *was* a scar. Oh my God, I told you the wrong guy. I saw his hand, how it was darker there." Vicki crying now. Guilt contorted her face and voice. "It wasn't the tattoo after all. Oh,

Jesus, it wasn't that guy in the casino, that Virdon. I ruined that poor guy's life."

"No," Teresa said. "It's okay. Some other things didn't check out. That's one of the reasons I came back. To be sure."

"But I was *wrong*. I might've picked him out in court, I was so sure. He could've gone to jail because of me and he didn't do anything."

Teresa stepped around the coffee table, sat next to Vicki on the couch. Put an arm around her shoulders. "It's all right. We would never have put him on trial with nothing more than your statement. Witnesses make mistakes all the time. It was dark, you weren't really paying attention till after it was over, you had some drinks, you were scared. I'm a cop, they train us to notice things, and I doubt I would've gotten everything right."

The crying over, Vicki sat with hunched shoulders, elbows on her thighs, a smaller woman than half an hour ago. "But still...I was so sure. What could've happened to him?"

"Nothing. Really."

"Nothing?"

"Not if we do our jobs. We searched his house and car. No gun, no bloody clothes. He stopped for ice cream on the way home and was recognized. He was probably at Wendy's, or on his way out, when it happened. The parking lot cameras show what looks like his car turning onto Leechburg Road a couple of minutes before the three of you left the casino. It wasn't him."

"What if he didn't stop for ice cream? Or if the camera didn't see his car? Of if you found a gun?"

"If he hadn't stopped for ice cream, or if the camera hadn't shown what looks like him leaving too early, we would've had to keep looking. If we'd found a gun, we'd still have to match it to the bullet that killed Doug before it would mean anything."

"But what if it did?"

Teresa re-positioned herself to look Vicki in the eye. "Then he did it. It doesn't matter if the witness who put us onto the right suspect made a mistake. If the evidence shows he did it, he did it. Finding a gun would be no big deal. Anyone can own a gun. If we'd found *the* gun...well, he would've had to explain why he had the murder weapon if he wasn't the shooter."

Vicki made eye contact at last. "So it didn't matter?" Almost sounded disappointed.

"It mattered. It added some urgency to things we would've had to check out sooner or later. But no harm done."

Teresa left, having confirmed two things. Bob Virdon didn't kill Doug Stirnweiss, and the only thing scarier than being eyewitness to a violent felony would be sitting in the defendant's chair when that witness testified.

18

"So." Stush folded his hands across his belly. "Back to Page One."

"Not quite," Doc said. "We would've had to check Virdon out sooner or later, as much time as he spent with Stirnweiss that night."

"What do we have?"

"Neuschwander looked at all the videos. People come, people go. The scene's near the edge of the lot, so we don't have video of all approaches."

"Why'd she park so far away from the doors?" Teresa Shimp said.

Doc knew. "Brand new car. Still has the smell. What I heard, she treated it like an egg. Probably more worried about a stray door dinging her than having it stolen, what with all the cameras they have there. Or, she thought were there."

Stush jerked his fist a few times. "Rance Doocy and I will talk about that later today. It's not going to go well for him." Leaned back, the leather chair creaking in welcome. "Shooter walked right up to Stirnweiss. No one thought twice about it. Did he know him?"

"I wish he had," Doc said. "Shrink the suspect pool. I doubt it, though."

"Explain why we both think so. Wait. Teresa, what do you think?"

"I'm with Doc. They didn't know each other."

"Okay. Explain why we're all so sure."

Doc read his notes. "Both witnesses agree the only thing the shooter said was to ask whose car it was. No hello, how you doing, where the hell you been lately. Just, 'Whose car is this?'

and *bam*!"

"Vicki Leydig told me Doug didn't appear to recognize the guy, either," Teresa said.

Stush kept at it. "Would the shooter say hello, make sure the guy he was about to kill recognized him? Maybe say his name in front of witnesses?"

"Why would an acquaintance shoot him?" Doc said.

"Why would a stranger?"

"Are we sure the shooter meant to kill him?" Teresa got it in quick, trying to sense the rhythm.

"Forty-four at that range, it's a logical assumption," Doc said.

"Then why not finish the job? Doug was alive when he left."

"Maybe he got scared. Someone never killed anyone before, might not have been like he expected."

"Someone afraid of being recognized might also be afraid of sticking around."

The cops thought for a full minute before Doc spoke up. "I thought we all agreed they probably didn't know each other. Why are we even having this discussion?"

"I know why I am," Stush said. "What about you?"

"Why are you having it?"

"I'm the chief. You first."

Doc ran a hand across his face and through his hair, left it to rest at the back of his head. "I hate to say it, but I want it to be someone he knows. Knew." A small smile from Stush. "And so do you."

"Guilty. But we have to assume he didn't know him."

Teresa looked half a step behind to Doc, the new kid on her first day inside the clubhouse. "This is how we work," he said. "We both know what has to happen, now that Virdon's clear, and neither one of us wants to go there. So we'll mess around for a few minutes, then we'll do what has to be done."

"Which is?"

Doc nodded in Stush's direction. "You're the chief. You tell her."

"We have to interview all the casino employees. Not just the ones who worked that night, but all of them, to see if they knew Doug Stirnweiss. Then we need to find every customer who was there that night. Credit card receipts will help, but we may have to get the employees to look at tapes, too. They all need to be talked to. Benny, that's your job." Doc nodded.

Stush turned to Teresa. "You get to interview the family and friends. I know, it's a shitty job, and I'm sorry. It has to be done. You did well with Vicki Leydig. I think we're better off with Benny working the casino side, and you building the known associates a circle at a time. Neuschwander can keep tabs on the evidence reports. You two talk often as you can and update me at close of business every day. We get a hit on a KA who was at the casino that night, we zero in until he's removed as a suspect. Questions?"

"What if the shooter didn't go into the casino?" Doc said. "Just waited for Doug outside?"

Stush rubbed a forefinger and thumb through his eyes, along his nose. "I'll burn that bridge when I get to it."

19

Sean Sisler and Katherine Burrows turned left onto Greensburg Road, headed for the Flats. Ulizio's day off, so she rode with Sisler, Snyder on her own.

"Why do they call it the Flats?" she said.

"Look around." Sisler gestured across the breadth of the windshield.

"I am. I don't think I could walk up that street," she pointed, "with my utility belt on. It looks like it's about a forty-five-degree slope."

"I mean right here. Where the road and these buildings are. This next few miles is the flattest stretch of road in Penns River. Except for what's built up, like downtown and that strip of Leechburg Road that runs from the station up to the bypass."

The radio interrupted. "PR-Six, what's your location?" Janine Schoepf, the dispatcher.

Kathy took the mike. "Going...east?" Sisler nodded. "On Greensburg Road. Just passed the Dairy Queen."

"We have a disturbance reported at Fat Jimmy's, 1425 Greenburg Road. Can you answer the call?"

Sisler nodded, mouthed "one minute." Kathy repeated it to Janine and signed off.

Calls to Fat Jimmy's were routine for Sisler, though he wondered who might be oiled up enough to fight at two in the afternoon. What he saw in the parking lot set him back. Not the man propped against the front left quarter panel of a truck, or the other applying what appeared to be a sleeper hold to the first. Sisler's amazement had to do with seeing Fat Jimmy himself standing outside the door. Only three feet away, to be sure, but Sisler had never seen Jimmy in natural light. He shut off the ignition. "Watch the crowd. This should be a milk run, but you never know around here."

Sisler slammed the door to announce his presence. The two principals gave no notice: one intent on his work, the other looked semi-conscious. Bystanders spread out to make room for Round Two.

Sisler stood so he didn't have to shout to be heard by the man applying the hold. "You're doing it wrong."

The man glanced over his shoulder. "Huh?" His subject sensed the break and made a token struggle.

"I said, you're doing it wrong. The hold. Your arm bar's in the wrong place. You'll never put him out like that. You could break his neck, though. That what you're after?"

The man relaxed and Sisler slid his baton between the elbow and the other man's neck. Spun around the assailant. "Aren't you Harley Hagenmeyer?"

"Yeah? So?"

"You're out on bail for stealing a bunch of city and county equipment, right?"

"Allegedly."

"You're allegedly out on bail?"

"I allegedly stole that shit. Nothing in my bail says I can't have a drink."

"The court takes a dim view of letting offenders strangle people while they're on borrowed time."

"I told you, goddamnit, alleged offender. Nothing proved."

"Sorry. Alleged offender. What's going on here?"

Hagenmeyer's opponent had recovered some wind, ready to launch into his description. Sisler showed him a hand. "Take a minute to make sure all the oxygen's back in your brain, sir. Let me hear what Harley has to say, then I'll give you plenty of time."

The guy gave a look and a gesture implying he'd hold Sisler to that, then put his hands on his thighs and sucked air. Sisler turned back to Hagenmeyer. "I'm all ears."

"This little runt," indicating the man rediscovering the art of breathing, "threatened to steal my truck here."

"Bullshit. I told him I was gonna *buy* his truck."

Sisler gave him the hand again. "What's your name, sir?"

"Art Bayless."

"Mr. Bayless, give me a minute here with Harley, and I promise you'll get all time you need." Bayless gave the same look as before, with less venom. "That true, Harley?"

"How come I'm Harley and that sawed-off cocksucker is Mr. Bayless?"

"Because you're the one I caught strangling him. Now, is what he said true?"

"Fuck no, it ain't true. Goddamn truck's not even for sale."

"It will be," Bayless said. "Soon as the county takes it."

"The county ain't taking my truck."

"Why would he think so?" Sisler said.

"That red-headed chick prosecutor said she was going to... seize anything I'd bought with money earned from those things I—she says I took. Like the new rims and my girlfriend's earrings."

"Good thing you didn't get her those tits yet," came from the onlookers, and Hagenmeyer pretended to try to break away. Sisler shifted his weight to make it look good.

"I just come out to take a look," Bayless said. "So's I know how much to bid."

"I'd drive the goddamn thing into the river before I'd let them sell it to you. And they're not taking the truck. Most they can get me for is the rims and those earrings. I had that truck way before I—before that stuff got stole."

Sisler released Hagenmeyer, poked his ribs with the baton. "Don't move." Turned toward Fat Jimmy, who showed signs of going inside. "Hey, Jimmy. What's your version of this?"

"I got no interest." Jimmy turned toward the door. "Settle it out here."

"Come on, Jimmy, work with me. One—or more—of your customers could be going to jail. Help me get it right."

"Harley's a jagov. Got about a dozen witnesses to that standing here. Bayless been egging him on about that truck the better part of an hour. How much he likes it, how it's gonna be his, knowing all the time it's the only thing Harley owns worth a shit. I was thinking about choking the little douchebag myself until he went outside for what he said was an inspection. Harley followed him out."

"Who called us?"

"Wasn't me." Looks and denials all around.

Sisler turned to the victim. "That right, Art? What Jimmy said? You been egging Harley on?"

"I been talking, is all. Asshole come out here and tried to choke me. Was choking me till you showed up."

Sisler lowered his voice, speaking only to Harley. "What about you, Harley? Jimmy's story about right?"

"Yeah. I shouldn't a grabbed him like I did. It's just, that truck's about all I have. They take that, I don't know what the hell I'll do. I'm touchy about it."

"I guess you would be," Sisler said, not without sympathy. "Absent a complainant, I'm willing to let this slide as a misunderstanding. Harley, he didn't do anything to your truck, and running your mouth isn't a chargeable offense. What about you, Art? You pressing charges?"

"Goddamn right. Son of a bitch was choking me, coulda broke my neck. You said so yourself."

"I only said that to get his attention. It would take a lot more pressure than Harley was applying to break your neck. Bear in mind, you press, he goes to jail, and not just overnight. This'll violate the conditions of his bail. He'll stay in till the trial. You good with that?"

Grumbling from the crowd. Harley Hagenmeyer had no admirers here—anywhere else, for that matter—the code said it was bygones time.

"You asked for it, Art."

"You never know when to let well enough alone, asshole."

"He should've just clocked you."

"All right! Fuck it! Let the bastard go." Bayless kicked dirt. "I'm the one gets choked and I'm the one has to find another place to drink. Somewhere safe."

"Jimmy's is safe," Sisler said. "Harley's going home, away from the temptation to do something that could get him locked up. Right, Harley?"

"Yeah. I guess." Harley looked in Art's direction. Spat in the gravel. "Fucking asshole."

"He owe you anything, Jimmy?" Sisler said.

"Fuck it. The floor show was worth the cost. Just get him out of here."

Sisler gestured toward the truck. Harley got in. Revved the engine, didn't kick up any gravel leaving.

In the patrol unit, still driving east, Burrows asked why Sisler played it the way he had, laid back so much.

"I thought about running up and cracking Harley across the back of the head with my baton, getting it over with."

"What changed your mind?"

"Things weren't out of hand. Our job's to calm the situation, not escalate it. We come in looking to kick ass and someone there decides Harley's getting a raw deal, we got a fight on our hands. Two against twelve? The balloon goes up, weapons may need to be drawn. Officer Needs Assistance call." Shook his head. "I don't want to have to explain that for a half-assed bar fight at two in the afternoon."

Passing the driver testing facility, Sisler said, "How'd you spend your time back there? While I was working?" Winked.

"Crowd control, like you told me. You didn't seem to need any help with Harley and Art."

"Had my back."

"You took the lead. I figured you'd let me know if you needed anything."

Sisler nodded, turned left on 380. "Okay, partner. Let me tell you the deal with Fat Jimmy's."

20

Rollison didn't like it. Committed now to full cooperation, he didn't have a lot of choices.

"I'll try not to be any more disruptive than I have to," Dougherty said. "Send people back to see me one at a time, somewhere out of sight. In a perfect world, I'd get their names and addresses and go to their homes, not bother you at all, but that's going to take too much time. Their jobs bring them to a central location. I need to take advantage of it."

"It makes sense, at least for those who are working while you're here."

"That's why I'm coming in across shifts. Catch the early crew on the second half of their day and the evening shift as they come in. If you get me a list of who was here that night, which shift they're on today, I'll take them in whatever order jacks you around the least."

"It'll take me half an hour, forty-five minutes to get the names of who worked that night and compare them to this week's schedule."

"I appreciate it." Rollison turned toward his office and Dougherty said, "There's one more thing."

Rollison stopped, turned his head to catch Dougherty in peripheral vision. "What?"

"We're going to need all the credit card receipts from that night."

"Why?"

"We're going to talk to everyone who might have seen Stirnweiss. Did he get into it with anyone."

"Just because he was killed here doesn't mean whatever got

him killed started here." Rollison still not turned toward Dougherty. "At least not that night."

"We have another cop trying to connect the dots from the other direction. Everyone who was here is still a potential witness. We have to clear them."

Rollison suspected before he volunteered full cooperation that at some point his definition and Dougherty's would vary. The problem, Dougherty did need to talk to the customers, and the credit card receipts were the best way to collect at least a partial attendance. Not the place to start drawing lines, though Rollison could see it from here. "I'll get one of the girls in the back working on a list while I pull the schedules."

"No offense, Da—shit. Which do you prefer? Dan or Daniel?"

"Dan's fine," Rollison said, though he could not remember the last time anyone other than that obsequious git Harriger had called him that.

"No offense, Dan, but a list of names isn't good enough. I need the actual receipts."

Rollison turned to face him, activated a glare that had intimidated men who killed for a living. "Why?"

Dougherty acknowledged the look, uncowed. "I really don't mean any offense. Your cooperation has been beyond anything I could've expected, even if we didn't have history. The thing is, I can't afford to work from an edited list."

"Why assume we'll turn over every receipt if you're afraid we'd hold back names?"

"Because I'm going to watch her pull them." Dougherty hurried on. "It's not you. It's Hecker and Doocy I'm worried about, having potentially embarrassing names left out."

Dougherty didn't lie well, as cops went. Given his history with the casino, he might well consider the previous cooperation a ruse in case such action was deemed necessary. Rollison could make him come back with a warrant, which would be no trouble to get. Dougherty would still have his list, and probably an attitude. This was not the hill to fight on. "Follow me."

"It wouldn't have to be an enemy, really. Someone he'd had a disagreement with recently. Maybe a friend or acquaintance things had gone wrong with."

Teresa Shimp hadn't expected Doug Stirnweiss to have had enemies his parents would know about. Everything she and Dougherty knew said Doug was easygoing with a quick sense of humor. A buddy. Someone his friends trusted.

"He was a grown man," Carl Stirnweiss said. "Not the age where we asked a lot of what he was doing, where he went, who he saw. It wasn't like we kept tabs on him."

"No, sir, I didn't mean it that way. When you talked, did he volunteer things about his life? How it was going? His work?"

"We weren't as close as we used to be." Patricia Stirnweiss shared the couch with her husband, Shimp in a wing chair across the coffee table. "He—we weren't as involved as before. With what he was doing."

"Were you estranged?"

Carl answered before Pat had a chance. "Nothing that serious. We got along. It was just more...superficial than things had been a few years ago."

"Any particular reason?"

"Is this necessary?" Pat said. "You're here to find who killed him, not to dig around our family business. Or so you said."

Shimp hadn't said a word about not digging around in family business. Not part of her original plan, still a legitimate topic if it led to anything relevant. "I'm not here to stir up painful memories. It's just, we have to ask about a lot of different subjects. Some little things he might have said, or you picked up on, might mean something in a different context. A name to check out, or a place. If it seems like I'm rambling, it's because I don't know in advance which questions are more important. I'm sorry to have to put you through this."

Neither Stirnweiss thought that merited a reply. "He was

divorced. How did he get along with his ex?"

"That was none of our business," Pat said.

"All right, I guess." Pat gave Carl a quick glance. "He loved his kids, did what he could to keep relations with Gretchen as friendly as possible. For their sake."

"Was Doug seeing anyone?" Neither knew. "What about Gretchen?"

"What difference does it make if Gretchen was seeing anyone?" Pat said. "It's not like Doug's suspected of doing anything to her or a boyfriend."

"Was Doug protective of Gretchen?"

"You mean, 'was he jealous?' don't you?"

Carl stepped in. "She's the mother of his children. He was protective of all of them."

"If Gretchen were seeing anyone, and Doug found out, would that bother him?"

"I think 'bother' is too strong a word. He'd be aware of it."

Shimp made a note, underlined "aware." Doodled to make it look like she'd written more than she had. "Why'd they break up?"

Carl and Pat exchanged looks. "That's pretty personal," he said. "Are you sure we have to go into that?"

"I understand, and I'm sorry." A pause for the air to calm. "Who left whom?"

"I'm not sure what you mean."

"Did Doug leave Gretchen, or did she leave him?"

"Well, look at it," Pat said. "She and the kids are still in the house. *He* left."

"Was it his idea, or did she ask him to go?"

"Doug never gave her any reason to ask him to go."

"Mrs. Stirnweiss, I apologize for asking these things. I can imagine how hard they must be. Please understand, I'm not asking just to tick a box off a checklist, or to make you uncomfortable. If Doug was asked to go and didn't want to, he may have been trying to get back in. If someone else was interested in

Gretchen, that person might have wanted Doug out of the picture. I know it's not likely and it sounds like the kind of thing you'd see in a bad TV movie, but it happens. We have to check."

"They just weren't happy anymore." Carl found something fascinating on the backs of his hands. "He never said more than that. I think they both agreed he should be the one to move, so she and the kids could stay in the house. It's the only place the kids have ever known to live."

"Was it true, what they say?" Pat said. "About there being two women in the car with him?"

"Yes, ma'am. They were friends of his, happened to bump into him at the casino that night. They both had a little much to drink. He was giving them a ride home."

"He'd do that," Carl said.

Doug Stirnweiss hadn't made much of an impression on the employees of Allegheny Casino. Some recognized him, coming in every couple-three weeks, seemed like a nice guy. Only two knew his name. One said, "So *he* was the guy got shot the other night."

Judy Abramowicz tended bar four to one, Tuesday through Saturday, the steadiest shift of any employee. Five-foot-ten, frosted blonde hair and ice blue eyes, high cheekbones. Worked the large bar closest to the gaming tables. Men preferred table games to slots, and Judy Abramowicz behind the most convenient bar had to be good for business all around.

Doc had been at it for three hours, nineteen interviews. Any potential to be entertained by proximity to who was, without doubt, the most attractive person in the casino had left him at least forty-five minutes ago.

"Ms. Abramowicz, do you recognize this man?" Handed her Doug's cropped DMV photo, showing wear at the edges.

"That's Doug Stirnweiss." Doc's hopes rose. "I saw him on the news." Doc's hopes fell.

"You ever see him in here?"

"A time or two. That's why I noticed him on TV. I knew the face, just never had a name to go with it."

"Ever talk with him?"

"No."

"See him talking with anyone else?"

"Well, yeah, but nothing that sticks out. He'd talk to dealers, customers, whoever was around. Seemed friendly enough."

"Ever hear anyone talk about him?"

"Not so it sticks in my mind. I know you're trying to get some idea of who might've wanted to shoot him, but he was just a guy. There's a hundred of them out there right now, just like him. Nice guys, no trouble. They come in once in a while and have a little fun. I don't want to sound like a bitch, but there's nothing memorable about them."

She did sound a little like a bitch, but she had a point. Doc handed her a business card. "Thanks for your time. Can you do me a favor and send..." scanned the list, "George Schaffer in?"

Judy would. Walked to the door—Doc not too tired to notice an ass with the rare combination of tightness *and* breadth—turned before she reached for the knob. "If I tell you something, can it stay just between us? No one else can ever know."

"Depends what it is. If you're about to tell me you saw who shot Doug Stirnweiss, then, no, almost certainly not. You're going to have to testify, at least in front of a grand jury."

Judy returned to the table. Doc gestured for her to sit. She rested her hands on the back of the chair, unsure, then swiveled around it and parked herself. "I could get fired for telling you this."

Doc said, "Then why are you telling me?" in a voice calculated to convey trust.

"There's a guy, drug dealer. He hangs around sometimes."

There didn't appear to be more. "Did you see him with Doug that night?"

Judy shook her head. "I don't think I ever saw them both together. This guy—he's nasty, you know what I mean?" Looked up at Doc like she wanted him to, so she wouldn't have to explain it.

"Nasty how? Like he stinks? Or he's dangerous?" Judy nodded. "You ever see him hurt anybody?"

"I heard stories. People owe him money, he hurts them. Bad temper. I saw him go off one night. Took three security guys to get him out."

"Was he here the night Doug Stirnweiss was shot?"

"He's banned from the casino since that other time. They found out he sold, so Rollison put him on the list."

"What made you think to bring him up if he hasn't been in?"

"He still hangs around. Does his business in the parking lot."

"You've seen him?"

She nodded three times, quick. "I heard he was, and...I think it was him I saw one night."

"You think?"

What little eye contact there had been disappeared. "There are some guys, you know, you don't want them to notice you."

"You know what he sells?"

"I ain't had anything to do with him, you understand?"

Doc stuck out his lower lip, shook his head. "I'm not thinking anything like that. You work at the bar. What do you hear?"

"Coke. Some grass. Crystal, of course. I guess he can get about anything."

"You have a name for him?" She shook her head. "Who else can I talk to? You can't be the only person here knows about him."

"No one else will talk to you. Not about this. They're either afraid of him, or they're afraid of the casino—you know, for bringing suspicion around the place—or they're doing business with him."

Doc leaned in, lowered his voice. "Why are you telling me?"

Judy looked away, then made eye contact for a second—damn, almost like Doc could see through the blue and there was white behind, they were so pale—swallowed once. "He scares me. I mean, really scares me. I kind of figured he could hurt someone bad. Now that someone's been shot—right outside, where I know he hangs out—I wonder was it him, and what else he could do. I don't want to sound like some conceited twat, but I know people notice me. I'm not complaining. I got the best job here, make the most tips, and I can go out with anybody I want to, pretty much. I know a lot of girls would trade with me. But, you know, people noticing you isn't always a good thing. Not if it's the wrong people. Or for the wrong reasons."

She looked at Doc again. He saw it this time, behind the blue. The fear. "Okay. We'll check him out."

"You won't let anyone know it was me that told?"

Doc shook his head. "Send Schaffer back. I won't say or do anything that might bring any suspicion until after I talk to everybody. There'll be no way to know where I got it."

Her smile was gone before it could take root, as if she were embarrassed to have done it. Doc spoke when she reached the door. "Thank you." She nodded and left.

Doc's cell phone in hand before the door catch clicked. "Teresa? Do me a favor. Find some subtle way to work drugs into the conversation with Doug's friends."

Doc kept his voice low as he could. No way to hide his irritation altogether. "Were you planning on telling me you recently ejected a violent drug dealer from the casino?"

Rollison gave away nothing, of course. "That was...three weeks ago. He's gone. It's not germane."

"Gone, my ass. He moved his operation to the parking lot, is all."

This time, displeasure flashed, disappeared like steam on a windy day. "I didn't know, and I should have. I'm sorry."

The apology ruined the speech Doc had worked on in the back of his mind ever since Judy Abramowicz mentioned the dealer. "It's all right. You've been bending over backward. No one's perfect. What can you tell me about him?"

"Bear in mind, I didn't know he was dealing until after we threw him out that night. My crack staff had suspicions, but no one thought I might like to know about it until I asked what the hell happened that brought me back an hour after I got home for the night. Then I find out it was a drug dispute. I had him banned, and the guy he beefed with. We don't want either end of that transaction hanging around here. Our reputation is tenuous enough as it is."

Doc listened, wondered what Dan Hecker or Rance Doocy would say about the new candor. "You have a name for him?"

"He was gone by the time I got back. You should understand, we have guys working here that couldn't handle security for an ice cream truck. I've asked if I could contract it out, hire some professionals. 'Why should we pay a middleman?' is what they tell me. 'It's your job to train them.' You remember Ken Czarniak, the guy who found the body here right before we opened?" Doc remembered. "He's a shift foreman now. My cream rising to the top." Rollison must have caught Doc's expression. "Yeah, I know. Out of character for me. Everyone has limits."

"You understand we're going to have to put that cop back on patrol in the lot. The one we said was leaving once we released the crime scene. We want eyes there in case this guy shows up again."

"Your chief get any flak from above on the police presence here?" He had. "Between us, I don't mind the cop being around. You and I both know the odds of anything else bad happening are negligible, but it makes the customers feel safer. They feel safer, they're not as likely to stay away."

Doc checked his watch, took a deep breath. Exhaled through his nose and stacked his wrists on top of his head. Already a long day, and he still had to compare notes with Teresa Shimp. "You stepped out of character, so will I. You've busted your ass so far. Is there anything I can do for you?"

Rollison took longer to reply than Doc expected. "Keeping that cop outside helps. We'll both catch heat, but I can handle it. Aside from that, the best thing you can do for me is to make an arrest. Between us, there are people interested in how this shakes out who will tell you any arrest will do. As a professional, I'd prefer it to be the right guy, if only as a practical matter. We both know how things went after your deputy tried too hard to pin that other shooting on Mannarino."

"Some of us more than others." Doc flipped his notebook shut and made for the door.

"Dougherty." Rollison's tone demanded attention. Doc turned to face him. "You understand, what we have here is a relationship of convenience. We're not friends, and we're not going to be. That being said, I want to tell you to your face I had no idea they'd come after your family. Those Russians. I'd have killed Yuri myself if I'd known anything about it."

Doc digested what he realized was an apology. Emotion did not overcome him. "Thanks. I appreciate you telling me." *You took your sweet-assed time getting around to it.* "I better hit the road. Best way I can show my appreciation is to catch this guy."

21

"I talked to his siblings, friends, people he worked with, and went back to Vicki Leydig and Mary Zelesko. None of them had any suspicions of Doug using drugs, not even a little pot." Teresa Shimp made eye contact with the other cops, no doubt in her assessment. "Even a couple of friends who admitted to using themselves said he never did. He was such a straight arrow, he only drank one beer a night."

"Either of that last group buy from the guy at the casino?" Doc said.

"Part of the deal to get them to talk was I didn't push them on their sources, but I did tell them I'd have to know if it was him."

"You believe them?"

"Even if it was him, what happened to Stirnweiss buys a lot of silence and bad memory." Willie Grabek, in a guest appearance as a working detective. Retired after thirty years in Pittsburgh, Doc's partner until an unattended gall bladder almost killed him over the winter. Contemplated retirement, stayed on as a house cat. Used his Detective Without Portfolio status to provide opinions on cases he had no direct knowledge of.

Teresa ignored him. "One told me Doug helped him out of a jam a few years ago. Said he wished he'd known if someone was coming after him. He would've stepped up, and brought friends. It didn't sound like just talk, either. This guy was hurting. I checked his record after. Nothing bad, but a few beefs for assault, all dropped. Self-defense. Seems like the kind of guy who wouldn't start something, but didn't mind finishing it."

"He have an alibi?" Jack Harriger's foot in the door before

Doc could lock it. Now they were imprisoned with his expertise.

"Yeah, he checks out." Doc smiled. Shimp didn't miss much and had a knack for anticipating questions. "Funny thing. He was at the casino that night, came in with a couple of friends about the time Doug was leaving. Didn't see him there."

"Check it out with the casino." Harriger gave up on his theories as often as dogs returned liver to the table. "He knew the victim and is known to be in the vicinity when it happened." Teresa made a note. Doc looked over at Grabek, who pumped the air with his fist.

"About this drug dealer," Doc said.

"Forget the drug dealer." Harriger in his version of command mode, bound to draw either exasperation or laughter from someone sooner or later. "The victim had no known drug connections."

"I was about to say, since we're keeping the increased patrol presence in the parking lot, it might be nice to pick us up a known drug dealer."

"Who authorized maintaining the increased patrols at the casino?" Harriger looked from Doc to Stush and back. "They asked to keep this as low profile as possible. Reminding people of a murder is killing their business."

Grabek lobbed his obligatory incendiary comment. "Last winter you were kissing ass for more patrols there. I wish you guys would make up your minds."

"Apples and oranges. Cars were being stolen. An increased presence would increase the chances of an arrest. This is different. More uniforms will remind them there was a recent event." To Teresa: "Did you get the names of the dealers the two friends use?"

"No. They weren't telling me much until I let them know I was working on a murder and didn't care about drugs today."

"And passed up an opportunity to take down a couple of drug dealers."

Teresa's posture retreated a step. "I doubt either of them does more than smoke a little pot. I thought the murder was more important."

"Obviously it is. That doesn't mean no other laws get enforced. Maybe Ohio State is willing to look the other way on what it considers victimless crimes. That's not how things work here."

Doc's eyes rolled up in his head. "Make up your mind, Jack. The last two things out of your mouth were, patrol units in the casino parking lot increased the chance of an arrest, and not to put one there, knowing there's a potentially dangerous drug dealer working it. Now these two guys are a crisis?"

Stush said, "Go back to the guy who said he would've stood up for Doug. Did he happen to say what it was Doug helped him with?"

Teresa checked her notes. "This friend—Randall Esch—had gotten into some trouble with a loan shark. Fell behind on the interest, started getting threats, the usual. Said Doug went with him to a meeting and talked the shylock into a more lenient payment plan. Didn't forgive any of what was owed, but gave Esch a chance to catch up."

"He told you Stirnweiss faced down a loan shark?" Harriger said. "And you bought it?"

"I asked around about Doug more specifically as I found things out. As far as I can tell, he had a way about him. Reminded the shylock Esch was even less likely to be able to pay with a serious injury."

"I still can't believe a shylock would roll over like that."

"Esch also said—and a couple of others confirmed—that Doug had what he called hard bark on him. He could get his back up when pushed, and he did it in a way that not too many were willing to test him."

"Small town shy, not connected...yeah, maybe," Doc said. "Not likely—definitely not one of Tommy Vig's boys—I've heard weirder stories."

Harriger had an argument ready. Stush beat him to it. "Let's not forget what put Stirnweiss in the position he was in the night he got shot: giving two friends a safe ride home. Take that with this Esch guy's story and we have someone who has his friends' backs and isn't afraid to go out of his way to do it, even at some risk to himself. What's to say he didn't have another friend in Dutch with this dealer from the casino? Maybe even one of the guys Teresa talked to, Esch could've held that back. Doug stepped up and the dealer didn't like some citizen sticking his nose in and decided to prove a point. We have multiple reports of what a mean bastard he is."

"That's a reach," Harriger said. "We have zero connection between the victim and this mysterious drug dealer whose name they couldn't even get."

Stush wagged a finger between Doc and Teresa. "Comparing your notes, do you have anything else?" Neither did. "Find the drug dealer."

22

Doc picked up Wilver Faison's trail near Jefferson West's house, by the tracks, when Wilver stopped to check on business. Didn't move on him right away. Watched the kid talk to his hoppers. Watched them listen. The situation as West had described it: Wilver called the shots.

The kid got into a gray Camry and drove to the corner of Fifth Avenue and Ninth Street, near the bridge. Parked and went into what looked like a small newsstand. Stayed fifteen minutes, drove south on Fifth Avenue, left onto Fourth Street, then right on Main. Slowed as he passed an apartment complex, right on Third Street, right again at Sixth Avenue, took his time passing along the back of the same complex. Right on Fourth Street, doubled back on Freeport, pulled into the parking lot of a beer distributor and drove around back, facing the front of the same apartment complex. Stayed in the car.

Doc about to pull in behind a Goodyear tire store when he noticed a patrol unit at the bank on the other side of the distributor. Drove over and parked next to the cruiser, leaned against the trunk to wait, an eye on the Camry.

Nancy Snyder came out of the bank five minutes later. Adjusting her sunglasses when she saw Doc leaning on her car, slowed her pace.

"Nancy, right?" She nodded. "Ben Dougherty." Pulled back his jacket to show the shield clipped to his belt.

"I know who you are. What's up?"

"I need you to do me a small favor. Won't take a minute." Handed her a note, folded over. "There's a young black man in a gray Camry parked at the back of the lot next door." He pointed. "I want you to pull in behind him and do a routine license and registration check."

"What's my probable cause?"

"Make something up. Loafing While Black will do. The registration check is for anyone who might be watching. He'll know why you tagged him as soon as he reads that note. Tell him I've been following him all day." Doc minded lying to potential felons less with every passing year. "Let him know if he's not where the note says to be in fifteen minutes I can pick him up at my convenience and make sure everyone knows."

"Is he a snitch?"

"Yeah. He just doesn't know it yet."

No one at the Little League fields at lunchtime. Ending the season before school let out always struck Doc as odd. He understood about the town all-stars and the tournament, how it was hard to fill rosters when families started taking vacation. He also knew summer brought better weather—spring in Penns River could be a brutal disappointment—and kids were out of school with time on their hands. A lot of Penns River families took their summer time off as staycations or visited family, inexpensive trips with flexible dates. Coaches and umpires also off more. At least the town left the fields open for neighborhood kids to play pickup games.

The ball fields—five, including the full-sized home of the high school team—were in an older neighborhood, halfway down the hill from an old dairy farm now sub-divided into two-acre lots; all-white without being exclusive: anyone could live there; only white people did. Tom and Ellen's house not a quarter mile from the concession stand where kids still got free snow cones for turning in balls fouled out of play. Wilver Faison no more likely to be recognized here than in Vancouver.

Showed some attitude, sitting in the Camry while Doc parked behind him and got out. "You followed me? For real?"

Doc gestured toward himself with two fingers. "Get out of the car."

Wilver tried for smooth and a smile. "We gonna play some ball? You should've said. I ain't got my glove."

"Get your ass out of that fucking car right now."

Wilver looked as though he'd been slapped. Recovered and eased his way erect with glacial speed. Doc saw the flash of amazement when he flipped the kid around and leaned him against the roof of the car for a thorough and unaffectionate frisk.

"Yo yo yo, Doc. What I do to deserve this?"

"Drug dealers are known to carry weapons. Now I know you're clean, let's get one thing straight: I'm Detective Dougherty. Or Mr. Dougherty. Call me Doc again and I'll bounce your head off this car."

"Really, man. No shit. What I do?"

"I told you not six months ago what would happen if you went down this road. Did you think I was bullshitting you?"

"Down what road, yo?"

The time Doc took to be sure no one would see him knock Wilver silly allowed the impulse to pass. "You're not just selling drugs, Wilver. You're running the show. Do *not* lie to me, or I *will* beat your ass."

Hard to say which left Wilver first, the piss or the vinegar. Why Doc worried about him, he lacked the hardness to succeed at his chosen profession. "It's not like I planned it this way. Things just kinda happened."

"Tell me."

"What, you want me to snitch off the whole operation? Someone else just come in. I know you know that whole 'nature abhors a vacuum' thing. You the one taught me."

"No one else interests me right now. I want to know how Wilver Faison, who was this close," held a thumb and forefinger an inch apart, "to getting his head blown off at Resurrection Mall, ended up as shot caller."

"This off the record?"

"It's unofficial. We can go to the station if you want, put the whole thing on the record, including the fact you were there talking to me."

"Weren't no one running—no one was running things. Fiends still needed their fixes, and the drugs was—were still available. Everyone left came to me for advice. I was in charge before I knew it."

"So you're the Avon Barksdale of Penns River, what? By accident?"

"I know how that sounds, but it's not like there was a plan or nothing." Sneaked a look at Doc. "You're not going to turn me out, are you?"

"I have bigger plans for you. For the time being, you can buy yourself some goodwill with a little help on a murder investigation."

"You mean that guy got offed at the casino?" Doc nodded. "No one I know had nothing to do with that."

"There's a guy we want to talk to. Drug dealer, works around the casino. White guy, so anything you tell me isn't likely to roll back on you."

"I don't know the white guys too good—well, but since it don't have anything to do with mine, I'll tell you what I know. He got a name?"

"That's what I'm hoping you can tell me. This guy sells some crank, coke, grass, and can probably get whatever you need. He's a mean motherfucker, too. Likes to threaten people and rough them up. Got himself banned from the casino a few weeks ago for making a scene. Been working the parking lot since. Any ideas?"

"Could be this dude named Scooter. He works out that way."

"There's a drug dealer named Scooter? You sure it's not Skippy, or Biff?"

"I didn't name the guy, I'm just telling you. I think he likes it because a lot of people have the same idea you got, so they underestimate him and shit. Gives him a chance to get physical, then they got to explain how they got they ass whipped by a Scooter. He's the guy I know best fits what you told me."

"Where can I find him?"

"I would say the casino, but sounds like you put the heat on there." Wilver thought. "There's bar in Butler he hangs at. Got some goofy-ass name, like it ain't a bar at all. Some other kind of business."

"What other kind of business?"

"No, man, really. It's a bar with a name like it's not a bar. I could tell you if I heard it, but it's not the kind of thing you be thinking about when you think of names of bars." Doc gave him a look. "For real. That's the serious. If I knew, I'd tell you."

Doc wondered why a Penns River dealer hung in Butler. Could be he didn't like to drink where he shit. "How sure are you?"

Wilver waggled a hand. "Not very. Ain't like I know this guy, like *know* him. Heard of him. Heard shit about him. Wouldn't know him if he walked up to us."

"All right." Doc considered options. "Thanks. I'll check it out." Turned for his car.

"Whoa, Do—Detective Dougherty." Wilver gestured between the two of them. "How are we?"

Doc turned to face him, about two-thirds as much of a prick as before. "I have better things to do right now than chase down penny ante drug operations. You want to stay off my radar, have any chance of falling through the cracks, you keep that shit off the streets down there by the Estates. I drive by and see anyone slinging by those goddamn train tracks again, I'm going to come looking for you. Personally."

23

Rance Doocy let Jack Harriger cool his heels in an outer office for more than half an hour. Made Harriger drive downtown to the Gulf Building after work, now left him to sit, gauge how bad he wanted the chief of police job. Knew Stan Napierkowski did the same thing in his own way. Assigned Harriger as many demeaning tasks as could be thought of in the hope the deputy would quit before the chief retired. So far, Harriger had eaten every bowl of shit handed him, regardless of flavor or smell.

"Have a seat, Jack. Would you like a drink?"

Harriger sat. "No thanks. I have to get back as quick as I can. The wife's holding supper."

Doocy hoped she was good at it. "I want to talk about the police department. What's going on up there."

"If you mean about this shooting at the casino, Napierkowski and Dougherty are freezing me out. I can't even sit in on their meetings or get a goddamned briefing. Far as they let me be involved, the case doesn't exist."

Doocy knew much of the blame resided in this office. Much as Napierkowski and Dougherty had personal reasons for wanting Harriger gone, they also had to know anything said in front of him might as well have been told to Doocy directly. Harriger knew it, too, in no position to complain. Any hope he had of the chief's job depended on staying in Doocy's—and, thus Daniel Hecker's—good graces.

Made himself a drink: Laphroaig eighteen-year-old single malt over two ice cubes. Not in the mood for one—didn't much like scotch even when he was—knew Harriger did and would appreciate the cost. A little disappointed he hadn't said yes; the bottle of Ballantine's twelve-year-old blended right there, ready to be served, remind Harriger he didn't rate the good stuff. "Do you still want to be chief in Penns River, Jack?"

"Yes." Said it too fast, the root of all Harriger's professional problems. If he'd been a kid and someone found a peephole into the girls' shower, Harriger would be the one to ruin it with over-eagerness. An open joke in the DanHeck offices, consumed by ambition for a job with little juice even by Penns River standards.

"Then you'd better start acting like it." Doocy sipped his drink, waited for Harriger to bite.

"What do you want me to do?" Exasperation woven through Harriger's voice like wire in a phone cable. "I stepped up when the casino came in and took the hit when things went bad, even though it wasn't my fault. Did what I could to get better security when the cars were being stolen last winter. Mostly I've been playing the good soldier." An edge appeared in his voice. "Like you told me to."

"You've done well, no argument from me." Another sip, and a moment to savor. "You know how Napierkowski got the job, don't you?"

"His brother-in-law was mayor and promoted him over a couple of more senior guys."

"One of whom was your uncle."

A pause, then, tight-lipped, "Yeah."

"How do you think he got away with it?"

"Mayor had a lot more authority over things like that in those days. The council has more say now, probably because of how that went down."

"I don't know what your uncle told you, but I've done some research." Sip. "Your uncle was a paper-pusher. No offense, he was apparently a hell of an administrator, but that's all he was. Napierkowski, on the other hand, was, by all accounts, a hell of a cop. Don't let that fat hick you work for now fool you. There was a time when he was a minor legend in Penns River. Born and raised there, state wrestling finalist, Silver Star and two

Purple Hearts in Vietnam. Shot it out with a robber leaving the old Pittsburgh National Bank on Fifth Avenue. I can show you the bullet holes in the bricks, if you'd like. I'm sure you heard the story of how he captured Jason Negley after he'd killed five people in three states, including two cops. Napierkowski got him three months before the previous chief retired. Your uncle never had a chance."

Not much to say to that. Doocy took another sip. "You didn't know, did you? I'm not surprised. For all the things I don't like about your chief, I have to admire his ability not to talk about himself. Can't say I agree with it, but he displays nothing that hints of his history. No awards, medals, plaques. I know. I look every time I'm in his office."

"Okay, he was a war hero. I'm a little old to volunteer for Afghanistan. What do you suggest?"

Doocy sipped, followed by a lengthy savor to give Harriger time to think. Better if he came up with the idea himself. Doocy knew he wouldn't. If Epiphany were a river, you'd have to hold Jack Harriger's head under to get him to drink from it. "You have to be a cop, Jack. You have to get out of the office and do police work."

"What I do *is* police work."

"Not the way I mean it."

"He won't let me out of the office to do street work."

"Do you want to be chief?"

"Yes. I told you already."

"Then get out of the office and at least look like a cop to the people in town. We can dress things up for you, but you have to give us something to work with. Napierkowski's a lame duck. He can't have more than two years left. What kind of man lets someone with one foot out the door deny him the job he wants? A job he's earned." Doocy knew what kind. A specimen sat across the desk from him.

"And do what? Drive around?"

This kept up, Doocy *would* need a drink. "An occasional arrest might be nice. Something we can play up in the paper. As much advertising as we buy, we should be allowed to write the articles ourselves."

A trickle of water from the River Epiphany slid down Harriger's throat. "You mean like this shooter from the casino."

"Let's not get carried away. That's a mature investigation, and you've been excluded. There's no good way to insinuate yourself back into it. You need something you can work from the start. Get out in the street more. Napierkowski happened onto that bank robbery going in to deposit his paycheck. Opportunities are available, but you're going to have to get out of the office." A thought flashed through Doocy's mind. "Not that I'm advocating shooting it out with an armed robber. We don't want to get you killed, now."

"There's nothing about the job says I *can't* spend some time on patrol."

"Or open an investigation you can run. We may even be able to generate some leads for you, avenues to explore."

Doocy took a sip. Harriger said, "You know, Rance, you don't mind, I'd like a drink after all. Scotch, please."

"Coming right up," Doocy said. Reached for the Ballantine's.

24

"Sisler's okay." Kathy Burrows sipped beer at Maguire's, choir practice night. "I wasn't sure at first. I heard how he killed that guy last winter and thought he might be all gung ho, but he calmed a situation down at Fat Jimmy's and never broke a sweat."

"You got called to Fat Jimmy's during the day shift?" Nancy Snyder let her visible disbelief linger. "What for?"

Kathy gave the condensed version. Nancy said, "He left the crowd to you? Never said anything about it?"

"Nope. Even now I'm not sure if he trusted me to have his back or if he thought he could handle it, even if I didn't. He's good and he knows it, but it's not like he plays super cop."

"Did he talk with you about it at all? Discuss how to handle it? Who'd do what?"

"It looked like he knew the one guy, from the way he talked to him. I mean, he would've handled it himself if I hadn't been there. You know, if I was riding with Ulizio like I usually do."

"Still, you were his partner, at least for today."

"I guess so." Kathy took a sip. "I never thought to ask about it. I figured, I'm on probation and he's the experienced cop."

"He has about a year's experience." Nancy warming to the task. "If that."

Teresa Shimp cut in. "Did you ask him about shooting that guy?"

"No. I'm curious—I mean, how many guys do cops shoot in a town like this?—there wasn't really a good way to bring it up. Sounds too much like something a cop groupie would ask."

"How come you never hear about male cop groupies?"

Nancy said.

Caught Teresa by surprise. "You mean men who want to sleep with woman cops?"

"Yeah. Seems to me we should get the same perks as they do."

"If I had to guess, I'd say it had to do with some women being attracted to dangerous men, with the added advantage of this breed of dangerous man is also a good guy. Men don't care much about those things in a woman."

"They would if her tits were big enough."

"You sound like you've thought a lot about this," Kathy said.

"Don't you?" Teresa swallowed. "I don't mean the sex part. I mean cop stuff in general."

"I think about the sex part a lot," Nancy said into her glass.

Teresa laughed. "No, I mean, really. There's a lot of weird stuff about being a cop. It attracts all kinds of people you wouldn't expect, but it also draws some the average citizen never thinks about."

"Not sure what you mean," Kathy said.

Teresa gathered her thoughts, more of a challenge now than two beers ago. "We're first responders, right? We're supposed to run toward things everyone else runs away from. Kathy, you're new, but I've worked with cops who are as eager to stay out of trouble as any citizen. Nancy?"

"Worse, some of them. To be fair, it's usually older guys. They've seen what can happen and don't want it to happen to them."

"I've seen it in young cops, too. I worked with a guy at Ohio State. I don't know if he thought a college would be easy or what. We had a fight get out of control after a bowl game a few years ago. Fifty drunken kids, picking up sticks and whatever was handy, wrecking the place and beating the crap out of each other. About ten of us waded in with batons to restore order the old fashioned way—"

"*Hoo*-rah!"

"And this guy lays back. Said someone needed to watch our sixes."

"Pussy."

"I wasn't sure at the time. But after that, I kept an eye on him. I think everyone who was there that night did." Glanced at her watch. "Sure enough, he was never the first one into a scene, or even the first one out of the car. I don't think I ever saw him subdue anyone. But he lived to face down kids when there was another cop handy. A real hard-ass then."

Nancy rose. "Like I said, a pussy."

"More like a bully." Teresa sighted Ben Dougherty standing in the doorway, scanning the room. She raised a hand. "Someone who liked to act tough when there was no risk in it. No one wanted to work with him. Where are you off to? Your glass is half full."

Nancy pointed to the back. "Restroom. You've been in there, right? It passes muster?"

"I guess. My standards may have suffered since everything looks good compared to Fat Jimmy's..." A second wave in Dougherty's direction, cut short by the look of disgust that crossed his face. Looking right at her. Nancy slid out of her chair, walked toward the restrooms, didn't see him. Kathy facing the bar, signaling for another round. The only worse response to seeing them would have been for Dougherty to turn around and leave. He paused, decided to brazen it out, came on in a straight line.

"Good evening, sister officers." Big smile, affable as hell now that he'd been caught. Pointed toward the restrooms. "Was that Nancy?"

"Yeah," Teresa said. Dougherty shook his head, turned up a corner of his mouth.

"Hi, Doc." Kathy scooted her chair over to make room. "Want a beer?"

Dougherty looked at his watch. "Sure, I can have one." Halfway into a chair, stopped and said, "Wait. Is it just you three cops?"

Teresa nodded. Kathy said, "Yeah."

Dougherty held his position, ass suspended a foot above the seat. "I'm not interrupting choir practice, am I?"

Kathy turned to Teresa looking like she'd learned a new handshake. "Choir practice is really a thing? I thought Nancy made that up."

"It's a police thing," Teresa said. Then, to Dougherty, "Actually, we are."

He stood. "Sorry. I don't want to interrupt."

"You don't have to go," Kathy said. "It's not like it's women's chorus or anything." Five-foot-two, a hundred pounds, over the legal limit from the fumes if she walked through a brewery. "We can pick your brain for Penns River dirt."

"It looks like Doc has somewhere else he needs to be." Teresa hoped her tone conveyed the message better than the words. "We don't want to keep him."

Dougherty's weight on his haunches, stopped in mid-sit. Gave a look that could have meant anything or nothing. "Another time, then." Stood all the way as Nancy returned to the table. "Here you go, Nancy. Kept it warm for you." Looked her over with a cop's scrutiny, more than was polite, not leering. "Sometime we have a minute, mention for me to tell you who you remind me of. There's a story there." Dipped his head toward the table. "See you guys tomorrow."

Nancy sat, tasted her beer. "What was that all about?"

Teresa glanced at Kathy. "I'll tell you later."

25

An internet search for bars and restaurants in Butler turned up a few places that could have met Wilver Faison's description of not sounding like a bar. The Crafty Butcher struck Doc as sounding least like one.

Not sure what happened at Maguire's. Teresa Shimp made it clear she didn't want him hanging around. Seemed pissed at him. Doc knew better than to attribute confusing female reactions to menstrual cycles, even to himself. They'd been joined at the hip on a case that had them both stressed; she might be sick of the sight of him. It had happened before.

The Crafty Butcher took some finding, part of a small strip mall off of Wayne Street, near a residential area the locals referred to as The Island. Basic neighborhood bar, a dozen cars in the unlighted lot. Doc lucked into a spot in front of the door. Out of his jurisdiction, he hadn't notified anyone in Butler. Didn't expect to find Scooter—his luck not that good—willing to take him down alone and sort out the consequences if it came to it. Stush knew every police chief in Allegheny, Westmoreland, Armstrong, Indiana, and Butler counties. Doc happened onto a good murder suspect, Stush would square it.

A bow had been made toward a butcher shop motif. Rolls of heavy white paper, cleavers, tongs, and assorted knives attached to the walls. Televisions the primary décor, at least ten, with baseball on all but a few, where soccer and what looked like rugby took up the slack.

Doc sat where he could see as much of the room as possible. Laid a twenty on the bar, nodded when the bartender held up a finger for him to wait. Pirates in Colorado and not on for another hour and a half, the Reds pounding some Mets pitcher Doc didn't recognize.

"What can I do ya for? I'm Eddie." Around forty, stocky, Eddie looked like one of those with a smile for every occasion. This one for someone he hadn't made his mind up about yet. Doc perused the taps, ordered a Yuengling. Eddie asked if he wanted to run a tab. Doc pretended to think about it before he said no. Eddie brought back the beer and change from the twenty. Doc said to keep the one, did he have a few minutes.

Eddie looked along the bar, nodded. Doc tasted his beer. Hard to believe he hadn't liked Yuengling before he left for the army. They must have changed something. "I'm looking for a guy."

"You came to the right place." Eddie extended an arm to take in the room. "The joint's full of them."

"I'm looking for one in particular."

"Aren't we all?"

Doc pulled back what he almost said, took inventory of the room. On closer inspection, he saw only men, some of whom sat closer than societal custom dictated. Turned back to Eddie, made eye contact, and broke up. "No, Eddie. Not like that." Still laughing when he took a sip, set off a brief choking jag.

Eddie's smile got a lot less friendly. "What do you want, buddy?"

Doc unclipped the badge from his belt, put it on the bar where his left arm blocked it from the sight of anyone but Eddie. "I'm looking for a guy goes by Scooter. Supposed to be a mean sonofabitch. You know him?"

Eddie's smile disappeared altogether. "This is the twenty-first century, pal. We work hard to be a good neighbor to the people that live over in The Island. You got no reason to come around here and try to roust us."

"Whoa whoa whoa." Doc held up both hands before Eddie worked up too much momentum. "It's not like that. This Scooter guy's a person of interest in a violent felony down Penns River.

I just need to find him."

"He a suspect?"

"Right now alls I want to do is talk to him."

"You understand, I don't want to cause any trouble for a customer."

"So you *do* know him."

Eddie made a face. "Yeah, I know him. He comes in a couple-three times a week. Later than this, usually."

"You got a name?"

"Scooter's all I know."

"Any credit card receipts?"

"I could look, not that I'd recognize the name if I saw it. Far as I can remember, he always pays cash."

Doc didn't mind hanging around if Scooter might come in. Give him time to call Butler PD, make it official. "He have any regular nights?"

"Not that I can tell. Like I said, he's in quite a bit, but not like he has a schedule."

"He ever cause any trouble in here?"

"Trouble, how?"

"I hear he has a mean streak. Ever seen any signs?"

Eddie nodded. "Tell the truth, I can live without the guy in here altogether. The owner hates to put people out. You know how it is, there's still places around here our usual customers can't walk into and not risk an ass kicking. I could be talked into asking him to make an exception for this guy. Always has an attitude, orders people around like the owner wouldn't dare to. I've never seen him get physical, but I've heard he threatened to."

"What reasons?"

"I couldn't say. Well, money, now that you got me thinking about it. A lot of people seem to owe him money, which strikes me odd, him not being the kind you expect to spot someone. Makes me wonder if he has something going on."

"What makes you wonder?"

Eddie rubbed a clean spot with a bar towel. "There's always

guys around him when he's here. No one stays long. I always figure they didn't hang around him because he's an asshole, but I keep seeing the same guys come in, go over and talk to him, then split."

"Is he dealing?"

"The boss'll put him out for sure then. He's zero tolerance when it comes to drugs. Like I said, that's a residential neighborhood over there. We try to be good neighbors, but we'll never win some of those people over. The best we hope for is live and let live from as many as possible."

"Any of the guys that come looking for Scooter here tonight?"

Eddie gave the room a good going over. "I don't see any, and that gets me thinking. He must have at least one regular night. How else would they know when to look for him?"

"If he's dealing, he may have one night a week he's here for sure, then others by appointment. I don't want to take too much of your time and maybe alert someone who might tip Scooter. What's your work schedule?"

"Wednesday through Saturday, four to one. Sundays four to twelve."

"You mind coming down to Penns River to look at some pictures? Maybe use the Indenti-Kit to draw one yourself?"

"All the way down Penns River? I live nearly to Slippery Rock. That's a hell of a drive."

About an hour, not on the way to anywhere Eddie would need to go. "It'll be easier there. Not only do we have the resources to help you look, it won't draw attention to the bar. Word gets out you're helping us find this guy and he doesn't want to be found, he might do some damage, if he really is as mean as people are telling me."

Someone up the bar hollered for Eddie. "Go ahead," Doc said. "I'll wait." Nursed his beer and decided what he first thought was rugby might be Gaelic football.

Eddie came back, slid a folded slip of paper across the bar. "Ralph up there says your next drink's on him, and to give you this."

Doc opened the note. A 724 phone number with "Ralph Nishan" written below it. Doc looked along the bar. Ralph smiled, tipped his glass in Doc's direction. Doc shook his head, tapped his watch, and mouthed "Thanks." Ralph gestured as if putting something into his shirt pocket. Doc held up a finger to buy a minute, turned to face Eddie. "You in?"

Eddie showed resignation. "Tomorrow?"

"Not too early. I'll need time to set up a few things, weed out the pictures you don't have to look at. You want to come in after lunch, you can stop here for work on the way home. Minimize the running around a little."

Eddie said okay and Doc gave him a card. "Come down 356 to 28, get off at 366 south. Cross the bridge and make a left at the first light past the Kmart. City-County complex on the right. You can't miss it." Eddie put the card in his shirt pocket. Doc palmed Ralph's note. "Where's the head?"

Eddie pointed along the bar, then jerked his finger to the right. "You're pretty open-minded, aren't you?"

"What can I say? Biological functions know no morals." Doc winked and Eddie laughed.

Stopped halfway along the bar, put a hand on Ralph's shoulder. "Thanks for offering the beer. I should let you know, I won't be calling. I'm kinda spoken for."

Ralph turned to look Doc up and down. "Why are the good ones always taken?" Both laughed.

Doc still chuckling when he opened the men's room door and walked into Sean Sisler.

26

Sisler had two Yeungling drafts at a table away from the flow of traffic when Doc returned from the men's. Doc tested his beer, pointed to Sisler's. Said, "Don't give up your Lime-a-Rita on my account."

Touch and go for a second how Sisler would react. Then he laughed with enough vigor to turn nearby heads. The laughter increased as the tension leached out of him, until he came up for air. Wiped tears from his eyes as he looked at Doc, said, "You're an assho—" Couldn't get the entire word out before they both lost it.

The look on Sisler's face coming out of the john, not knowing how or what to feel; Doc understood. He knew he'd had gay friends in the past without knowing who they were. Never assumed he didn't have any gay friends now, undismayed at having been proven right.

The catch was, how to convey to Sisler it not only didn't matter to Doc; he didn't care. One of his friends in the Army had been diagnosed with cancer. The first sergeant called the outfit together one day to ask them, as a favor, to treat the poor bastard as they always had. Bad enough he might die—and he did, two years later—without everyone making him feel like a dead man walking, too careful of his feelings. Treat him as they'd treated him ten minutes before they found out he was sick. Doc thought of this in the men's, washing his hands, then felt guilty. Reconsidered, decided the lack of a direct parallel didn't demand a different remedy.

They sat sipping beer, two friends in a somewhat unnatural silence, each waiting for the other to go first, for a hint on how

to play it. Doc took the plunge. "I guess I owe you a partial re-
fund for Chet Wagenbach's bachelor party last month."

"Just because I don't indulge doesn't mean I couldn't appreciate the...talents of those two who came over the house before
the bus took us to Pittsburgh. The food was good, too." Swallowed beer. "Lime-a-Ritas would've been nice, though."

They drank beer and watched baseball, the tension slipping
away without conversation. Two friends who had each other's
backs. The waitress came when their beers were almost empty.
Doc ordered two more, asked Sisler if he was hungry.

"I could eat."

"What's good?"

"Marlene," Sisler said to the waitress, "does Len have any of
those good crabs today?"

"Sorry, no crabs for me. Allergic. Don't let me stop you,
though."

"It's not you that'll stop him," Marlene said. "No crabs today.
Len is making some of those sliders you liked a while ago, Sean."

Sisler held up a menu. One laminated page, front and back.
"Where are they? I would've ordered some when I came in. I
love those things."

"Don't read the menu. Len makes what he feels like back
there. You want to know what to have, ask me."

Doc had thought of several things to ask Marlene during the
conversation. Tall, dark hair and eyes, her standing so close reminded him of New Orleans in August. No exclusionary jewelry.
Doc looking for a conversation starter when it occurred to him
there was one obvious reason a woman who looked like Marlene would work in a gay bar. "The sliders sound good. You
have onion rings?"

"Good ones, too." She indicated their glasses. "What are you
drinking?"

"Yuengling for me," Doc said. Pointed to Sisler. "And a—"

"Two Yuenglings. Thanks." Waited for her to get out of ear-
shot. "I figured you to take more notice of Marlene."

"I'm leveraging the circumstances to work against my inherent heterosexist tendencies."

"She lives in Sarver, you know."

"Please. I'm only human." Sarver halfway between Butler and Penns River.

Marlene brought their beers, the food would be ready in five minutes. Doc drank off the head, said, "I'm going to have to apologize to Ralph Nishan."

"How do you know Ralph?"

"He passed me a note and tried to buy me a drink. I told him I had someplace to be, and that I was spoken for. Now I'm eating and drinking with you, slut that I am."

"Me and Ralph go way back. I'll square it for you." Stopped himself halfway into a drink. "What *are* you doing here?"

"Running down a lead on a drug dealer named Scooter." Made a "go figure" face. "I heard he drinks here."

"You mean Scott Wheeler?"

"You know him?"

"To see. I didn't know he was dealing. If assholery was a crime, he'd be doing fifteen-to-life. You waiting for him to show?"

Doc shook his head, glass at his lips. "The bartender— Eddie—says he comes in late, if he comes at all. Eddie's stopping by tomorrow to look at pictures, try to get us a name so we can grab an address. All I had coming in was Scooter." Doc filled in the background from the casino. Mentioned a snitch, not who it was.

"Sounds more like Wheeler all the time. He lives down that way, but not in Penns River, I don't think. Tarentum, maybe? Natrona?"

"Take a look tomorrow when you sign in. I still want Eddie to come down, but it'll be nice if we can get confirmation."

"Sure. First thing."

Marlene brought their food. As she walked away, Doc chided himself over his newfound sensitivity. After further review, he decided the heightened awareness came from being shot down in too many similar situations. This somehow made him feel better.

"Her defenses will be down," Sisler said. "She doesn't expect to get hit on in here."

Doc flashed him the finger, irritated for being so obvious. The sliders and rings were as good as advertised. They ate and drank and bantered, two guys out for beers and baseball.

The food eaten and beer drunk, Doc called for the check. Sisler reached for his wallet. Doc waved him off. "It's on me." Took a minute. "I want to get something out there. I'm probably going to phrase it badly, but...well, okay. What I found out here tonight, it doesn't change anything about us being friends. It's another aspect of you, like your height, your weight, and being the best fucking shot I've ever seen. I hope you know me well enough to know I'm down with the two consenting adults thing. Whatever disgusting perversions you want to do in the privacy of your home..."

Sisler snorted through his nose. "You really are an asshole."

"That being said, I'm not going to mention this to anyone. Literally. Not because it's anything to be ashamed of or anything to be anything about. Because it's *your* business. You want to tell someone, or not tell them, that's your call. Anyone ever says anything to you, acts different, they didn't get it from me."

"Thanks, Doc. I appreciate that."

They left together. Sisler took Marlene aside on the way out, whispered something in her ear. She laughed and tossed a quick look in Doc's direction.

"What was that?" he said outside. "With Marlene."

"I told her you were a breeder." Doc made a face. "What? You didn't say I couldn't tell anyone about you."

27

Doc got a sinking feeling the instant Sisler identified Scott Wheeler's photograph. Seeing Wheeler in person didn't help. Stepped out of the interview room, put a hand on Teresa Shimp's arm to keep her from entering.

She stared through him. "What?"

Doc tapped the square window cut into the door at eye level. "Remind you of anyone?"

"What?" Shimp didn't appear to be in any better mood than the night before. "Remind me of who?"

Doc held up a hand. "Humor me." Pointed again into the interview room. "Who does he look like?"

Shimp glared for a second, made a show of peering through the window. "Okay, I looked, now who..." Returned her attention to Wheeler. "Oh, fuck." First time Doc had ever heard her say it. "Doug Stirnweiss."

"Yep."

Wheeler also hadn't been at the casino the night Doug was shot. Spent his evening at The Crafty Butcher and could prove it. Never occurred to Doc to ask Eddie, not that he had any reason to at the time.

They left Wheeler to wait, knocked on Stush's door. "We have a problem," Doc said.

Stush gestured to his visitors' chairs. "Tell me it's a small one." Doc's expression must have implied otherwise. Stush turned to Shimp. "Okay, then. You tell me." Shook her head. "All right. How bad?"

"The drug dealer we brought in?" Doc said. "The one people from Penns River to Butler and probably points beyond are lined up to say is a miserable lowlife piece of shit they'd all love to be rid of? He has an airtight alibi."

"Such is life. He's only here for questioning. We didn't expect to beat a confession out of him."

"It gets better."

Stush held up a hand to stop Doc, fished half a dozen jelly beans from the bowl on his desk. Shook them in his hand, put two in his mouth. "How much better?"

"He's a dead ringer for Doug Stirnweiss. Our victim."

"Fuck an underage duck."

"Yeah."

"How close is the resemblance?"

"In bad light, like that night? Brothers. Twins, maybe, you weren't paying attention."

"God *damn* it."

"Anyone in a potentially drug-induced state with a hard-on for Wheeler could easily have shot our boy by mistake."

"I don't suppose there's any way he'll give us the names of his customers to add to the suspect list." Stush's fake smile showed his opinion of his own suggestion. "What do you want to do?"

"Follow him. He's a drug dealer, let's try to roll up his customer base. Watch him at the casino, see who he talks to. Run their plates if we can, get their names and addresses. Look them up later so they don't know how we made them."

"You worried about offending the dealer?"

Doc shook his head. "We don't want them bitching to him. Then he changes up and we lose any leads we might've got."

"I hate to be the killjoy here," Shimp said.

"Then don't." Stush caught her expression, smiled and waved her on.

"Isn't someone who wants him dead more likely to be a former customer?" Talking to Stush, Doc might as well be in another room. "A current customer needs him around."

Stush and Doc exchanged looks. "Yeah," Stush said, "but

they're still related to him. Only way I can think of to find who used to be a customer is to find who buys from him now and see what they know."

"We do it right, find a guy who needs Scooter bad enough and thinks someone's after him, maybe he steps up," Doc said.

"Does Scooter move so much weight that anyone needs him that bad?" Shimp said.

Stush deferred to Doc. "I really don't know."

Stush's chewing the only sound. Doc reached over, took two green jelly beans. Stush offered the bowl to Shimp. She declined. Stush reached with his hand, pulled back, then took three black ones. "Does anything else look promising?" Neither detective spoke. "It doesn't sound like there's any low-hanging fruit around this Wheeler, but he's all we have for the time being. I'll tell Eye Chart to keep that extra unit on the casino parking lot. Plain clothes, if possible. Wheeler has money waiting for him there. He can't afford to stay away too long. While I'm at it, I'll call Rollison, tell him not to chase the guy off for the time being. Benny, you have any informants might be able to tell us if anyone has it in for Mr. Wheeler?"

"Hard to say, but worth a try."

"Well, try." Doc and Shimp halfway out of their chairs. "Either of you hear the news this morning?"

"About?" Doc didn't read the morning paper, watch or listen to news before work. Whatever bad might have happened overnight knew where to find him.

"I listened to the radio driving in," Shimp said. "What in particular?"

"Mike Mannarino and his crew were shot beside the first hole at Oakmont last night."

"All of them?" Doc said.

"If we consider Mike, Stretch Dolewicz, and Buddy Elba to be all of them."

"Dead?"

"Buddy, yeah. Head damn near blown off. Shotguns at close

range. Back door was open on the driver's side and they found him next to the car, so he must've got out and tried to do something. Whatever he did, it bought some time for Mike. He's shot up pretty bad, but it looks like he'll live. Stretch was in the front passenger seat, got out the door. He's least hurt."

"How'd it go down?"

"Who's Mike Mannarino?" Shimp said.

"Pittsburgh mob boss, lives here in PR." Stush pointed to Doc. "Him and Benny have history."

Doc made a "get on with it" gesture. Stush rocked back in his chair. "Way I heard it, Mike and his boys had dinner at Bilotti's. Driving into Oakmont, a car blocked the road in front, another behind. Hulton Road's narrow there, country club fence comes right up to it, line of trees on the other side. Looks like two cars, two shooters in each by the tire marks and shells. They'll know for sure after the firearms report."

"Sounds like pros," Doc said. "How come Mike and Stretch aren't dead?"

"Dumb luck. Oakmont town cop dropped off some flowers for his grandmother in that assisted living place next to the country club. Came out just in time to see the shooting start. Hit the siren and lights, did what he could to come on like Gangbusters."

"Mannarino should send the cop's kids through college. Sounds like the guy saved his life."

"Did he pursue?" Shimp said.

"No." Stush leaned forward, resisted the jelly beans. "He had a practically headless body and a disabled vehicle in the road. He preserved his scene, stopped traffic, and waited for the cavalry. They almost missed Dolewicz, over by the fence under the trees. If the passenger door hadn't stayed open he might still be there."

"Any word on the shooters?" Doc said.

"They found the cars on fire at a gas station a mile back this way."

"Pros. Definitely."

Shimp looked confused. Appeared for a second she might not speak, then said, "How did they get away if they burned the cars?"

"They stole three cars," Stush said. "Or, more likely, had three cars stolen for them. One they left at the gas station as the escape vehicle. They'll find it a few miles away, sooner or later."

"Why burn them? Wouldn't it be better if it took longer to find them?"

"Destroy the trace evidence," Doc said. "They didn't care when the cars were found. They knew they'd be gone. Probably left the weapons there, too. Better than getting picked up with them."

Shimp grew antsy and it occurred to Doc Ohio State probably didn't see a lot of gangland executions. Doc and Stush in no hurry to end their reverie. Mike Mannarino not a friend, still a familiar presence at least since Doc had returned to Penns River. Even longer, counting back to Mike's days as second team All-State pitcher for the high school baseball team, a twelve-to-six curve ball the origin of his nickname, "The Hook."

Doc in his thinking pose. "Why the hell was Mike going toward Oakmont? If he was at Bilotti's, that's dead-ass the other way from home."

"No idea," Stush said.

They all sat, the room somber, until Shimp's fidgets got Doc's attention. "Let's go work on our case for a while."

In the hallway she asked, "What's with this Mannarino guy? Stush said he's a mob boss and you two look like you lost a friend."

Doc leaned against the wall to be out of the flow of traffic. "We all have friends, and even relatives, we don't really like, but who've always been around. I do, Stush does, you do." Doc scratched his thumbnail against the insides of his fingers, "Mike Mannarino was a big deal pitcher when I was on the JV team. Batted against him in intra-squad games a couple of times. His curve was unhittable. He went away to college. Auburn, I think. I joined the Army. By the time I came back, he was the boss for Pittsburgh. He's just always been there. Feels weird without him."

Stopped moving his fingers, made a fist. "Besides, I don't want some asshole to kill him before I get to arrest the bastard."

28

Mike Mannarino threw the pillow from his hospital bed at Ray Keaton. "Here, you cocksucker. You want me dead so goddamn bad, just smother me. Not like I can stop you."

Keaton caught the pillow, tossed it on the bed at Mike's feet. "Keep your voice down. The FBI paying its respects to a mob boss after a botched hit is routine. They'd take it funny if I didn't come."

"Like they don't know already." Mike reached, came up empty-handed. "Give me the fucking pillow."

Keaton slid the pillow behind Mike's head. "Mike, swear to Christ, even if they did find out, they didn't get it from us. I am the only person who knows your CI number. I even fudge the reports you give me so there's nothing too identifiable in them."

"That could be what tipped them: you were too careful. They figured someone big, and I'm the biggest fish around."

"It would still have to be someone from inside the Bureau, Mike, and I can't believe they have a source in the Pittsburgh Field Office. The only other people who know about you are SOG."

Mike made a face. "Stop trying to impress me with your bullshit jargon. Speak English."

"Seat of Government. Washington, DC. The J. Edgar Hoover FBI Building. Pennsylvania Avenue. That English enough for you?"

"Fuck you."

"Do you want to know what we know, or do you want to bust balls? I'm staying at least half an hour. We can spend it however you want."

Mike lay back, closed his eyes. Hadn't touched the morphine button all day, had no interest in giving Keaton the satisfaction of prompting the first hit, even if he had no way to know. Or did he? Fucking feds monitored everything else, wouldn't surprise Mike if they knew how often he clicked for relief. "All right. What?"

"The order came from Sal Lucatorre."

"Bullshit. It's not bad enough working with you almost gets me clipped, you don't listen. Sal is out of it. He doesn't know what the fuck he's doing. From what I hear, half the time he doesn't know where the fuck he is."

"Fine. Have it your way. Tino DeFelice pushed the button. Whoever thought it up, it had Sal's blessing."

That made more sense. "All right. Anything else?"

"We're pretty sure Carmine Valentinetti got the contract and put a crew together."

"They gave the job to The Saint? Jesus."

"That's what I'm trying to tell you. He's as good as it gets. Three of you in that car and only Buddy Elba dies. Are you sure it was you they were after?"

Mike's eyes squeezed shut. He'd known Buddy since they helped out with Tommy Vig's collections, two young humps on the make. "Buddy got out of the car. I don't know why. Maybe he thought he could face them down, four guys with shotguns, him with his dick in his hand. It was like they no sooner started shooting and I heard sirens. Tino's fussy about civilians and paranoid about killing any law. They probably had orders."

"Are you sure it couldn't have been Buddy they were after?"

"Why would they want him dead?" Mike reading Keaton's face when it dawned on him. "You mean they figured someone flipped, and they thought it was him?"

Keaton raised a finger. "If they figured out on their own there was a snitch—*if*—they might've guessed wrong. I told you our security has been tight. Maybe they thought Buddy had a grudge and was looking to take some people out."

Mike started shaking his head halfway through Keaton's speech. "If Buddy had the goods to rat anybody, it would be me. I'm the only local guy who'd have even second-hand knowledge of what goes on up there. Anything he'd have would be third-hand, at best."

"Do they know that?"

"They should, after all these years. If they don't, Tino's as bad off as Sal."

Keaton slumped in his chair. Filled his cheeks, exhaled. "I didn't really think so, either. I had to run it past you." Tapped the bed's guardrail with a finger. "There's a task force in New York. Our guys, DEA, New York and Jersey state cops, and some NYPD detectives."

Mike wanted a nap. "Everyone knows that."

"We think Tino has someone on the inside. Probably NYPD."

"So? You just been telling me about this legendary security you have for me."

"Think about it. The pressure's gone up on them since we started working together. If Tino suspected you and has a man on the inside, what's to say he didn't plant some information with you, then wait to see if it came back? Something only you and he knew, so it couldn't've come from anyone else."

"That's a lot of assumptions."

"I know. We're doing background on all the NYPD guys, just in case."

"Can you get me a list of their names? Maybe I'll recognize one from before."

"I'll have it for you tomorrow. In the meantime, I'm going to show you what kind of a friend I am."

"You want the pillow?"

"We have a wire in a social club owned by a made guy in the Lucchese family. We're going to bust some people the day after tomorrow and let it slip we've been getting a lot of good shit from that wire, stuff we actually got from you. We're sacrificing an asset we worked hard for, and it's going to cost us. Not just in that club, but in how careful everybody's going to be for a while. That's to get the heat off you."

A lot more than Mike had expected. "I know it ain't free. What do I do?"

Keaton waved in dismissal. "Get better. You're not worth much more to us here than if they really had killed you. You heal up, maybe we get them to think they made a mistake, then we'll let you know how to play it."

29

Doc lunched alone at Long John Silver's. Asked Shimp if she wanted to come. She had a salad in the station refrigerator and would see him after. Abrupt about it, her manner somewhere between off-putting and irritating. He considered asking what the issue was, decided against it. A lot going on, Doc not the kind of person to ask such a question even when things were quiet. Someone didn't want to talk to him, they didn't have to. What did Yogi Berra say? People don't want to come to the game, how you gonna stop them? Something like that.

Refilling his root beer—A&W, best root beer in the world—when he heard the sirens on Tarentum Bridge Road. Long John's not five hundred yards from the river and town line; where the hell were they going? Giant Eagle? The Clarion? Doc dug out his cell and called in.

"There's a jumper on the bridge," Janine Schoepf said. "Stush was just about to call to see if you were handy."

Doc told her he'd be right over. Went out the back way behind Giant Eagle to avoid the parking lot on Tarentum Bridge Road. Found Sisler and Nancy Snyder working crowd control. About to ask what was up, shaded his eyes and saw the figure halfway across the bridge. Pointed, said, "I guess he's the show."

Snyder kept her attention on the crowd, people getting out of their cars for better looks. One guy had binoculars. Sisler said, "That's him. Some passing motorist innocent bystander called it in."

Doc shifted his line of sight from the man to the cluster of flashing lights and tiny figures on the far bank, then back. "He's on the Tarentum side, isn't he?"

"That's what I thought. Tarentum says no."

Doc exhaled resignation. "I wonder if he'd be willing to move twenty yards that direction for a hundred dollars."

"I doubt a hundred bucks makes much difference to him, if he's serious about jumping." Sisler squinted. "Maybe he was walking across the bridge and stopped to enjoy the nice day."

"How long's he been out there?"

"Gotta be at least fifteen, twenty minutes."

"And no cars getting on the bridge from either side for— what? Five minutes?"

"At least."

"And he hasn't noticed anything? It's not *that* nice a day." Doc judged the distances again. "Tarentum doesn't want him?"

"Nope."

"Well, hell." Another measuring look. "Anyone call for the boat?" Pittsburgh had a police river unit, helped out when needed.

"I think so. Still be half an hour till they can get here."

Doc unclipped the holster from his belt. Handed it, gun included, to Sisler. "Don't do anything with this to get me in trouble." Stepped onto the bridge roadway, hands away from his body, started walking. Noticed how flimsy the bridge seemed, like walking on a forty-foot-wide concrete and steel tightrope.

The man stood on the footpath to the right of the road. Both hands gripped the safety fence, not moving. The breeze blew wisps of thinning brown hair. Quiet on the bridge with no cars. Doc wondered how close to get, stopped five feet away, a Jersey barrier separating them. The potential suicide paid no notice.

Doc spoke in as conversational a tone as he could manage. "You okay over there, buddy?" No response. "Do me a favor, would you? I'm not crazy about heights, and I'm a lousy swimmer. Bridges are not my favorite places, is what I'm trying to say. I really don't want to have to crawl over this barrier to talk to you. Can we do it from here?"

"Stay over there."

"That's what I want to do. Why don't you tell me what we're doing here?"

The man glanced toward the Penns River side, then returned to looking straight ahead, north along the river. Doc not a huge fan of small talk under the best of conditions; no idea where to start. "What's your name, buddy?"

"Mitchell."

Doc hadn't expected such a quick answer. "Okay, Mr. Mitchell, how about—"

"My first name's Mitchell. Mitchell Tomczek."

"You prefer I call you Mitchell or Mr. Tomczek?"

"I prefer you fuck off, okay?" Squeezed the fence. "I said 'Mitchell,' didn't I? What do you think I prefer?"

"I'm sorry, Mitchell. I'm a little nervous. This isn't an everyday thing for me."

"Oh, really? I come out here and think about jumping three or four times a week."

Doc re-evaluated his position. Came out expecting someone depressed, not this asshole. At least he knew for sure this wasn't someone walking across, got a cramp. "I wouldn't jump if I were you."

"You're a cop, right?"

"Yeah…"

"Good. I always wanted to tell a cop to go fuck himself. I guess today I get away with it."

For the time being crossed Doc's mind, stayed there. "Let's understand one thing right away: I'm not coming over there. You're on your own far as that's concerned. I told you I'm a shitty swimmer. I'm not taking a chance of getting tangled up and going over with you. I have no idea when that fence was last inspected."

"It's not the drowning that'll kill you."

"Sure it is. That fall's not going to do it, unless you're damned lucky."

Mitchell gave Doc a quick peek. "Like hell. That's at least a

147

hundred feet."

"More like seventy-three." Doc had no idea. Looked like half a mile from where he stood. "That'll only kill you if you land head first and at just the right angle. Miss a little, and you'll live a normal life expectancy...as a vegetable. Not to mention, bodies have a natural tendency to fall feet first. Have to force yourself to hit the water with your face."

"You're full of shit. Divers go head first all the time."

"Divers go *hands* first. Break a hole in the water for their faces. Try to land face first, break the water with your nose, take a superhuman effort not to flinch. Turn the wrong way, even an inch, and it's the difference between fishing a dead body or a live paraplegic out of the river."

"Then I'd sink and drown."

Doc shook his head. Didn't speak until Mitchell turned to see. "Paralyzed, all relaxed like that? You'll float. Not indefinitely, but there's already guys scrambling boats in the marina over in Brackenridge." Brackenridge a little far to see with that kind of detail, the truthfulness of Doc's comment at less risk than if he'd mentioned Tarentum, where not a goddamned thing was going on at river level. "They'll fish you out in a heartbeat. Get themselves on TV as heroes."

Mitchell kneaded the fence with his hands. Red crept out of his collar. Doc not done yet. "You want to kill yourself jumping off this bridge, the time to do it is winter. January or February. Remember all the ice last year? You land on that from here, you're sure as shit dead. Even if you break through, end up in that thirty-two-and-a-half degree water? Die of exposure in a few minutes, and no one will come hauling ass across dangerous ice to pull you out. You missed your chance this year. Wait till the holidays. Those depress a lot of people. You'll be in the mood again then."

Mitchell turned to speak. "What the hell kind of suicide negotiator are you?"

"I'm not. I'm a cop who was eating his lunch ten minutes

ago. I don't know you. Don't know anything about you, so I have no idea what to say. I don't want to lie to you, though. If I talk you off this bridge by lying to you, you'll be back in a week. Or try some other way. Why don't you step over here and we'll walk back together?"

"Because I want to jump."

"No, you don't."

"You think I'd lie about that?" Mitchell took one hand off the fence, turned like he had an argument ready.

"You'd have no reason to." Doc listened for the boat. "You strike me as a decisive person. I mean, so far you haven't pussy-footed around anything you've said to me. If you really wanted to jump, you'd of done it before I even heard about you. You ever try to kill yourself before?"

"No."

"You're up here trying it on, see if it'll work. You're not a hundred percent sure. Tell you what, though. You think you have problems worth killing yourself over now, try solving them paralyzed. They won't go away, you know, just because you're paralyzed. The problems."

Indecision replaced anger on Mitchell's face. Examined Doc, then turned to face upriver. Hands looser now. Hefted himself up a foot and stretched his neck to look straight down and Doc's stomach pulled into his throat. "Can you answer a question for me?" Doc's voice no louder than necessary.

Mitchell still looking into the river. "What?"

"Why?"

"Why what?"

"Why are you going to kill yourself?"

"You mean why do I want to kill myself?"

"I mean, why are you thinking about it?"

The reply took time. "Haven't you ever thought about it?"

"No. Honest to God, I haven't. I'm not a real introspective person." Doc looked over Mitchell's shoulder, pretty sure he saw activity on the river. Not sure how he felt. Last thing anybody needed was some asshole hollering, "Jump!" On the other hand, good Samaritans often more trouble than they were worth. Want to be helpful, pull too close, this guy could land on a boat. Kill himself for sure, maybe even take someone with him. Go right through a smaller boat, far as Doc knew about boats. "So tell me why. I'm genuinely curious."

Mitchell's hands flexed and loosened. Alternated between looking upriver and down into it. Doc gave him all the time he wanted. "It's hard to say. I mean, to put in words."

Doc took time, to give Mitchell the impression more of it went into his reply. "This is kind of an irrevocable decision not to be able to describe, isn't it? I don't mean to be argumentative, but do you want the last thought that runs through your mind to be, 'I hope I'm not making a mistake?'"

Mitchell leaned against the fence, slumped his shoulders. "I get so goddamned frustrated sometimes. You know what I mean? Nothing goes right, nothing's ever good enough. Take a walk, get drunk, punch a wall, doesn't matter. I want it to go away."

"What kinds of frustrations?"

"No." Mitchell's voice went flat. "I've been to a counselor. Waste of time. One more thing to be frustrated about."

"I'm not a counselor. Think of me as like a bartender. A guy you don't know and won't see again. What would you say to him?"

"I'd tell him to leave me the fuck alone."

Mitchell looked as if he had more to say, then tightened his grip on the fence and started to climb over. Doc moved before he could think, flung his torso across the Jersey barrier to grab Mitchell's belt and pants with both hands. Realized he had a bigger man than expected, the bed of the footpath a foot lower than the road. Felt Mitchell twist, then stop. The belt loosened, the pants slipped. Doc let his arms slide along Mitchell's legs, tightened them to draw the knees together, a classic tackle. They hit the surface hard, momentum driving Doc into the base of the fence. Mitchell's hands on Doc's head, pushing away, Doc's arms squeezed tight around Mitchell's knees, back pressed against the fence, the breeze cooling his shirt. Skin crawled behind his knees and thighs, working up, the sensation not of falling, but of being about to fall, the solid surface on which he lay sliding away beneath him, the fence pulling loose of its anchorage. The impotence came even with his eyes squeezed so tight all he saw were stars, knowing what was behind him. Mitchell beating him with fists now, yelling something. Doc unable to defend himself, not trusting whatever held him place to do so indefinitely, his mind begging for Sisler or someone to please get this asshole away from him and help him off the bridge when Mitchell hit him again and Doc shifted position, no more than an inch, to let the blows land on a different spot. Mitchell wriggled and the pants came free, Doc's arms wrapped around a cotton and polyester envelope of air. His head twisted up of its own accord, along the walkway to see Mitchell flip himself over the fence. Didn't make a sound until he hit the water, Doc still grasping the empty slacks.

30

Rasheed Mason didn't look like much to Wilver. Stereotypical street nigger, far as he could tell: white tee shirt four sizes too big, jeans hanging halfway down his ass, stuffed into the tops of his unlaced Timberlands. Thick gold chain suspended a gold cross four inches high around his neck like he was Jesus's personal drug dealer. Not a Penns River boy, which explained why Wilver knew so little about him.

Parked in the beer distributor's lot and walked across the street to where Rasheed stood near the north entrance to the Stewart Tower Apartments. No action there, hoppers on the corner to Wilver's left. Someone approached Rasheed, directed toward the corner as Wilver crossed the street. How Wilver knew who to talk to. No drugs or money anywhere near the boss.

"Yo, you Rasheed, right?" They slapped and slid hands in Penns River's current shake.

"My boy down the corner take care of you, yo." Rasheed whistled through his teeth, raised his arm and pointed downward toward Wilver.

"No, man, not like that. I ain't looking to buy."

Rasheed's eyes narrowed. "Then you looking to step off." Walked toward the non-sales corner.

Wilver followed, not too close. "I'm here to talk. Might have a business proposition for you."

Rasheed let Wilver catch up. "What proposition you have might interest me?"

"We both in the same line of work. Word is you have a solid supply of product. Wondering if you might put me onto your connect."

"Why the fuck would I do that? Give away my advantage to the competition."

"We ain't in competition, not really. You selling down here at the Towers. I'm up the other side of town."

Rasheed sized Wilver up. "What's your name, boy?"

"Wilver Faison."

"You the nigger runs that raggedy-ass crew up past the bridge?"

Wilver bit down to swallow the insult. "We sell up that way. By the tracks and into town a little."

"I got no need to work with you. Fore long you be working for me, or you be gone. I ain't looking for no half-assed partners."

"I ain't talking partners. More like borders. You get your territory, I get mine."

"Why I want to split with you, when I can take whatever I want, anytime I want?"

Wilver looked up and down the street. "This Penns River, man. Ain't like them bigger towns like Pittsburgh, or even Wilkinsburg. The bidness not that embedded here yet, and the po-po takes a special interest of anything in the open. I been here all my life. I know how to run things, keep them on the down low, not draw no special interest. I help you with that, you hook me up with your connect, we draws our lines in advance so's we don't go to tussling over corners. I even give you points on my package for being the broker."

Rasheed listened with humor in his eyes. "You small town niggers the cutest things, you know that? Coming to talk with me like we's equals or some such shit. Now here's my counter-offer: fuck you. Once my operation consolidated, and word done getting out where we at and the kind of product we got, we'll come for you. Then—maybe—you can work for me. Wash my car, you ax nice.

"I know why's you here. I ax around, too, you know. You getting that stepped on shit from Ike the Barber. Hell, what Ike selling you been cut at least twice before he got it. I work with the same connect, cept I gets it direct from him, with protection besides. When I'm ready for you to wash my car, get me a cold drink from Sheetz and be my general-purpose bitch, I know where to find you."

Three months ago this would have sent Wilver running. No faster than he could and save face, but running all the same. He'd taken the time since he found himself de facto head of Donald Woodson's old operation to learn the structure from the bottom up. Ike the Barber's connect got his drugs from a guy who got them from Mike Mannarino; Wilver knew that for a fact. Rasheed either lied about who his connect was—a distinct possibility—or Mannarino didn't know Rasheed had set up shop in Penns River. Way Wilver heard it, Mike Mannarino busted people up, and worse, for a lot less than selling dope in town. Rasheed maybe talking out his ass, Mannarino not knowing what was going on here. If it even mattered, what was on the radio about Mannarino and his crew all shot up.

Wilver made a tactical retreat. Hadn't lost a thing—not yet—learned a lot. On balance, a good day.

31

"We're running down leads, Rance. What can I tell you?"

"Running down leads could mean anything." Rance Doocy used the supercilious tone that led Stush Napierkowski to fantasize of grabbing him by the tie and pounding his face into the desk a half dozen times. Stush, whose initial response to learning of Ben Dougherty's near abduction by a Russian gangster had been, "I guess we'd better ruin some people's evenings and get them in here." Oh, and Doocy hadn't finished. "More likely it means nothing. Who's in charge of the investigation?"

"Benny Dougherty." Stush knew Doocy had that information walking in the door, and that he and Benny had history.

"Are you sure he's the man for the job?"

"Yes, and I'd say so even if he wasn't my only viable option, which is where I figure you're going next."

"I'm not qualified to argue whether he's competent." Not that qualifications to argue anything had ever stopped Doocy before. "His animosity toward the casino is well known. I question his motivation."

"Ben Dougherty was born and raised here. Could've lived anywhere he wanted when he got out of the army. He came back, and takes violent crime in this town as a personal affront. Ran down his two leads as vigorously as anyone could have, and they blew up in his face. It happens. Right now he's regrouping his team to move forward."

"What, specifically, do you mean by 'regrouping his team?'"

"What I mean is, he's planning what to do next. More than that is police business not to be discussed with a civilian. Even a civilian with a vested interest in the investigation."

"Can I at least talk to Dougherty?"

Stush's first impulse, tell Doocy to pound salt. Manhandling him out the door came to mind, as well as the ever-popular tie grabbing and face slamming. Knew he couldn't prevent Doocy from getting his chat—he'd go to Benny's house if he had to—thought the best option was to control the conversation. "Can it wait until tomorrow? Benny's having a rough day."

"I'm sympathetic to his personal issues, of course, but I cleared time to come up here. If he's available, I want to see him."

"Did you listen to the news on your way up?"

"I was on the phone. What happened?"

"Benny tried to talk a jumper off the bridge around lunchtime. Guy decided to go anyway and Benny wrestled with him until the guy broke loose and jumped."

"Dead?"

"No." Stush looked at Doocy, thin-lipped and chinless, wondered how he'd look taking the express ramp off the bridge. "Broken foot, sprained ankle, hairline fracture of either the tibia or fibula. I always confuse those two. And a dislocated hip. He's resting up at Allegheny Valley till he's fit to be moved to Western Psych."

"Was Dougherty injured?"

"Bruises and scrapes."

"Is he here, on duty?" Stush nodded. "Then I'd like to see him."

Stush fixed Doocy with a look that would have caused a less oblivious person to reconsider. Pressed a button on his phone and told Ben Dougherty Rance Doocy wanted to chat. He didn't want Benny to be surprised when he saw Doocy, hoped "chat" conveyed the seriousness in which Stush held the conversation.

Benny took his time, which Stush spent not speaking. Read reports, made notes to himself. Considered cleaning his gun, which he thought was in the bottom desk drawer, didn't want oil on his blotter.

Two raps on the door before it opened and Benny came in. "You wanted to see me?" Stush nodded toward Doocy. Benny said, "What is it, Rance? I'm pretty busy today."

"I heard about what happened on the bridge. I hope you're all right."

Benny might have smiled. "That's not why you're here, Rance. What do you want?" Stush suppressed a smirk of his own every time Benny said, "Rance," which came out sounding like "dickhead."

"How close are you to making an arrest in the casino shooting?"

"Closer than we were a few days ago."

Doocy shot Stush a look. "Really? I was under the impression your leads weren't panning out."

"They're not."

"You said you were closer."

"We are."

Doocy gave the look. Benny made him say it. "I'm confused."

"We now know of two more people we're sure didn't do it." Waited for the irritation to show on Doocy's face, added, "I didn't say we were a *lot* closer."

Christ, Benny was a pistol. Stush felt guilty sometimes, loving him as if he were blood, a bond between them not even his own kids could duplicate.

Doocy's expression showed his opinion of Doc's perceived insubordination. "Your chief says some leads haven't panned out. What can you tell me about them?"

"They didn't pan out."

Doocy seemed surprised there wasn't more. "I'm not asking out of idle curiosity. Mr. Hecker wants to know."

"Then Mr. Hecker can call me and I'll tell him the leads didn't pan out. Not why, though. That's information we're holding back. It might be significant later, when we have to evaluate other stories."

"This is for internal use only. It's not as if we're going to seek out the suspects and tell them."

Doc turned to Stush. "Permission to speak frankly?"

"Be my guest."

Back to Doocy. "Your office leaks like a sieve. I don't think it's you—I really don't—but someone you're telling in good faith is telling someone else and every time we give anyone at DanHeck the time of day I get a phone call from a reporter asking to confirm. You've gotten all you're going to from me today." To Stush: "Am I done here?"

Stush nodded, knew if he spoke he'd laugh.

32

"PR-Four, what's your status?"

"I'm ten-eight on 780 eastbound, coming up on the college."

"We have a vandalism complaint, F and M Motors, 115 Stevenson."

Jack Harriger on the way to work, keyed his mike. "Dispatch, this is PR-Two. I'm three blocks away. I got it."

Lester Goodfoot's voice came over the speaker. "You sure, Deputy? I'll be there in five minutes."

"I can see it from here," Harriger said. "I'll take it."

He pulled his personal Crown Victoria into the lot. Reached back into the car for his hat. Walked into the showroom. Two guys with ties stood around bullshitting. The younger man approached. "We're not open for an hour or so yet, buddy. Take care of whatever you need then."

"Someone here call the police?"

"Yeah, we—oh, shit, I'm sorry. I was expecting a *cop*. You're all dressed up."

"Deputy Chief Harriger. I was in the neighborhood. What's wrong?"

The older man stepped forward. About sixty, suit coat over his shoulder, short-sleeve shirt, tie loose an inch. "It's out back, Officer."

"Deputy."

"Huh? Oh, sorry. It's back here. I'll show you."

They passed through the showroom to the parking lot behind the building. Cars lined up in tight rows, white plastic on the flat surfaces, price stickers on the windows. They walked to the chain link fence in back, where a dozen new cars had every

159

piece of glass broken out of them.

"When did you notice it?" Harriger said.

"When I come in a few minutes ago. I got a guy might've wanted to buy this Regal, so I came out to pull it around so the kid could prep it. Ruined now."

The salesman leaned on the hood of a vandalized Encore across the aisle. "Don't touch anything," Harriger said. "We may want prints off all these cars."

The salesman went from zero to condescending in a heartbeat. "Do you have any idea how many people have touched these cars? Test driving, or just walking by, run their fingers over the finish? Come on. Alls I need is for you to write up the report for the insurance. Quicker the better, so I can look for another car this guy might like."

Harriger shielded his eyes, scanned the lot. The salesman was right: unless the vandal left behind an implement of destruction with his prints on it—or, even better, his wallet and driver's license—not much could be accomplished here. Worst part, he didn't have the form he needed to write this up. Goodfoot would have to come, anyway.

Walking back to the showroom with the salesman—Butch Gorman—something on the lip of the roof caught Harriger's eye. "That a camera up there?" He pointed.

"Yeah," Gorman said as if cameras had never occurred to him. "We got two back here. One for each half of the lot."

"Can we take a look at the tapes?"

"I don't know if they have tapes."

Harriger glared. "You keep a million dollars' worth of inventory overnight on an unsupervised lot and the cameras don't record?"

"What? Oh, yeah, sure they record. I don't think they use tapes, is all. Floppy disks or DVDs or something. I can show you."

Security office in a small windowless room near the back of the building. Four cameras altogether, each with its own monitor.

Harriger found the one that best showed the damaged cars, pointed. "Can you roll this one back?"

"I can't record a show off the television since my kids moved out. Donnie might be able to. Hey, Donnie!"

Donnie, in his forties, could work the equipment. "How far back do you want to go?"

Why Harriger didn't leave the office much. "Just till you see something happen."

Something happened at twelve forty-one. A man climbed the chain link fence, cut the barbed wire that ran along the top—no one had noticed that—let himself down the other side. Picked up what looked like a small slab of concrete and broke the windows with vigor.

"Either of you recognize him?" Harriger said.

"Uh-uh," Donnie said.

"Can't see much of him from here," Gorman said.

Donnie thought they should be able to zoom in. "Mitch had this system put in a year or so ago after a couple cars drove themselves off the lot. Spent good money on it." Inspected the control panel. "Too bad my kid's in school. He could probably let us count this guy's nose hairs."

Harriger checked his watch. Neuschwander the department computer savant, should be in the office or close to it by now. Dougherty supposed to be pretty good, too. Harriger wouldn't call him for help if stuck in a collapsing well with a broken leg and five poisonous snakes.

"Hey! What'd you do there, Donnie?" Gorman all excited. "It moved in."

Donnie had found the magic button. Zoomed in, out, focused on various areas of the screen. Happy as a kid playing Pac-Man or Donkey Kong or whatever the hell it was kids played now.

"Let it run until he's looking right at the camera, then zoom in as close as you can get." Harriger said.

Donnie feeling cocky now, slow motion when the angle looked promising, regular speed when the vandal turned his back. "Let's see...how's that?"

Harriger leaned in. "Let him complete the motion...slow... slow...there! Can you take it back two or three frames?" Donnie could. "Now, can you print it?"

Donnie futzed around, fired off a dirty look when Gorman said, "Don't erase the goddamn thing" under his breath. Paused his index finger over each button, then smiled and pushed one. A mechanical sound behind them as a printer fired up.

Harriger took the printed page as it fell into the tray. The quality was disappointing. Guy looked white, hard to make out much of his face. Borderline homeless-looking, stringy hair almost to his shoulders. Hooked nose. Tattoos peeked out from beneath what appeared to be a denim shirt rolled halfway up his forearms. "I don't suppose either of you tried to sell him a car in the past few days." Neither had. "Print up another copy. Show it around when everyone comes into work. Maybe someone saw him."

"What about that one?" Gorman sounded like he was afraid the cost of the page would come out of his pay.

"I'll get copies made at the station. Hand them out to the patrol units." Harriger looked at his watch. "I'll send someone back with the paperwork you need for the insurance, too. I don't have the forms in my personal car. Should be here in less than an hour."

Gorman and Donnie looked disappointed no action was imminent. They grunted something that sounded like grudging acceptance, and Harriger went back to his car. Drove less than a block when he noticed a sign, hit the brakes and made a hard left into the parking lot of Ink in the River.

A little surprised to see a tattoo parlor open at eight thirty. Morning commute the time least likely for crime to occur. Harriger didn't consider tattoos to be a crime, but, since crimes were the result of bad judgment—by definition, in his eyes—and fewer crimes were committed in the morning, Harriger—being a morning person—associated mornings with good judgment. He did not associate tattoos with good judgment, thus his surprise at seeing an "Open" sign hanging in the main door of Ink in the River.

Guy behind the counter where the cash register lived had short hair, large, sinewy arms, and a ring in his left ear. No visible tattoos, which struck Harriger as odd. They exchanged good mornings, and Harriger held up the printout from F&M. "Do you know the man in this picture?"

That was when the man who'd been standing with his back to the door perusing the books of standard tattoos turned to see what was up and Harriger found himself looking at the man in the picture. No question about it. Harriger said, "You're under arrest," reached behind himself for handcuffs that weren't there. The guy saw Harriger's hand come back with nothing in it and broke for the door. Underestimated the narrowness of the aisle and Harriger's quickness, tripped over an extended foot. Harriger jumped on the suspect's back. Looked over his shoulder, yelled for the man behind the counter to call the police.

"I thought you were the police."

"I am. I need help."

"To arrest Brian Fitzhugh? Seriously? What'd he do? Piss on the sidewalk or something?"

"He broke the windows out of about a dozen cars at F&M up the street. I don't have any handcuffs. Now either call for help or get me something to restrain him with."

Fitzhugh's struggles were less than desperate. "Yeah, I broke their fucking windows. Cocksuckers wouldn't even talk to me about buying one of their used pieces of shit. Like I didn't have money and all."

The Ink in the River employee appeared to be having the time of his life. "You don't have money."

"Fuck you, Phil. I ever come in here and ask for anything I didn't have money for?"

Phil handed Harriger two cable ties. "Can't say you have, but we're talking considerably different amounts of money. I mean, you're a good customer and we're sort of friends and that, but, I gotta tell you, you don't smell like somebody with the scratch to buy a car."

The situation defused, Harriger realized the man he knelt on smelled like a garbage truck in August. Jerked him up by the wrists. "Are you homeless?"

"Fuck you, cop. I ain't no bum. I got an address."

"What is it?"

Awkward pause. "I don't know the exact number. It's up the street there." Moved as if he would have pointed had his arms not been bound behind him.

"Jake Malobicky lets him sleep in a room he has over the garage at his car repair joint," Phil said. "I don't think there's any running water up there."

Harriger tried not to breathe, couldn't help himself. "Where's he go to the bathroom?"

"Out the window, from the looks of the grass," Phil said. "I don't want to think about where he shits."

Harriger looked at Fitzhugh, shifted his eyes toward the Crown Vic parked in the lot. Gave Phil the non-emergency police number. "Tell them Deputy Harriger has a suspect for transport." No way that smelly son of a bitch got in Jack's personal vehicle. Made a mental note to be better prepared if he planned to be a more active participant in Penns River law enforcement.

33

Sally Gwynn's office always impressed Doc, how she managed to make it look like it had been dropped from the set of *SVU* or *CSI* or some other show that tried to pass off models as cops. Sometimes thought about sneaking in when she was out, see if that made a difference.

Sally herself looked like she'd walked off the set of one of those shows. Tall, with lustrous red hair and a small pulse that showed in the hollow of her throat, legs that—in Stush's phrase—went all the way up to her ass. Doc nicknamed her The Red Baroness for all the potential suitors she'd shot down, him not one of them. The way she acted sometimes, he wondered if she wanted one more penis to paint on her fuselage before she retired to married life in July.

She met him halfway to shake his hand, closed the door. Sat in the other visitor's chair, no desk between them. Crossed her legs right over left, cut right to the chase. "Did you really run Alvin Crenshaw out of the station the other day?"

"How'd you hear about that?"

"He was over here bitching to Don Michelosen in the Solicitor's office not five minutes after you ditched him. Said he wanted a *habeas corpus* hearing and an injunction against any questioning or polygraph until the judge ruled."

"What'd Don tell him?"

"Pretty much the same thing I guess you told him. Didn't matter who paid him or sent him over. The prospective client has the final say, and he said no. Case closed."

"And that did it?"

"Oh, he threatened to sue the city and talked about civil

rights violations and a bunch of Constitutional amendments. First, Fifth, Sixth, and Fourteenth, I think. Those are his favorites. Don listened politely—you know how he is, wouldn't say shit if he had a mouthful—told him the right to counsel didn't mean any ambulance chaser who showed up with a briefcase, and asked him to close the door on the way out."

Doc snorted through his nose. "Don really call him an ambulance chaser to his face?"

"*Everyone* calls him that. Hell, his initials are A.C. It's almost too easy." Sally looked as if she were relishing the moment, playing it over in her mind. "That's how Don told the story in the lunchroom. I doubt he was that specific in person. You know how he loves to make his stories interesting." Let the smile pass, said, "Haven't seen you on this side of the building lately."

"Willie Grabek takes care of the warrants and paperwork now. Most of my cases pled out. No need for me to come over."

She gave a look he couldn't measure. Sally's passion for cutting deals a point of contention between the police and prosecution sides of Neshannock County law enforcement. Rumor had it she hoped for a United States Attorney job, with a ninety-eight percent conviction rate at the top of her resume. That number might do it, if no one looked at how many of those convictions were pleas. Her record with juries far less stellar. "How are your new cops working out?"

"The women? Fine, far as I know. I really only work much with the detective. Shimp. She's good, and she learns fast."

"How much does she have to learn?"

"Practical stuff, mostly. She knows the theory from working at Ohio State. Hasn't had much experience with some of what we get here. This Stirnweiss business is her first homicide."

"Why'd Stush hire her? I know of half a dozen experienced female detectives off the top of my head. I even sent him some names."

"We talked to them. They were good. The best wanted to be

a detective sergeant or lieutenant, run the shop."

"You mean, have you work for her."

"Yeah."

"How'd you feel about that?"

"I didn't sabotage the application, if that's what you're asking."

"I know you didn't. Besides, Stush would never let anyone get between the two of you on the chain of command. You know that." Had to give her that one. "I'm just curious. How would you feel about working for a woman?"

"I had a woman CO in the Army for a while. A year, maybe a little less. I had worse. And better."

Sally showed an ambivalent grin. "What made her worse or better than some of the others?"

"This what you called me over to talk about?"

"What if it is?"

Doc caught himself before he engaged, sat back. "Sally, you are a piece of work."

"What?" They both laughed.

Doc rubbed his lower lip with a finger. "What made her better than some was she took things at face value. Didn't try to read more into them than was there. She'd call you into her office to discuss an investigation or sort out an action, and she was a good sounding board. Able to distance herself from whatever emotion or psychology might have you missing something. Or misinterpreting it."

"What made her worse?"

"She didn't think a woman could do the job." Let Sally absorb it. "She was one of those who thought she had to be twice as tough as any man to get her command to respect her." Saw Sally breathe, held up a hand. "I know, some of that's true. What she didn't recognize was the men were more likely to respect her as her than as whatever she thought she should be, and she had a First Sergeant who'd make goddamn sure they did. She didn't see it." Rubbed his lip and thought. "Always struck me as ironic, how she recognized things like that so well in others and missed it in herself."

"Did the First Sergeant ever tell her about it?"

"We didn't have that kind of relationship." Doc stopped rubbing. "Is that why you asked me over? To talk about ambulance chasers and women's rights?"

"Would you mind so much if it was?" Her expression changed as if a switch had been thrown. "How are you doing on Stirnweiss?"

"How long we known each other?"

"About five years."

"So I'm not talking out of school if I speak frankly. Whatever I say stays between us."

She looked almost hurt. "You know it will."

"We have dick. Our best lead is a drug dealer who looks a lot like the victim. We're running down his customers and known associates to see if someone might have mistaken this dead citizen for the dirtball drug dealer."

"That's it? Really?" Doc nodded. "Wow. That's not just dick; that's puny dick."

Doc laughed in spite of himself. Sally could be a great broad when in the mood, "broad" not always a pejorative in local vernacular. "Practically Irish," Doc said.

Sally reached over, put two fingers on his knee. "I might be able to make it bigger for you."

Her blouse hung free when she leaned in to touch him. Doc caught a glimpse of oft-discussed breast in a low-cut bra, lifted his view to her eyes. She looked straight at him, gave nothing away. "I'd be a fool not to listen," he said.

She removed her hand, leaned both elbows on her knees. Direct eye contact, at an angle where Doc need only shift a few degrees downward for a show that would have been cut from a movie when the Hayes Office had the juice. Doc held the eye contact, not out of chivalry. To peek would make him the lesser of the two. He'd seen breasts before; he'd see them again.

"I had a kid in here this morning, Tom Kurpakis. Not bad, not really. Sort of a knucklehead in training. On probation for underage drinking, in a car with a couple of guys. Car gets pulled over, cop smells pot, everyone out. He's not holding, but, because he's on probation—"

"He has to pee in the cup."

"Exactly."

"And he flunked the test." Maybe a little peek wouldn't make him too weak. "So?"

"He panicked. He's terrified about going to jail—which he wouldn't, though he would have to plead to community service and a fine—says he knows stuff about that guy who got shot at the casino."

Doc lost interest in the soft dusting of freckles on Sally's chest. "Where is he?"

34

Tom Kurpakis looked about how Doc expected: hair somewhere between groomed and stylish, average height, stocky, not
quite out of the pimple years. Homemade tat on his left wrist.
An apprentice loser.

"Tell me about this party," Doc said. Kid already scared,
Doc saw no reason not to run with it. Shimp in the corner,
looking no friendlier, but quiet. He'd let her be the shoulder to
cry on if needed.

"It was like, you know, a party." Kurpakis looked from cop
to cop. "You're not gonna make me say where, or who was
there, are you? Lot of these guys is friends of mine."

"You know why you're here?"

"Yeah. 'Cause of that guy that got shot at the casino."

"That's right. Today we don't give a shit about the precise
location where you saw this mystery man showing off his gun,
or who else was there. Not today. Now tell me about the party."

"That lady lawyer said this would clear me up. On the viola-
tion. That right?"

"If that's what she told you. She's the prosecutor. I'll bet she
also told you there were conditions. Like how cooperative you
are and whether an arrest results from what you tell us. Right?"

Kurpakis looked defeated. Nodded. "Yeah."

"So, start earning your way out."

"What do you want to know?"

Doc shot a look over his shoulder to Shimp, standing expres-
sionless. Turned back to Kurpakis. "About the party. Where
you saw the guy with the gun."

"Like I said, I was at this party down the Flats—shit."

Blushed, squeezed his hands together. Doc rolled a hand over in a "continue" gesture. "Lots of people there, but this one guy, he was acting all badass. You know, 'let's rob a bank,' or 'let's steal a car.' Bragging how he'd shoot anyone who messed with him."

"This guy have a name?"

"Steve."

Doc arched his eyebrows. No response. "Last name?"

"I'm not sure. Might've been Martin."

Another glance to Shimp. Still no reaction. "You're telling me Steve Martin shot the guy at the casino?"

"It was Martin or Miller or something like that." Kurpakis saw Doc's expression. "No, man, not *that* Steve Martin. This is a young dude, local. Big mother. I think he used to be a Marine."

Doc heard the interview room door open and close behind him as Shimp left. "Ever see him before?"

"Once or twice. He runs with these two guys I used to pal around with."

"Used to?"

"They hang with him now."

"And you don't."

Kurpakis lowered his head. "No."

"Why not?"

Head stayed down. "This Steve guy, he's a scary dude. I could imagine bad things happening around him."

"What's the attraction for your old buddies?"

"He's legal, so he can buy beer."

The door opened and closed. Doc looked to Shimp as she resumed her position. She shook her head twice, no more than an inch.

"Okay, Tom," Doc said. "Tell me why you think Steve Martin—or Miller, or Carrell, or, hell, Blass for that matter—why you think this Steve shot the guy at the casino."

"Well, we was all there, you know, hanging. I was trying to stay as far away from this guy as I could, 'cause, you know, he likes to do shit to me."

"What kind of shit?"

"He don't hurt me or nothing, but, you know, he, like, he picks on me. Because I don't run with Greg and—fuck—those guys that hang with him now. Says I'm a pussy. Likes to make me look bad in front of everyone else. You know, slaps my cheeks, or pinches them like I'm a little kid."

"So you stayed away from him."

"Yeah, right, like I said. So I'm talking to these two girls I know and I hear some noise over the other side of the room, and I go check it out. There's this other guy I know a little, and he's giving Steve lip. How he's all talk and big man at a party where maybe he can impress some chick into going home with him, but it's different out there, you know?" Looked to Doc as if asking whether he'd explained enough.

"I know."

Kurpakis took a few seconds to shoulder the conversation again. "So this is getting kind of heated, and all of a sudden Steve pulls a gun and sticks it right in Bill's face. *Damn* it."

"Bill's the guy who'd been giving him lip?"

"Yeah."

Shimp stepped up, sat across from him. "Don't worry about it. We're not going to do anything with these names unless we know enough that people can't assume it came from you. This isn't like some cop show where we're going to holler at you until you break and not care what happens when we're done."

Kurpakis shot Doc a look when Shimp mentioned not hollering, though Doc hadn't raised his voice. Took the level down another notch, kept the intensity. "Where'd Steve have the gun? Before he pulled it?"

Kurpakis ran the scene through his personal screening room. "I didn't see it before. He had on a flannel shirt over his jeans and a tee shirt. Must've had it stuck in his pants."

"What kind of gun?"

"I don't know anything about guns."

"How big? Automatic or revolver?"

Kurpakis shrugged, opened his hands. Doc and Shimp drew their weapons in unison, ejected the magazines, and laid them on the table. "Bigger than these?" Doc said. "Or smaller?"

"I don't know man. I don't see guns, not for real, and it wasn't laying on the table like these are. He was pointing it, you know?"

Doc picked up his Sig Sauer P-226, racked the slide three times, stuck a finger in the breech. Pointed it in Shimp's direction, a foot to her left. Earned Kurpakis's immediate attention. Shimp never flinched. "Bigger or smaller?"

"Bigger."

Doc brought the gun down to Kurpakis's eye level, not pointing it. "Was it an automatic, like this? Or a revolver?"

Kurpakis sweating like a pedophile in a prison shower. "What's the difference?"

"This is an automatic. Revolvers have a cylinder here." Showed him.

"What's a cylinder?"

"A round thing." Doc pointed the gun between Kurpakis's eyes. Rotated a finger where the cylinder would be. "Here."

"Revolver." Kurpakis jumping out of his skin. "Point that thing away from me."

Doc raised the Sig to inspection arms, returned the magazine, and re-holstered. "So, a revolver bigger than this. What color?"

"Silver, man. Shiny."

Doc looked over at Shimp. They both nodded. "Then what'd Steve do?"

"He told Bill he'd better shut his mouth. Said he'd shot men before and didn't mind shooting another. Pushed the gun right up against Bill's nose and cocked the motherfucker, man. I mean, you could hear a pin drop, you know?"

"What did Bill do?"

"What the fuck you think he did? Nothing. Froze. Shit his pants, maybe. I would have."

"Steve's got the gun against Bill's nose and Bill freezes. What did Steve do?"

"He pulled the trigger! He pulled the fucking trigger, man, right in Bill's face."

"The gun didn't fire?"

"It wasn't loaded. Steve started laughing his ass off. He thought it was fucking hilarious."

"What did Bill do?"

"Ran like hell. What the fuck would you do?"

Doc sat and stretched. Hadn't meant to press the kid so hard. Went where the rhythm took him. Time now to let the tension drain away.

Shimp asked Kurpakis if he was all right. "Yeah. I'm okay. It's just—I never seen anything like that before. Don't want to again. It ain't like on TV at all."

"We're going to have to look for Steve," she said. "Do you know where he spends his time?" Kurpakis went pale. "We're not going to run right over there. We need to know a lot more before we confront him. Makes it easier for us, and less obvious that we got anything from you."

Kurpakis shook his head. "I only run into him at parties and stuff. You know, like events where people get invited. I don't know where he hangs."

"Your old friends do, though. Don't they? The ones that dumped you because he can buy them beer."

35

Sophie Dolewicz had several choice things to say to Mike Mannarino when he came to visit Stretch at HealthSouth rehab. You almost got my husband killed, you got a lot of nerve showing your face around here, go to hell you miserable son of a bitch who almost got my husband killed, you bastard. Kissed Stretch's forehead and left for the snack bar to get him a milkshake.

Mike turned the padded chair to let himself in easier. His first full day out of the hospital, bummed a ride from Stretch's nephew Ted to visit. Nodded toward the door. "She's taking it well."

"Yeah, well, you know how it is."

"How's the hip?"

Pure dumb luck, Mike all shot up, nothing vital damaged. Stretch only grazed, but pellets wedged in his hip had to be removed. Weeks of rehab in front of him. "I'd say it's a pain in the ass, but it's around the side a little."

They sat for a minute, friends as well as business associates, neither sure how to start. Mike trying to shape his thoughts into spoken words when Stretch said, "She won't be gone long."

"Your nephew's down there. I told him to keep her busy until I came back."

Stretch opened his hands. "Go on."

"It had to be New York." Mike paused to decide how it sounded, in the air now where he couldn't take it back. "They're catching heat. Must figure someone's talking out of school, had an idea it came from here." A pause before the plunge. "They must've thought it was Buddy."

"Buddy?"

"He's the dead one."

"That cop was right there. Buddy's all they had time for."

"Valentinetti got the contract. He wouldn't leave without whoever he came for. You know him. An Oakmont cop would've been collateral damage."

"How'd you hear it was Val?" Stretch a little too casual when he said it.

"Not from anyone in New York, that's for sure. I got friends in Buffalo, Philly. Word gets around."

"I can't believe Buddy flipped."

"He didn't." Stretch shot Mike a look. "No one did. They're panicking. Things are fucked up there, the feds are leaning on them, and they're looking for witches under the bed. Everyone's too busy sucking each other's dicks to push the button on one of their own, so they looked outside. Buddy drew the short straw."

"You hear that from Buffalo, too? Or Philly?"

Mike shook his head. "I don't need to hear that from anyone. That, I know."

Stretch sipped from a straw in a cup of ice chips. "So, what? We're clear now that they think they got the rat?"

"No, because they didn't. Even if there is a rat—which I doubt—they clipped the wrong guy. Things aren't going to get any better and they'll realize that, send someone back. Hell, they may send Valentinetti back just to clean up the mess he left."

"So, what now? It's not like we can slug it out with them. Look at what we got. I can't walk on my own, and I'll bet you can't tie your shoes."

Mike gestured toward the door with his head. "We got the kid downstairs."

"A twenty-something kid that never fired a gun in his life definitely tilts the odds in our favor. They can't have more'n a hundred guys. You're as fucked up as Sal. Worse, maybe."

Mike looked at the far wall like it had something interesting on it. "I got things in play."

"Like?"

"The feds come to see you?"

Stretch made a face as he repositioned himself. "Yeah. That douchebag Keaton was here the other day. Once in the hospital, too. I'd hate for one of them to have my back. First thing goes wrong, they think people bail. I told him to shit in his hat." Stretch stopped fussing. "Why do you ask?"

"He came to see me, too. I told him the same thing."

"So, what do you have working?"

Mike made him wait. "Chicago."

"You thinking about moving there?"

"I'm thinking about switching."

"To Chicago?"

"Yeah. We can kick up to them same as we been kicking up to New York. We might actually get some service." Stretch looked skeptical. "There's history there, too. My uncle was tight with those guys years ago. The Outfit don't forget who their friends are." Stretch looked as if he'd speak, didn't. "What?" Mike said. "You got something?"

"No. Just thinking." Mike's turn to wait now. "You think Sal and Tino are just going to let bygones be bygones?"

"No, but I don't think they'll do dick about it, either. Chicago says we're with them, Tino's not going to make waves. Him and Sal were afraid to help us against a handful of Russians. They're gonna face down the whole Outfit?" Stretch still wore the face like he had something to say. "You have a problem, tell me."

"No, no problem. Playing around with the idea." Stretch not sounding convinced at all.

"You think of something, let me know. I'm going to have to rely on you a lot more now, with Buddy gone. You're all I got."

"What about Tommy Vig?"

Mike waved a dismissive hand. "Tommy's too old. Don't want to work anymore, just sit in his house and wait for people to bring him money. Never had the belly for heavy work even when he was younger. Way he talks and acts anymore, I'm thinking he's about half a fag." Made eye contact with Stretch. "It's you and me now. And the kid downstairs."

36

The rest of the morning spent checking out Tom Kurpakis's former friends while Doc scanned the mug books and identified Steven Malick as the scary dude with the gun. Lucky with that, Malick's sole arrest for vagrancy, and then only because he mouthed off to Lester Goodfoot when asked to move along. Lester at the end of his shift, eight in the morning and not in the mood for banter with someone who didn't smell any better than Malick. Doc and Shimp on their way to Subway to discuss Malick's record over lunch, stopped at PNC Bank in Hilltop Plaza so Shimp could deposit a birthday check from her parents in Ohio. Doc came with her, took the inventory all cops are compelled to make when entering a bank, dropped his head in disgust. An obscene sound—not even a word—escaped.

"What?" Shimp said.

"That woman in line. The next one to go."

"Where? In the shorts?" A quick look. "That looks like Nancy. I thought she was working today."

"It's not Nancy."

"Are you sure?"

Doc put out an arm to stop her from going over. "Nancy banks at First Niagara. I saw her there the other day." Shimp gave confused. "Look at the hair."

"She has it all pulled up into that comb."

"It's too light. Nancy has darker hair than that." Doc paused, deciding how much to let out. The hell with it. "That's Marian Widmer."

Marian's hair darker now than it had been when she and Doc first met a couple of years ago. Her physical condition hadn't changed, everything as taut and well-proportioned as ever, in remarkable shape for a woman of forty-two, as he knew her to be, Doc the world's leading authority on all things Marian Widmer.

"Marian Widmer?" Shimp paused as the realization dawned on her. "*That's* Marian Widmer?"

Marian finished her transaction, turned to leave the bank. Doc put on his sunglasses. Marian walked toward the door. Within five feet of him when she stopped. Her face distorted as if she'd touched a rotting corpse. "I thought it was agreed you'd stay away from me."

Doc stood almost at parade rest, eyes locked straight ahead. "Good afternoon, Mrs. Widmer."

"I'm going to report this." Marian with the arrogance of privilege, sensing an advantage. "I agreed not to pursue the harassment claim, and you agreed to stay away from me."

"I'm here with a bank customer, ma'am, and did not approach you. It was you who stopped to speak to me."

"Just because you didn't say anything doesn't mean you aren't intimidating."

Shimp stepped in front of Doc to create a triangle. "Go on about your business, ma'am. Detective Dougherty has done nothing intimidating." Doc kept his vision on the rest of the bank. A slow day, people with nothing better to do than watch the scene developing near the doors. He banked here, too. He knew these people.

"Who are you?" Marian said to Shimp.

"Detective Shimp. Penns River police."

"It figures. Where's your fat friend? Grabek, is it? Or does this one provide a better way for you to channel your aggression?"

"That's enough." Shimp rounded on Marian.

Doc saw the color in Shimp's face. Put a hand on her shoulder. "Teresa. Let it go." His head still and steady, not looking at Marian. Spoke *sotto voce*. "Mrs. Widmer, I appreciate your situation. I'd feel uncomfortable, too, if I had a conspiracy to murder charge hanging over my head every day for the past three years. All that time wondering when that one piece of evidence will drop into place. Several witnesses and the bank's security cameras will establish I in no way approached you, nor did I speak until spoken to. There's no harassment claim to be made. Move along."

Marian shuddered with rage. Doc went on. "I *will* arrest you if you spit on me again. Move. Along."

Doc couldn't see what expression Marian threw him on her way out; she didn't speak. Shimp watched her leave, gave Doc a look, and walked to the teller's window.

"Nancy had a hat on that day in Maguire's. I couldn't see her hair." Doc bit into his Big Philly cheesesteak. "Where she was standing, I couldn't see you or Kathy until she turned. That's why you got that look. I promised Stush I'd leave her alone, but I also didn't have to avoid her. I wasn't in the mood that day."

"She actually kill those people?" Shimp's lunch a roasted chicken breast on seven-grain.

"Not Carol Cropcho. She set up her goofball husband for that. The second one, she may have helped, but all we'd be able to prove was she hired it done. If that. I'd say the odds we ever get her back in court are three-to-one against, and that's only if Sally Gywnn gets another job."

"If Sally stays?"

Doc chewed, swallowed. Took a drink. "Sally Gwynn will never prosecute Marian Widmer again."

They ate in silence for a minute, Doc's foot-long disappearing at a rate proportional to Shimp's six-inch. "I owe you an apology," she said.

"Not necessary. You didn't know."

Shimp raised the sandwich to her mouth, let it sag. "I'm afraid I told Nancy about it, too. I think it colored her opinion of you."

"That explains a few things." Another bite. "Don't worry about it. I'll live."

"I'll talk to her later."

"I'd rather you didn't."

"Why not?"

More eating business to buy time. "I get along with people, or I don't. If Nancy holds a mistaken impression, and my conduct doesn't change her opinion, that's on her. I don't care if you tell her if she asks, but I'd prefer you not bring it up." A drink, then, "Malick."

"Kurpakis was right: Malick was a Marine, for about seven weeks, I think. Got into a fight with his drill instructor on Parris Island and they threw him out."

"Physical fight?"

Shimp chewed and nodded. "Malick spent a week under arrest in the base hospital while they did his paperwork. He was escorted off post directly from his room."

"So, combining this with what we want him for, Malick isn't just violent, he's not too bright. Who the hell picks a fight with a DI?" Licked mayonnaise from a finger. "What's he been up to lately?"

"Nothing criminal. At least not that showed on NCIC. I haven't had a chance to look at his employment or education records. If Lester Goodfoot hadn't picked him up on that vagrancy charge a few months ago, we wouldn't even have a mug shot."

Doc rolled his wrapping into a ball while Shimp ate her last Sun Chip. "How do you want to play it?"

"We have his address from DMV," she said. "We could just go over and see if he's home, but that looks bad for Kurpakis. I'd also like to know more about him first."

"Agree. Let's get the rest of his background and look into those other two jagovs he hangs with. See if Grabek can find time in his busy schedule of playing switch with his thumbs to get us a warrant to search Malick's place. Once we go to see him, the cat's out of the bag. He'll ditch anything we might want."

Shimp rolled her debris into a ball, stuffed it into the Subway plastic bag. "I *am* sorry. About that Marian Widmer confusion."

"It's forgotten."

"I was kind of a bitch, I guess."

"Well, yeah, you kind of were, and I'm not about to forgive you for it." Saw her expression, went on. "Nothing to forgive. You thought I was a phony, and with reason. We're partners. Not trusting your partner is as bad as it gets in this job. You had a right to be bitchy."

At the car, Shimp offered her hand. "Friends?"

"Hell, let's take the relationship to the next level." Doc took the proffered hand. "Partners."

37

The Dougherty family plus Ellen's sister at PNC Park, watching the grounds crew chalk the lines. Upper deck, front row, halfway along the first base line. Tom knew a guy from working on the zoning board. He pointed as Doc took a bite from his sandwich: roast beef on thick-cut white bread, fries, and coleslaw on the sandwich. "Those any good?"

Substantial chewing had to occur before Doc could speak. "Oh, hell, yes. They put a Primanti Brothers in Penns River, I might never eat anywhere else. Except your house, Mom." Ellen turned back to her primary conversation, the need to comment gone.

"That could put Mike Knipple out of business at the Edgecliff, you not going there anymore."

Doc chewed and thought. "I'd still get the fish sandwiches. And wings. Aw, hell. I guess I'd just get fat."

Doc ate his sandwich, Tom and Ellen and Shirley their hot dogs, watching the players stretch and run sprints. Tom sipped his beer, made a face. "I hate these aluminum bottles. Makes the beer taste funny. I miss the paper cups."

"Doesn't the beer stay colder in the metal bottles?"

"I guess." Doc chewed, Tom drank, Ellen pointed out to Shirley a riverboat coming down the Allegheny toward the Point. "Reminds me of those glasses your grandmother had for iced tea."

Doc's turn to grimace. "Why'd she insist on using those nasty things?"

Tom screwed on the lid, looked at Doc. "You don't know? Really?"

"No. Everyone hated them."

"They were aluminum. Your granddad worked thirty-three years at Alcoa. Aluminum paid for the house and every car they ever owned. She found something made of aluminum, she bought it. I used to thank God there was no aluminum toilet paper."

Doc snorted through his nose, forced his jaws together to keep from spitting out a mouthful of meat/fries/slaw/bread. "No shit?" Tom nodded.

Ellen leaned in. "Shirley says they're closing the fire hall on Burgly Avenue."

"I heard the other day, Mom."

"I don't like it."

"Why not?"

"What if there's a fire up on the hill?"

Doc slid the empty food tray under his seat. "It can't be more than an extra couple of minutes to get a crew over there from Leechburg Road, across from the school. There's one on the top of Edgecliff hill, too. Next to my place."

"How do you figure?" Tom said. "Those are both three-four miles away."

"Edgecliff is more like a mile and a half. Besides, we're talking fire trucks. It's not like they wait for lights or follow the speed limits. The other thing is, consolidating the firehouses, they can have enough of a crew on duty to dispatch right away. Burgly's closer. But you still have to get a crew together." The smaller firehouses in Penns River still depended on sirens to alert the volunteers when needed. "I was a little surprised. Last I heard, they were talking about hiring a couple of guys to beef up your crew."

"That money got spent on the woman cops."

"The feds paid for that."

"They paid the salaries and benefits. Some extra equipment and those new radios. Then, after everyone thinks things are settled, Stush up and decides he's got two extra patrol officers, he needs a new car. You can't just go over to Nick's and buy a cop car off the lot. They cost."

"I knew we got a new car." Doc unsnapped the lid from his Coke, took a sip. Replaced the lid. Didn't drink beer at ball games—"I like to be kissed when I'm getting fucked"—had an idea pop tasted colder without the straw, drinking off the top where the ice was. Straws drew liquid from the bottom and insulated it on the way up. "I can't believe a cop car costs as much as two jobs. It's not like they paid cash for it."

"Revenues are flat, and that goddamned winter hurt us bad. Overtime for the road crews, gas for the plows, salt." Unscrewed the lid of his beer, held it without drinking. "The company where we get road salt called the other day. They're suspending the contract until we get current with what they're owed."

"I thought we caught up with that."

"We were close until that big snow came in March." Took a swig. "Things are tough, Benny. The wrong business lays off, unexpected road or bridge repair comes up...we could default."

The men lapsed into silence while the women discussed whether a nearby infant was adequately clothed, down here by river, that wind's cold. Five minutes before first pitch they left for the restroom.

Doc, looking at the field, said, "Mom talk to you about her eyes?"

"Yeah."

Doc turned his head to see Tom in his peripheral vision. "And?"

"And we went to the eye doctor the next day. He didn't have much to say except she needed to see an ophthalmologist. So I called. They'll take her week after next."

"Optometrist have any ideas?"

"He seemed to, but he played it close. Said it could be a couple of things he didn't have the equipment to diagnose, get her to the specialist soon as we can."

"And two weeks was the best they could do?"

"It was three when I called last week. I probably could've got her in someplace sooner, but Dr. Walker says this guy's good, and he takes our insurance. Way the hell down Oakland, though, a block or two from where Forbes Field used to be." Oakland twenty miles from home, Tom acting like it was in Ohio.

"Well, let me know what he says." Doc took another swallow.

"It ain't like we been keeping it a big goddamn secret." Tom pointed to a player trotting through the diamond to right field. "That's him, huh? Polanco."

"That's him," Doc said, applauding. "He's the goods."

"I hear he's the best they've had here since Bonds. Even better than McCutchen."

"We'll see. They also used to say it was a toss-up who'd be better, McCutchen or Tabata. McCutchen's a hell of a ballplayer."

They watched Polanco and McCutchen play catch, tossing the ball a hundred feet with the ease and accuracy of handing it to each other. "He's bigger than I expected," Tom said.

"Six-four, about two-twenty, I think."

"I didn't think those Spanish boys got that big. Where's he from? Puerto Rico?"

Doc shook his head, cup to his lips. "Dominican."

The first Atlanta batter walked. The second hit into a force play. One out, runner on first. The three hitter sliced a drive down the right field line. Polanco cut it off, spun, and threw a strike on the fly to erase the runner at third by three feet. The ballpark exploded.

"Jesus Christ," Tom said. "Bonds never threw that well in his dreams. I ain't seen anything like that since…at least since Dave Parker. Maybe not since Clemente."

"I saw a game from Detroit, I think it was, couple a weeks ago. Those three," Doc gestured to the outfielders, "put on a real show. I don't think a ball landed on the outfield grass all night, it didn't roll through the infield first."

They watched the replays on the scoreboard. Tom finished his beer, put the bottle under his seat. "You know how to tell when you're old, Benny?"

Doc half turned, a smile forming. "No."

Tom pointed toward right field. "When you see a kid like that come up—already good, but the potential, my God—and you come to realize you're not going to be around to see how his career plays out."

Not what Doc had expected at all. The smile felt stupid, frozen on his face. "What the hell, Dad? You don't think you'll last fifteen years?"

"I'm almost seventy now. What's life expectancy for a man? Seventy-eight?"

"That includes all the people killed in car wrecks and wars and fights in their teens and twenties. Once you hit seventy, that number goes way up."

"To eighty-five? Eighty-seven?"

Doc doubted it went up that much. Stuck for something to say now. "Well, look on the bright side. Maybe he'll get hurt, won't last as long as you expect."

Tom glared for a few seconds, then broke up. "You...are an asshole."

Ellen settled into her seat, a small Jolly Roger pennant in her hand. "Who's an asshole?"

"Your son."

"He gets it from your side." She waved her little flag.

38

Doc and Teresa Shimp picked up their warrants along with Sisler and Snyder for backup and drove to 1396 Fourth Avenue, Steve Malick's address of record. Found a rectangle made of the tops of cinder blocks at ground level, weeds a foot high, across the street from the Ukrainian Club.

Doc let his head sag no more than a couple of seconds. "I knew this place burned down. Hell, it was two or three years ago. I've driven past a hundred times. It didn't occur to me it was 1396." Took another look. "Shit."

Sisler's voice came over the radio. "What next, Kemosabe?"

Doc looked to Shimp. "Where's Szczesny live?"

"Hastings Drive."

Doc arched his eyebrows. "That's all middle-class single-family homes over there."

"He's nineteen. He's probably living with his parents."

"And he's unemployed, which makes his nineteen-year-old ass unlikely to be up yet. Let's hope he's more conscientious than Malick about keeping his license current."

The drive took eleven minutes. Doc made a note to ask his father about the condition of Chester Drive, torn up like the Ho Chi Minh Trail after a B-52 run, ruts and grooves and depressions running along and across for what looked like new water lines, but, Jesus. Bel Air rehab down that way, ambulance coming out in a hurry could shake some old biddy's kidney loose.

At 2804 Hastings, Sisler trotted around behind, Snyder stood backup at the front door. Doc pounded cop style, with the side of a closed fist. "Jeffrey Szczesny! Penns River police!"

Nothing. Doc pounded and called again. Same nothing. About

to send Snyder around the side to check the garage when the door opened a crack, the chain set. Half a face could be seen. "What?"

"Jeffrey Szczesny?"

"Yeah. What?"

Doc showed his shield. "Penns River police. We need to have a few words."

"What time is it? Come back later." The door started to close.

Doc got his right foot in the crack. "*Now*, Jeffrey. We can do it here, or we can do it at the station. Your choice."

"What'd I do?" Whiny.

"Far as I know, nothing. We just want to talk. You don't answer our questions, make me come back with a warrant, then you can explain to your parents why we had to kick the door down."

Thought pulsed from the other side of the door. Then, "Okay, but you have to move your foot so I can get the chain off."

Doc and Shimp stepped into a front room that could have come out of half the homes in Penns River. Couch, small recliner, and one wing chair faced across a coffee table to the corner with the television. Kitchen down a short hallway to the back. Stairs led up to the bedrooms; down to the cellar would be in the kitchen.

"How old are you, Jeffrey?" Doc curious how the kid would play it.

Jeffrey rubbed his eyes. Wore shorts past his knees, no shirt. Hair styled by entropy. "Nineteen."

"You know that means we don't have to have one of your parents here when we question you."

"She's at work, anyway."

"Where's she work?"

"Kmart. Where they keep the lipstick and makeup and shit. What do they call it? Health and Beauty Aids, or something?"

"What about you?"

"What about me, what?"

"You working?"

"No. You know how it is. No one's hiring."

"You graduate last year?"

"Yeah."

"Worked at all since then?"

"Some. You know, around. Part-time stuff."

Doc wrote what he planned to have for supper in his notebook. Shimp asked if Jeffrey had any hobbies.

"I watch TV, hang around."

"I'll bet you help out around the house. The place is immaculate."

"Uh, yeah. You know. When I can. My mom works hard all day. Whatever I can do to help."

"Watching TV and hanging around must get boring after a while. What do you do for fun?"

"When I say 'hang out,' you know, it could be anything. I got lots of ways to spend my time, just not like I have a regular routine so things come to mind, you know?"

"Spend much of it hanging around Steve Malick?" Doc said.

Jeffrey's heart landed in his stomach so hard Doc heard it splash. "Who?"

"Were you at a party in the Flats last week when Malick drew a gun and pulled the trigger on someone?"

"No, hey, what's this? I never saw him shoot no one."

"I didn't say he shot anyone." Doc stepped into Jeffrey's personal space. "The gun was empty."

"Jesus. What was that for? What are you doing coming in here and making like I was there when some guy got shot?"

"You hang with Malick because he buys you beer, don't you? You and your little buddy Delahanty."

"No, man." Jeffrey took half a step back. "I told you, I'm only nineteen." His appearance lost a year every time Doc opened his mouth.

"That's why Malick buys. You're not legal."

"I ain't legal to drink it, either." Another small retreat.

Doc feigned surprise. "Is that why you think we're here? Talk about underage drinking? You're what we call a person of interest in a homicide. We don't care if you drink a fifth of Jack on the front steps of St. Margaret Mary's Sunday mornings when church lets out. Not today we don't." Turned to Shimp. "We better take him in. Make sure he appreciates the seriousness of the situation."

"Shouldn't we let him get dressed first?"

"What about it, Jeff? You want to get dressed?"

"I don't want to go to the police station."

"I didn't ask if you wanted to go. I asked if you wanted to get dressed."

"Yeah, I want to get dressed. But then we can talk here."

"No, then we can talk at the station."

"But I said I didn't want to go to the station."

"No one asked if you wanted to. Now get your ass dressed."

"No, man. I said I'm not going." Doc took Jeffrey by the arm and nodded to Shimp, who put a hand on the doorknob. "All right, all right. Let me get dressed. My clothes are in my room."

Doc let go. Jeffrey started up the stairs, stopped when he noticed the detectives following. "I'll *be* right down."

"I know you will," Doc said. "We're going with you. Persons of interest in a homicide investigation don't leave our sight."

Jeffrey trudged up the stairs. Paused in front of an open threshold. "I'm getting dressed, man."

"So do it."

Jeffrey gestured toward Shimp. "She can't come in. I'll be naked while I'm putting on my underwear."

Doc turned to Shimp. "Detective Shimp will avert her eyes at the slightest chance of seeing your, uh, manhood. That clear, Detective Shimp?"

Shimp gave Jeffrey a less than enthusiastic once over. "I'll do my best."

Doc pointed into the bedroom. "Get a move on."

191

Jeffrey must have used all his energy helping Mom with the rest of the house: his room made baseball dugouts look like operating theaters. Pop cans and pizza boxes, clothes everywhere except in the hamper. And two standard .44 hollow point bullets on the dresser, next to the television.

"Skip the belt and shoelaces," Doc said. "You're under arrest."

39

"I told you I have no idea how those got in my room. I never saw them before."

The worst part of the job. Dishonest people who were either too stupid or too lazy—or both—to lie any better than that. "Then I guess you don't have any idea what else we found after Officer Snyder showed you to her car."

"You looked in my room? Don't you need a warrant or something for that?"

"Constitution says we don't need a warrant for anyone who doesn't lie any better than you do. It's in the Eleventh Amendment: 'The provisions of the Fourth Amendment are hereby waived in the case of obvious jagovs who lack the sense to make up a decent lie when caught red-handed.'"

Jeffrey Szczesny gathered himself for a moment. "No, man. The Eleventh Amendment, that's the one that freed the slaves. They call it the Emancipation Amendment."

Shimp's voice, calm and measured. "We're allowed to search the immediate area after an arrest. The murder was committed with a .44, so the .44 bullets on your dresser gave us what's called probable cause."

"For real? It works like that?"

"Yes," she said. "It does."

Doc put a piece of paper on the table. Pointed to a section of text. "Read along with me." Recited the Miranda warning from memory. "Do you understand your rights as I've explained them to you?"

Jeffrey in a daze. "Yeah. Yeah, I understand."

Shimp touched his arm as if waking a baby. "Jeffrey. Are

193

you sure?"

Jeffrey collected himself to look at her. "I ask for a lawyer now, you'll think I'm guilty."

Doc started to speak, caught himself. Shimp said, "It's your right. Anything you say here can be used against you if charges are filed."

"We already know what we think," Doc said. "It's a jury you have to worry about."

"You can change your mind." Shimp handed Jeffrey a pen. "If you say stop, we have to."

Jeffrey looked from cop to cop. An expression more like resignation than decision passed across his face, and he signed. Doc folded the paper, put it in his pocket. "You ever eat ice cream in Kittanning, Jeff?"

"Huh? What?"

"It's a simple question. Did you ever eat ice cream in Kittanning?"

"What's that have to do with anything?"

Doc pointed to his own chest. "*I* know what it has to do with. Now, have you ever eaten ice cream in Kittanning?"

Jeffrey turned to Shimp. "What's he talking about?"

"It's a simple question," Doc said. "Did you ever eat ice cream in Kittanning?"

"Tell us how you know Steve Malick," Shimp said.

"Hold on a minute. I want to know what's so fucking difficult about whether he ate ice cream in Kittanning."

"He started showing up places I like to hang," Jeffrey said to Shimp. "We talked, joked around. Like you said, he's cool about buying beer."

"It's a binary question," Doc said. "He did or he didn't."

"So it's you and him and your buddy Greg Delahanty?" Shimp said.

"Yeah, pretty much. Tom Kurpakis for a while." Jeffrey spreading the joy. "Not so much lately."

"Tell me about Malick," Shimp said.

"They got a nice little place up there," Doc said. "Block or so off of 422."

"He's just a guy we hang with, you know. To drink with."

"Tell me about him and the gun," Shimp said.

Jeffrey swallowed hard enough to hear. "I don't know anything about a gun."

"You been to Kittanning, right?" Doc said. "You've been that far, haven't you?"

Jeffrey scooted as far away from Doc as the bolted chair allowed. Said to Shimp, "I really don't know what gun you're talking about."

"Hey. Asshole." Doc leaned in. "Don't talk to her. Talk to me. I asked you a question. Did you ever eat ice cream in Kittanning?"

Jeffrey on the edge, eyes wet. "What does ice cream have to do with anything, man?"

"I'll tell you what it has to do with anything, you lying sack of shit. Now answer me."

"What did Malick tell you about the gun?" Shimp's volume less than half of Doc's.

Doc stood to tower over Jeffrey. "You ever been to Kittanning?" Slammed a hand flat on the table. "*Answer me!*"

"Yeah, yeah, I been to Kittanning."

"You ever been to that little ice cream place up there, in West Kittanning?"

Shimp's voice almost a whisper. "We found the gun."

Jeffrey's eyes flicked to Shimp, then down. Doc six inches from his face. "*Have you ever been to that soft serve place in Kittanning?*"

"Yeah! Everyone goes there."

"So you were in Kittanning and you went to that soft-serve place—"

Shimp calm as a frosty lawn. "It was in a shoe box under a pile of clothes in your closet."

"You took your cone to a table and sat down—"

"I didn't put the gun in the shoebox!"

"And you took a lick. So, yeah, you ate ice cream in Kittanning."

"You need a better explanation than that."

"Yeah, *Yes!* I ate ice cream in Kittanning!"

"Then why didn't you just say, 'yes,' you weaselly little cocksucker?"

"That gun we found in your room is being tested right now—"

"I didn't shoot anybody, I swear to God—"

Doc gripped Jeffrey's arm, made to hoist him from the chair. "You're going to jail, motherfucker."

"If it matches the bullet we found at the casino that night—"

"What'd I do?"

"Get your ass up."

"It was Steve shot that guy. I didn't even know he had a gun. I swear to God I had nothing to do with it."

Doc let go his arm. Jeffrey crying for real now. "He's always talking about what a badass he is. Some kind of Special Forces shit in the Marines. Said he wanted to rob a bank or steal a car or kill a cop or something, show them he wasn't afraid. I always figured he was full of shit, talking big in front of the underage assholes. Said he knew a chop shop would give him a grand for certain models. We were out shopping—that's what he called it, shopping—at the casino that night for a car to steal."

"You were with him?" Doc said.

Jeffrey wiped his nose with a sleeve. "Yeah. We were just supposed to boost a car, you know? I thought it might be fun. It was, for a while. Walking through the lot like we was in Giant Eagle buying apples or something. Not this one. What about over there? Shit like that."

"Did he show you the gun?" Shimp said.

"I swear to God I didn't know he had a gun. I didn't know he even owned a gun until that night. We were sticking to the part of the lot where the light wasn't too good." Sucked snot.

Shimp gave him a tissue. "Weren't you worried about the cameras?"

Jeffrey blew his nose. "Half those cameras are dummies. Everyone knows that."

"He know which ones?" Doc said.

Jeffrey shook his head, rolled the tissue into a damp ball. "He said it didn't matter. If we stayed where the light wasn't too good, or got right under one, no one would be able to make out our faces, and we'd get rid of the car before anyone could find it."

"How long were you there?" Shimp said.

"I don't know. Seemed like all night. Steve would look a car over and find some reason it wasn't right. Too old or the wrong model or the wrong color or something."

Doc and Shimp exchanged eye contact. "The wrong color?" he said. "For a chop job?"

Jeffrey nodded. "I know, right? I'm no GTA expert, but I'm figuring by this time, unless we're stealing custom expensive jobs—which we ain't—Steve's looking for excuses not to steal anything."

A long silence, then Shimp, quiet as cotton. "What happened next?"

Jeffrey's sigh bordered on a sob. "I...I was starting to bust his stones. You know, are we gonna steal a car, or what? I was good with calling the whole thing off. You know how it is, when you get all worked up over something, but if it doesn't come off right away you lose interest? It was like that. So I'm giving Steve grief and Greg—he didn't want to be there in the first place—"

"There were *three* of you there?" Doc said.

Jeffrey looked up like he was surprised Doc didn't know. "Yeah. It was Steve, Greg, and me. I thought I told you we hung together." *In more ways than you can imagine*, Doc thought.

"What happened next?" Shimp patient as a spider.

"Steve got the red ass. Saw this sweet little Malibu in the next row. Said, 'Okay, assholes. We'll see who's serious.' We got to about thirty feet away and we see these three people coming so we slide into a dark spot and damn, if they don't go right to that Malibu."

Jeffrey watching things play out in his mind now, curling himself up as if hiding from a snake on the floor. "We should've just stayed quiet. Just shut up and not said nothing. But Greg couldn't let it alone. He said something like, 'Well, I guess you're off the hook now,' and Steve told him to go fuck himself, he was driving *that* car off the lot, and pulls this fucking massive gun out of his pants, you know, from around back? I about shit, swear to God. If I'd a known he had a gun—I mean, I thought we were stealing a car—I'd a never gone with him if I knew he had a gun. You gotta believe me." Paused for acknowledgment.

"We believe you." Shimp sounded like a kid had scraped his knee.

Jeffrey sat with his hands over his eyes as if he could block out the sight. "Steve walked over to the car while they was getting in, you know, had the gun down alongside his leg. The people was talking inside like they was having a good time, and Steve, he knocked on the window so the guy'd open it. I thought he was gonna tell them to get out and get lost, maybe show them the gun to scare them. He just said something and the guy in the driver's seat pointed to one of the women and Steve...he just...oh, fuck, he shot that guy."

Jeffrey's eyes wide open now, staring as if watching the scene take place in the interrogation room. Hands clasped tight between his legs. Took short, shallow breaths with a yipping sound Doc hadn't heard before. He shook the kid by the arm, worried he'd hyperventilate. "What did Steve say to the man in the car?"

Jeffrey had to recover first. "I don't know. I could hear his voice, but not what he said."

Quiet now, the silence made more profound by what had come before. The way Shimp said, "Then what happened?" made Doc wonder if she had kids. He should know that by now, working with her a month.

Jeffrey dropped his head to stare at his hands. "We ran.

Across the street and past the bowling alley. Back into that neighborhood behind the library and the Legion."

"You stayed there all night?"

"We waited for the sirens to stop, then we split up and walked home. It's only a mile or so if you go through yards and the woods. Greg had to cross Leechburg Road, so it must've been harder for him."

"How did you get to the casino in the first place?"

"Greg drove. He parked in the casino lot but we...I guess we panicked and ran. By the time we calmed down enough to go back for the car, cops was there and we were afraid to go for it."

"Where did Steve go?"

Jeffrey looking at his hands, hair forming a tunnel around his face. Shook his head. "I don't know. I really don't."

"Do you know where he lives?" Doc said.

"Nowhere, I don't think. Sleeps with friends or in cars or vacant buildings. Said he found a camper closed up for the winter he could get into, but he can't sleep there now that the weather's nice and the owner uses it. I think he has an aunt or something lets him crash once in a while if he's really hard up and brings her some beer or grass or something."

"How's he get around?"

"Walks, mostly. Me and Greg give him rides sometimes."

The room went quiet again. Air conditioning kicked on and cool air whispered across the back of Doc's neck from a ceiling register.

"What happens to me now?" Jeffrey said.

Shimp's voice, not unkind, but definite. "For now, you're going to jail. If you make bail you could be out as late as tonight or tomorrow morning."

"I didn't kill that guy." Crying now, a little kid who'd broken something valuable and realized too late there were consequences. "I swear to you I didn't."

"You were there, and you were there to commit a felony. You also didn't come to us. You're at least an accessory." Doc knew that depended on what Sally might be willing to let Jeff plead to if it meant no trial for Malick, stayed quiet.

"He told me he'd kill me if I said a word to anybody, and after what I saw that night I believed him."

Doc nudged Jeffrey's shoulder. "Come on, kid. Things were quiet last time I looked. You'll probably get a cell to yourself. Tomorrow you could be out."

Jeffrey scuttled across the chair till one ass cheek hung in the air. "What are you charging me with?"

Doc and Shimp exchanged glances. "For now," she said, "accessory to murder?" Doc pursed his lips in assent. Close enough for government work.

"You mean like I helped? I told you, I didn't even know he had a gun. After that, alls I did was run." A thought brightened his face. "Alls you have against me is what I said here. I have a right not to incriminate myself, don't I?"

"You have a right not to tell us anything incriminating." Doc tapped the folded paper in his pocket. "You waived that. We told before we started you didn't have to talk, but anything you did say could be used against you. You're going to jail, at least till the DA decides what to do."

Jeffrey deflated as though his ribs had left his body. Doc took his arm to stand him up without resistance. Stopped at the door. "Let me ask you one more question, for my own curiosity. Why did you keep those two bullets in plain sight? We'd of never searched your room and found the gun if we hadn't seen them."

"It didn't seem real, you know? None of it. Sometimes it was like I saw it all in a movie or something. Then I'd remember it was real, and what Steve'd do to me if I messed up, or said anything." Jeffrey licked his lips. "I kept them there to remind me to keep my mouth shut. I should have brought the fucking things in here with me."

40

"If he thinks Chicago's the answer, he's as delusional as that syphilitic nitwit Lucatorre," Stretch Dolewicz said to his nephew, Ted Suskewicz. "Unless he's the rat and he's trying to cover up."

"Mike's the boss," Ted said. "I thought the whole point of getting guys to flip was to get to the boss."

"First off, this mafia ain't like in the Godfather." Stretch adjusted himself in the chair. Home now, getting around the house more or less on his own. Took half as many pain pills as prescribed. He'd seen too many fuck themselves up with them, get dependent. Addicted, even. "Bosses are just as likely to flip as soldiers. More, even, since they have the most years inside hanging over them. Things get tight, they'll give up the whole operation to skate into that program."

"But why Mike? You said yourself he's the smartest guy you ever worked with. They got nothing on him."

Stretch sat back, Ted getting to the crux of the matter. "You're right: he is smart. He's also as vindictive a son of a bitch as I ever knew. Couple a years ago—before we brought you in—he had some Russian trouble."

"I heard about that. Real psycho, wasn't he? Tried to kill a cop's whole family?"

"Mike asked New York for help. That regular kick we send is supposed to pay for protection, right? They were afraid of the Russians. Left Mike out on his own. Buddy Elba was so mad when he told me, he almost broke the back off the chair he was leaning on."

"What does that have to do with Mike flipping?"

"Take a step back." Stretch sipped iced tea. No booze until

he was off the pills. "Word is New York thinks there's a rat, which is why they tried to hit us. Mike's telling me the contract was for Buddy, why the shooters left us alive, which is bullshit for reasons I'm not going into right now. So now Mike figures New York is gonna come back to clean up the mess."

Ted gave confused. "If New York thought Buddy was the rat, and Buddy's dead, why come back for you and Mike? Haven't they sent enough of a message?"

"Exactly. And this Chicago allegiance is a pipe dream unless he's flat-out lying. Why would they take on that kind of trouble for an operation that wouldn't earn as much as a decent crew there? No, that's bullshit. Now, who else can protect him and might have an interest in hurting New York at the same time?"

Obvious Ted knew the answer, having trouble bringing himself to say it. "The feds, I guess, but, Christ, Uncle Stretch. I can't believe Mike would fuck us like that."

"Me either." Stretch saw the confusion on his nephew's face. "Mike wouldn't look at it as fucking *us*. He's fucking New York, and more power to him for that. The catch is, New York figured it out. Now, whether they suspected Mike or Buddy doesn't matter so much. What matters is, Mike's good with letting people think it was Buddy. Like he told me, he has friends in Philly and Buffalo. Might've steered them that direction. Here's the thing: if New York's trouble doesn't go away and they suspect someone from here is the problem, who's the next person in line for Mike to tee up, if that's what he's doing?"

Stretch felt for the kid. Only a few years removed from petty crime, ran his collection route as well or better than anyone in Mike's crew. The occupation of "organized criminal" wouldn't seem too risky to someone with Ted's experience. The Oakmont shootings had to have been a serious jolt to his perception. "You think they're coming after you next?"

"Hard to say. If there is a rat, the only person who knows for sure who it is right now is the rat. I know it's not me, so, with only two of us left in a position to cause that kind of trouble, it has to be Mike."

"If there is a rat."

"Right. If there is one. But if there is one, and it is Mike—and it has to be—he's going to steer suspicion my way. We've been friends a long time, but I ain't taking a bullet for that asshole."

"But there was only you and him and Buddy. With Buddy gone, even if he gets rid of you, won't they come for him next?"

Stretch shrugged, opened his hands. "Depends on how long until the feds are ready to go to the grand jury. They'll bring him in then. Remember, we don't know how long this has been going on."

"If it's been going on."

"Right. If."

Ted nursed a beer. Stretch cracked a soft ice cube with his teeth. "Mike wasn't happy with my attitude when he stopped by the other day. If he is the rat, and he thinks I'm onto him, he'll come after me."

"What do you want me to do?"

"What you been doing. Make the collections and report direct to him while I get back on my feet. Pay attention to what he says and how he acts. If he is going to make a run at me, it'll probably be through you."

Ted's eyes got big. "He'd try to get me to whack you?"

Stretch swallowed ice. "Not that directly. He'll try to get to me through you some way you won't suspect. See what he says about how I'm doing, when I'll be up and around. He asks me to go somewhere, I'll say no at first. If he doubles back to you to talk me into it, that's a tell."

"Aren't you worried he'll come for you here, while you're laid up?"

"Nah. Say what you want about Mike, he does precision work. He won't want to make a move when your aunt or one of your cousins might be here. Besides, I always have one of these handy." Pulled a nine-millimeter Smith and Wesson M&P Shield from a bathrobe pocket. "There's a shotgun under my side of the bed, charged and ready to go."

Ted finished his beer. Sat with his elbows on his knees, bottle dangling from his fingers. "So, what if he does come to me?"

Stretch maneuvered the glass to get the ice cube he wanted into his mouth. "Keep me posted every time you two talk. It comes to it, we'll do him first."

41

Steve Malick jogged across Leechburg Road to McDonald's parking lot hoping to hit up Greg Delahanty for a double Quarter Pounder and fries when the manager wasn't looking, then a ride to Malick's aunt's house on Dutchman Run Road. She'd let him sleep there as long as he didn't abuse the privilege, a good place to go to ground: out in the woods, semi-bedroom and bathroom in the cellar, direct access to the backyard. He'd have to spring for a six-pack to get the ride—irritating how these kids used him sometimes—finances dictated either a free meal or walking four and a half miles; he couldn't pay for a burger and a six-pack both.

Across Leechburg Road, slowed to a walk when police cars pulled into McDonald's lot. Two cruisers and an unmarked, two cops in each. Two uniforms went around back. The other two covered the doors. Plainclothes walked to the counter. Malick checked traffic, jogged without hurry back across Leechburg Road to watch.

The cops came out with Greg Delahanty in handcuffs between the two plainclothes, a man and a nice-looking older woman. Malick didn't bother watching them put Greg in the car. Showed his back to Mickey D's and walked away on Jefferson Drive.

Jeff Szczesny might give him a ride, his house a hell of a lot closer than Aunt Jess's, only a half mile or so out of the way even if Jeff wasn't home. Thought of calling—have Jeff pick him up—knew his phone was almost out of minutes. Sent a text and started walking, keeping to side streets.

He could only think of one reason the police would arrest

Greg Delahanty, unless the kid had something going on Malick didn't know about. Doubtful, Greg about able to tell a nickel from a quarter in good light. If the cops were on to him, only a matter of time before they knew about Jeff and Malick, and it would never occur to Greg they'd all be fine if everyone kept their mouth shut.

Halfway to Jeff's house and no reply to the text. Sent another. Malick wanted to talk to Jeff before the police had a chance, keep their stories straight. Should have tightened them both up before now, they'd been hard to find since that night at the casino. Both of them egging him on then, called him everything but a pussy while he tried to find the car that would get the most cash from the chop shop in Apollo. Tough guys that night, Malick imagined them folding like the bitches they were the first time a cop threatened to call their parents.

Across the street from Jeff's house, still no response to any texts. Jeff's blue Tercel in the driveway. House looked empty, the mother's car either in the garage or out. Didn't want to ring the bell on the chance the police had been there and told her told to keep an eye out. Risked a call to Jeff's cell, got voicemail. Almost out of minutes, fewer than ten dollars in his pocket, took the chance and called Jeff's house landline. His mother answered on the second ring. Sounded like she'd been waiting by the phone, the way she said "Hello" before she had it all the way to her mouth.

"Is Jeff there?"

"No, I'm sorry. This is his mother. Can I take a message?"

"Do you know when he'll be back? This is his friend, uh, Cletus. I know where we might be able to get some work next week."

"He's away for a few days, Cletus. He should be back tomorrow or the next day. Give me your number and I'll have him call you as soon as he gets home."

Malick left her a random number with a Penns River exchange and hung up. Jeff was in jail trying to make bail sure as

Lucy Halladay would give you a hand job after two beers.

He stayed on side streets, hung out in a half-built house near Rabbit Foot Lake until full dark. Walked back to Jeff's house and waited in the woods behind until all the lights were out, then another hour. Went to the back door and took the key from under the fake rock Jeff didn't think he knew about. Mrs. Szczesny often had trouble sleeping and took something. If she had tonight, she'd be out cold. If not, well, he'd run. Not like he was there to inspect the place. Thought about getting the gun, decided against it. No idea where Jeff put it, and he'd be exposed every second he looked.

Turned the key in the lock and opened the door slow as he could and be sure it moved. Stepped into the kitchen and removed Jeff's car keys from the hooks hanging off a cabinet. Closed the door with as much care as he'd opened it, held his breath as the latch caught. Hoped Jeff's car started better than it had last time. It did, and Malick crept up Hastings and away.

He drove through near-deserted streets to the Sheetz on the corner of Leechburg Road and Craigdell. Took the tire iron from the trunk, pulled a baseball cap low and walked inside. Smashed the glass counter next to the register, screaming for the cashier to open the till and give him everything in there. The girl no more than seventeen, eighteen years old, probably her first job, panicked. Stared at him and shook, too scared to cry. He reached across and opened the cash drawer himself, obscured his face as best he could going back to the car. Drove down Craigdell to the Ice House to count the $247 he'd taken. Ripped with adrenaline, he drove the bypass to Seventh Street and robbed a Valero on the corner of Constitution. The Middle Eastern-looking guy working there made of sterner stuff than the Sheetz chick started yelling in what might have been English until Malick broke his arm and a couple ribs with the tire iron. The hero gave up $182 and the .38 he kept under the register. Steve could run a ways on $429 and a gun, and this robbery business was easier than people made it out to be. He'd need to dump the car before too long, but that could be arranged by a man with the skills his new-found confidence imagined him to have.

Too late to show up unannounced at his aunt's. He parked out of the way somewhere to shut his eyes for an hour or two, catch her before she left for work. He needed a few things before he could beat feet, and some sleep and a decent feed were among them. Aunt Jess would have both, and the car made gathering everything else much easier.

42

"Two smash and grab convenience store robberies within hours of us picking up Szczesny and Delahanty." Doc sipped his Dunkin Donuts coffee. Still too hot. Bit into the powdered-sugar doughnut instead. His day to uphold tradition, bought an assorted two dozen of nothing he didn't like, tired of eating jelly-filled concoctions that looked like they were oozing out of fresh road kill. "Think it's a coincidence?"

"No way." Teresa Shimp chewed on the earpiece of her glasses, the pollen count too high for her contacts. Couldn't help covetous glances at the box of doughnuts. "Malick knows we're on to him and he's making a break for it."

"Agree." Doc brushed sugar from his shirt. "Any luck finding KAs?"

"He has no criminal record, so we have no known associates. We only know about the fight at Parris Island from his military record."

"Let's do what we can to find local relatives. And get his photo distributed to all conveniences stores, beer distributors, small groceries. Anyplace that might have cash and not much security."

"Liquor stores?"

Doc caught himself in the middle of giving her a funny look, remembered she was recently arrived from Ohio. Liquor and wine sales in Pennsylvania were conducted through state-owned stores. "He robs a State Store, he'll have state police on his ass. Of course, we're not talking about the sharpest picket on the fence. He may not think of that, so hit them, too. And lottery outlets." After a second's pause, "Nice catch. Thanks."

Shimp tapped her front teeth with the glasses. "Do we know what he's driving?"

"He doesn't own a car, but the second robbery was too soon for him to have walked. He didn't tell some cab driver 'wait for me while I rob these convenience stores,' so it's a safe bet he stole one. For Christ's sake, eat a doughnut before I have a stroke from watching you."

"It's that obvious?"

"I'm afraid someone will slip on the drool and sue the city."

"I shouldn't. I gained half a pound last week."

Doc looked at her, a pound-and-a-half heavier than "skinny." "Eat the doughnut. We may have to chase a guy and you'll need your carbs." Her hand hesitated over a chocolate glazed before moving to a plain cake. "You're welcome," Doc said.

The phone rang. Janine Schoepf, the dispatcher. "Doc, you said you wanted to hear about any stolen cars."

"Thanks, Janine. What do you got?" Doc listened, his face placid. Wrote on a pad as Janine spoke. Thanked her again and hung up. "Stolen car. Want to guess whose?"

Shimp in mid-bite. Thought for a few seconds. "Don't tell me it's either Delahanty's or Szczesny's."

"Okay, I won't." She stared through him, a tiny crumb on her lower lip. "Szczesny's. His mother just called it in."

"So Malick is running."

"Yeah, and he might be gone already. I'm going to publish a BOLO for our guys and surrounding jurisdictions. State police, too. Approach with caution." Fixed Shimp with a look until she made eye contact. "If you're done eating, maybe you could round up as many local relatives as you can find and we'll start paying them visits in case he touched base or stopped by to pick something up. Not much else left for us to do. I'll check to see if the warrant's ready, ask Stush to detail Neuschwander and Grabek to help us. Maybe a couple of uniforms. We'll start with that aunt Szczesny told us about."

Steve Malick had parked in Logan's Ferry Heights. Figured even if Penns River police were onto him, surrounding jurisdictions wouldn't get the word right away, and he didn't want to burn Aunt Jess's place before he had to. Adrenaline draining away, satisfied with his hiding place, he overslept. Woke up at seven thirty knowing he had to get the car hidden before Mrs. Szczesny noticed it was gone. Might be too late already.

Debating whether he needed to see Aunt Jess or not when he noticed the warning light on the gas gauge. Hadn't occurred to him to fill up before robbing either of the gas stations last night, and he had no idea how much Jeff's tank held when the light came on. Cursed his bad luck for a second, then remembered the Sunoco where Stevenson split off from Freeport Street. The detour wouldn't even be half a mile.

Jack Harriger heard the BOLO over his radio as he gassed up on his way to work. Turned to disengage the nozzle from his car when the exact blue Tercel described pulled into the next row of pumps. Almost brained himself getting into the car to snatch his microphone.

"Base, this is PR-Two. Over."

"PR-Two, this is Base. Go ahead."

"I have visual contact with the blue Toyota Tercel, Pennsylvania Hotel Foxtrot Zulu 5473 at..." scanned the convenience store door for a street number, "it's the Sunoco on Freeport Street, about a block up from Arby's."

"I copy, PR-Two. Stand by, please." What seemed like three hours passed before Janine Schoepf came back. "All units, officer needs assistance at the Sunoco station, two-nine-eight Freeport Street. Suspect vehicle is the blue Toyota Tercel described in the BOLO. Seal off the station but do not approach pending further instructions. Driver is a suspect in a recent

211

homicide and should be considered armed and dangerous. PR-Two, come in."

"PR-Two."

"You are instructed to maintain a position of cover and good visibility on the station lot and report any movement. Do you copy?"

Great. Deputy Chief, taking orders from the dispatcher. "PR-Two, copy."

Doc ran so fast out of the station he skidded past his car. Started it while Shimp strapped in, hit siren and lights before he cleared the lot. A slight delay negotiating the left turn in morning traffic at Tarentum Bridge Road, then drove a hundred down the by-pass. Slowed as the road merged into two lanes, heard the converging sirens. Less than a block away when Sean Sisler's voice came over the radio, flat as wet sand. "Base, this is PR-Six, requesting an ambulance to two-nine-eight Freeport Street. We have an officer down."

"Copy, PR-Six. Dispatching paramedics now."

Doc keyed his mike. "Where's the Tercel?"

Sisler: "Suspect vehicle is not visible."

Doc burned rubber stopping in the Sunoco lot. "Anyone? All units: does anyone have eyeballs on the blue Tercel, PA HFZ fifty-four seventy-three?" No reply. "Son of a *bitch!*"

Slammed down the mike and opened the door, Shimp already halfway to where Sisler knelt on the other side of the nearest island of pumps. She came up short and drew a hand to her lips as Doc rounded the island and saw Sisler covered in blood next to Jack Harriger, who lay on his back staring with dilated pupils into the bright morning sun.

43

Local cops. Not just stupid: unprofessional. Steve Malick had been surprised when the uniformed cop approached him, hand on his gun. No marked cars in sight, no sirens heard; who the hell was this guy? Weren't cops supposed to wait for backup? This sawed-off dipshit walked between the islands like he expected his mere presence would bring Steve to his knees. Grabbed the .38 he'd taken at the Valero, hoped the piece of shit worked. The cop said, "You! In the Toyota! Get out of the car with your hands up!" Steve stepped out and in one quick motion used the car roof as a platform and shot the cop three times in the chest before the dumb shit drew his weapon.

The good news, Steve had the presence of mind to take the cop's gun. The bad, he drove away without getting the gas he'd come for, sirens approaching as he started the car. Resisted the urge to run away fast, observed the speed limit driving to the old hospital converted to an outpatient care clinic on Fourth Avenue. Took a ticket from the machine and parked in the lot, thinking the police would check roads out of Dodge, not parking garages downtown.

Felt not bad considering how the day had started. Two guns now, the cop's a sweet Sig Sauer that became Steve's weapon of choice the first time he hefted it. Something would have to be done about the car. He couldn't believe how fast they'd picked up on it and it would only get worse with a cop down. Safe for now, he could hang in the clinic for a while like he was waiting for someone. All he had to do was stay off the radar until the sun went down. He'd been a Marine. Darkness was his friend.

Every time he calmed himself by thinking of how well he'd

done, the car situation nagged at him. Never stolen a car before last night, and that didn't really count, having the keys and all. Didn't know how to hotwire one. Thought of going to a car lot—there were a couple in easy walking distance—ask for a test drive. Even if the salesman insisted on going along, hey, he was Two-Gun Malick. No salesman would argue if Steve told him to get the fuck out a mile down the road. That plan fell apart when he remembered they'd make him leave his license, might recognize the name once word got out a cop had been shot.

He could jack one. Wait here in the garage for someone to open their car, show the guns, grab the keys and go. People were here because they were sick, and sick people were often old, and old people weren't going to fuck with a man holding two guns. They'd give him the keys and call Jake from State Farm. Right after they called the police. No point trading one car the cops knew about for another they'd know about before he left the garage.

Aunt Jess would take him in for sure, this kind of emergency, no matter how he got himself into it. Guilt over family issues extending back before Steve was born available for leverage. Shooting the cop might even help: if he died, no way would Aunt Jess leave him in the wind for a possible hot shot. He could walk there in a couple of hours, but not in daylight. Wait till dark, keep his head on a swivel, be aware of headlights from either direction, into the woods before he registered as more than a possible deer. "Stealing" her car would be easy. He could even tie her up if she wanted, make it look good for the insurance.

Left the car, took his money and guns into the clinic, asked if there was a waiting room; his uncle was upstairs. Lasted fifteen minutes before he realized the hardest part of his plan would be killing time waiting for dark.

44

"This is good, kid. Lots of collections have been down since we got shot up, but yours have been steady. I appreciate how you're keeping the cash flow flowing."

Mike Mannarino's first day back at the Aspinwall Hunter's and Fisherman's Club. Handed Ted Suskewicz a beer, took one for himself. "*Salute*—er, *na zdrowie.*"

"Thanks, Mr. Mannarino." Ted waited for Mike to drink before tasting his Bud. Okay, but Ted preferred Rolling Rock. "Just doing my job."

Mike turned a chair around so he could straddle it. "How's your uncle?"

"I thought you saw him yesterday."

"I did. I don't trust him to tell me how he feels. You know how it is. He doesn't want to sound like a complainer."

"He does love to play the stoic."

"I figure you probably have a more accurate picture. You know, your aunt, she don't talk to me at all. Acts like I smell when I come to the door. Between him not complaining and her not talking, you're my source for how he's doing. I'm not asking you to talk out of school, but I kind of need to know when to expect him back. So I can plan how we're going to crack the whip, get these other guys back in shape before one of them gets ideas about taking over."

"I guess some days are better than others, but he's coming around. I know he's driving Aunt Sophie crazy, home all day like he is. She says he's ruining her stories, picking them apart the way he does."

"I can see that." Mike held his beer by the neck to sip it, real casual-like. "I wonder how many times he's told her they need to throw someone a beating."

"Or worse."

Mike laughed. "Or worse."

A quiet minute of drinking passed as easily as pushing a wheelbarrow full of bricks up a sandy hill. Ted tried to suppress his discomfort, wondered if Mike picked up on it.

Mike broke the silence. "Probably why your aunt's so pissed at me." Ted gave a questioning look. "Fucking up her stories."

Like damn near getting him killed wouldn't be enough. "I think everyone will be happier when things get back to normal." Wanting to hear what Mike had to say about the new normal, with Buddy gone.

"I tried to help the old broad out, get Stretch out of the house the other day. Take him up to East Brady for a ride on the boat. I know he loves that, especially this time of the year. Told me he didn't want to go."

"I wouldn't take it personal. Like I said, he has good days and bad days."

"I guess I do, too, now that I think about it." Another casual tipping of the bottle. "That's when I can most use a change of scenery." Brought the bottle halfway, let it down. "It could be he's pissed at me a little, too. You know, blames me for what happened. Wasn't my fault, but it sure as hell wasn't his, and I'm the boss. Gotta take the bad with the good, right? Why don't you ask him? Bring him up one day, your choice, and I'll meet you there with some beer and sweet sausages and that pasta salad my wife makes he loves so much. Ride down to the woodsy spot around the other side of Brady's Bend, drop the anchor and have lunch. Get away from everything for the day."

Ted felt his hand squeeze the beer bottle, forced himself to relax. "Yeah. I'll mention it to him."

45

Doc and Shimp approached the house on Dutchman Run Road with their jackets already clear of their Sigs. Doc stood to the side when he knocked, where he wouldn't be seen by anyone not right at the door. Shimp at the base of the stairs. Jeffrey Szczesny confirmed the aunt Steve Malik used as a security blanket lived on Dutchman Run, which was not overpopulated by any means, out past the Flats in an area most people weren't sure was still Penns River. Stopping at every house wouldn't have taken long, became unnecessary when the address check turned up a Jessica Malick at 169.

No answer to knocks and shouted identification; no car in the driveway. He and Shimp walked the property, looking in windows where possible. Open shades all around the ranch-style house showed no activity. Malick could be in the basement: glass block windows admitted light, but no external visibility.

Around to the front again. Doc stood, arms akimbo. "If Malick is in town, I think this is where he'd come. Szczesny seemed pretty sure, and I have a feeling."

"It's a perfect place to lay low, especially with a relative to cover for him."

"Let's check the next few on our list, then we'll come back here later. Or find out where she works and talk to her there, though that's not my preference."

"Afraid she'll call him?"

Doc nodded, scanning the terrain. "What I'd like to do is stick a car here for about forty-eight hours. See who comes and goes."

"I'm sure Stush will approve the overtime."

Doc spread his arms to indicate the surrounding landscape. "Where would we put it? There's not a hundred yards of straight road within a mile of here and the tree cover is so thick we almost drove right by the dump and we were looking for it. In daylight. The unit would have to park right in front of the house. Hell, even then, Malick might be able to get in around back if he knows the terrain, which there's a good chance he does."

Shimp followed Doc's hand cues, nodding. "I see your point." Took her time to form the next comment. "Maybe I'm out of line saying this…"

"No, you're not." Doc turned on her with a look he'd been told could be disconcerting, couldn't help it. "I know some people look at me as the favorite son or prodigal son or whatever. That's bullshit. You don't work for me; we're peers. You're still new and I've lived here damn near all my life, so I know things and places and people you don't yet. Pick my brain when you need to, absolutely. But never—not ever—be bashful about expressing an opinion. I'll take all the help I can get. It was Jack who didn't want to listen to anyone. You saw where it got him."

Shimp spent a moment digesting. Said, "Sean Sisler. Wasn't he a recon Marine or something?"

"Sniper, and a damn good one. Why?"

"Wasn't he trained to sit concealed for long periods of time and observe? Sure, he's not going to shoot Malick, but he could call for backup if he saw anything he didn't like."

Doc pursed his lips, locked his fingers behind his head to open his chest. "That has potential." Looked around again, this time at specific places. Spoke to himself as much as to Shimp. "Snipers work with spotters…he wouldn't really need one for this, since he's not looking for a shot. For that matter, I could help him. I have some similar surveillance training, though not at his level. Cover two angles, or split the shifts…" Exhaled and let his shoulders sag. His face eased into its normal configuration. "I like the idea in principle, but it's not practical. He's working a double already, and I doubt I could stay awake all night after the day we're having. Plus, Malick almost certainly knows the terrain better than we do, so we still could miss him." Took thirty seconds to try to talk himself into it. "No, not with a force our size. We're only guessing Malick will come here. It's too low percentage to tie down our two best cops—" smiled and winked, "two of our three best cops when there's so much else going on."

The first two names on Sisler and Snyder's list weren't home. They caught Al Turner backing out of his driveway, pulled over to block his way. Turner sat in the car like someone who knew his way around a traffic stop.

Sisler and Snyder approached on different sides. Sisler said, "Albert Turner?"

"Yeah?"

"Mr. Turner, I'm Officer Sisler. That's Officer Snyder over there. Is Steven Malick your grandson?"

"Yeah." Turner looking straight through the windshield.

"Have you seen or heard from him recently?"

"No."

"If you'd like to get out of the car, talk to us eye-to-eye, that's fine."

"I'm good right here. You're in my way."

"We just have a few more questions about Steven."

"I already told you I haven't seen or heard from him. I have things to do, and I want to get to Busy Beaver for a toilet kit before they close."

"It's eleven o'clock in the morning, sir. We're not going to hold you up that long."

"I told you all I know about him."

"Do you know any of his friends? Places he might go if he was in trouble?"

"The kid comes by here once or twice a year to borrow

money. No, for me to give him money I'll never see again. I don't know where he goes, I don't know who his friends are, and I don't care. Can I go now, or are you going to arrest me for not knowing anything? Wouldn't be the stupidest thing cops have harassed me for."

Sisler smelled it now, the alcohol seeping through Turner's pores. Looked closer, saw the broken veins in his nose, the unsteady hands. Turner might be going to Busy Beaver, but he'd stop at Galli's or a State Store somewhere along the way. "Sir, would you turn off the engine, please?"

"Goddamn it, I got to go. You think because I'm retired my time isn't valuable to me?"

"Mr. Turner, Steven is a suspect in a felony. We'd like your permission to ask a few more questions and take a look inside for him. Now, you can let us in, or we can sit here and ask for a warrant, which will arrive with half a dozen other cops and we'll turn the place upside down. Officer Snyder and I will be as considerate as we can, and it'll go a lot better if you can guide us around. Either way, we're going in."

Turner's view shifted to his hands, still on the steering wheel. "Is this about that guy that got shot at the casino?"

Sisler hesitated, decided what the hell. "Yes, sir. It is."

"Aw, Jesus." Turner's head sagged. Spoke almost as if to himself. "That goddamn kid. We should've figured." Then, to Sisler: "Yeah. You can look at anything you want."

Doc and Shimp caught up with Jessica Malick at a quarter to six. Found out where she worked, what time she got off, timed their arrival for fifteen minutes after they expected her home. Went to the door in the same formation as before, safety straps unsnapped.

She answered on the first knock. Still wore her uniform from Dick's Sporting Goods in Pittsburgh Mills. Quizzical expression, pulled a strand of blonde hair due for a refill out of her left eye.

Slender in a raw-boned, white-trashy way. Took a quick look at Doc and Shimp, said, "Sorry, I ain't contributing to nothing today."

Doc badged her. "Jessica Malick?"

"Yeah."

"I'm Detective Dougherty, this is Detective Shimp. Penns River Police. May we come in?"

"What do you want?"

"Ask a few questions, look around a little. With your permission, of course."

"What for?"

"Are you Steven Malick's aunt?"

"Is he in trouble?" Curled the stray wisp of hair around her finger.

"Not necessarily. We do need to talk to him, though."

"What if I don't let yinz in?"

"We'll get a warrant, ma'am."

"He's not necessarily in trouble, but you're willing to get a warrant to search my house for him. Bullshit."

Doc felt busted, didn't let it show. "We still need to talk to him, ma'am. Is he here?"

"No."

"Have you heard from him?"

"No."

"Do you know where he might be?"

"No." Jessica leaning against the doorframe now, settled in for the duration.

"Do you know any of his friends? People he might go to if he was jammed up?"

"No."

Doc tried not to show his exasperation. Jack Harriger dead not ten hours. He and Shimp had left the crime scene to Neuschwander and Grabek to spend a ninety-four-degree day trying to develop non-existent leads. "Would you prefer to do this at the police station?"

"No."

"Then you might want to stop breaking my balls, lady."

"I don't go with you on my own, you gonna arrest me?"

"No."

"Then kiss my ass."

Doc rubbed sweat from his brow, felt grit come with it. Spoke to Shimp. "Call for a warrant. One-six-nine Dutchman Run Road. Searching for the person of, any articles pertaining to, or signs of a recent appearance by Steven Malick. Grabek knows what to do." Shimp turned for the car.

"Whoa! You really gonna get a warrant?"

"That's right," Doc said. "And then we're taking your bony ass in for questioning."

"Aw, for shit's sake, yinz might as well come in, then. If you're going to be assholes about it."

No sign of Steven Malick, aside from two book boxes of possessions in a spare bedroom that didn't appear to have been disturbed. Doc paused at the door on his way out. "Do you mind if I ask one more question, Ms. Malick?"

"Yeah."

"Why'd you make a federal case out of this when you were going to let us in, anyway?"

Jessica pulled the recalcitrant strand of hair out of the way for at least the fiftieth time. "Why should I let any cop that wants to, poke around in my personal stuff? Go through my drawers and touch my things and that? I got rights, too. But if yinz're really gonna get a search warrant, I couldn't stop you if I wanted to. I got nothing to hide here, anyway. So..."

In the car, Doc started the engine, tapped his thumbs on the steering wheel. "Do me a favor. Call Eye Chart and ask him to have patrol units drive past here on an increased schedule for the next few days. And have Grabek draft the warrant. We can sign the affidavits in the morning. We might have to come back here, and we're not going to want to fuck around about getting in if we do."

46

It took a few knocks to get Aunt Jess's attention.

"Who's back there?" Sounded like she was a few beers into her evening. Aunt Jess could be a surly drunk. "I got a gun in here for guys need to sneak around, not come in the front door like they should."

Steve got there later than he wanted. Hadn't taken the time of year or his nervousness into consideration when he'd planned to wait until dark. Set out at eight when he hoped the light had diffused to the point where someone would have to get right in his face to identify him, which he had no plans to allow. Made it out of town and walked fifteen feet or so into the woods to stay out of sight. Passed Dutchman Run Road to circle back through the woods in case the police were watching the front. Be damned hard for them to watch the back, thick as the trees were.

"Aunt Jess, it's me. Steve," he said in a stage whisper. "Let me in."

"Aw, Christ. I shoulda knowed." Unlocked the door. "Come on in, then. Police already been here looking."

"What time?"

Jessica yawned, scratched the back of her head. "Six? Somewhere around there. I was home but hadn't ate yet. Maybe a little before."

"What did they say?"

"Said they wanted to talk to you. That you weren't necessarily in trouble, which I knowed was bullshit soon as they said it, or they wouldn't of been talking about no warrants."

"They came with a warrant?"

"They said they'd get one if I didn't let them in. I didn't and they got serious, so I did. I didn't have nothing to hide." Saw the sweat and dirt and scratches on his face, burrs on his pants and socks. "You hungry?"

"Starving."

"Go get cleaned up and I'll fix you a plate of leaveovers."

Ten minutes in the bathroom got him somewhat less disheveled. In the kitchen, a chicken leg, mashed potatoes, and a cut tomato with salad dressing were on the table next to a glass of ice water. "You got any beer, Aunt Jess? I'm dying for a beer."

"Let's hear what you have to say about all this before you get any beer in you. My mind's not made up about if you're staying or not."

Steve ate like a starving coyote while he told his aunt how things had turned bad for him. Hanging out one night around the casino when these two guys he thought were his friends decided they wanted to steal a car. He'd come with them and didn't have a way to get anywhere, figured he'd lay back and maybe disappear when they made their move. They found a car they liked, but there were people getting in it and the one guy, Greg, got so pissed he shot the guy in the car and killed him. Steve didn't even know anyone there had a gun or he never would have gone, and, jeez, do you have any more of that chicken?

He ate the thigh cold while he drank a PBR and told her how Greg and Jeff—the other guy's name was Jeff—got caught by the cops and both said Steve did the shooting, so he had to lay low.

"I seen on the news a cop got shot today," Jessica said.

"I don't know nothing about that."

She took a long time to come up with her next comment. "Well, you came here for something."

Steve took a pull off the PBR. "Well, mostly, right now, I need a place to sleep. I can't believe how tired I am."

"Sleeping will get you through the night, but you're going to need to do something longer term."

"I was hoping maybe, tomorrow morning, I—Aunt Jess, I

need a car bad. It's my only chance to get away. Can you lend me yours?"

"Lend you? You're running away from a killing and expect me to believe you're going to bring my car back?"

"I been thinking about it, how I can get away and you can get a new car out of the deal."

Jessica lit a cigarette. "I'm listening."

"You'd let me take your car. Then you call the police and tell them it was stolen. You can blame me, even. Tell them I stayed here sometimes and knew where the extra keys are hid. I must've let myself in while you were asleep, got the keys and took off. The car was gone when you woke up. I can even leave real early so that part won't be a lie."

Jessica blew smoke from the side of her mouth. "Why don't you call a lawyer in the morning? Clear this up. Since it wasn't you shot anyone." Looking right into his eyes when she said it.

"It don't matter." Giving it right back to her. "Law says we're all as guilty as if we'd pulled the trigger."

They held each other's gazes. Jess said, "I wish I could help you. God knows I could use a new car, and that's why you're screwed. Mine's in the shop. I guess you didn't see it missing, coming in the back like that."

Steve felt sick to his stomach. "It's in the shop? How long?"

"The guy at Bender's says at least another day. They're waiting for a part, a—I don't know. Something for the transmission. Gonna cost me a fortune, so they're trying to find me one in a junkyard first."

"How are you getting to work?"

"Linda Petrone, lives over by the golf course. She works at the Hallmark store in the mall and is giving me rides so's I'll keep watching her bratty kids."

The perfect end to the perfect day. Considered walking back into town for Jeff's car. *If* the police hadn't found it. Thought of who else would help him. Grandpap Turner acted as if he'd given up his annual booze budget every time he handed over a twenty.

Hadn't seen his mother in so long he doubted he'd recognize her. Maybe, if she was on her knees. Rather go to prison than ask his old man for the time of day. Greg and Jeff already locked up. Ron Oddis a possibility. Have to make it worth his while, though, and Steve didn't have much to barter with.

"Why don't you go on downstairs and get some sleep?" Aunt Jess's voice surprised him. "You look like you ain't slept in a couple days. We'll talk in the morning. See what we can come up with."

47

The American Legion donated its function room for Jack Harriger's wake. Split the cost of the open bar with the VFW. Neighborhood Market sent over chicken wings, kolbassi and sauerkraut, potato and macaroni salad, cold cuts, rolls, lettuce, tomato, onions, ketchup, mustard, mayonnaise; whatever they'd need for a nice spread. Whole town closed ranks, Jack Harriger two days dead and no sign of Steve Malick. Flyers everywhere: businesses, schools, churches, telephone poles, neighboring towns, state police, FBI. Malick had shown more skill in running than anyone expected, which didn't lift the mood.

Doc's first wake as a Penns River cop. A disappointment. None of the boisterous telling of stories and lies with accompanying laughter he'd expected. Jack's name not mentioned much at all, considering the party was for him. His sudden death had made everyone sad, then when the time came to tell heartwarming Jack Harriger stories people remembered his defining quality had been the stick up his ass

"I feel bad," Rick Neuschwander said. "I mean, the poor guy's dead and no one has anything to say about him."

Stush and Doc exchanged glances, two beers into the evening. Stush raised an eyebrow. Doc made a point of taking a drink, no intention of breaking the spell.

Stush rose. "I know this is awkward, but there's a lot of food here, and a lot of beer. A cop's dead, and in the line. It's a tradition when a cop passes to drink to excess and tell truth-optional stories. Part of why it's so hard is because we haven't caught the bastard who killed Jack, and we don't know if we will. *Someone* will—that miserable little cocksucker's too dumb to run for long—but I'm afraid it's not going to be us." Stush had refused to use Malick's name since he heard about Jack. "Another part is—and God forgive me for saying this—Jack was pretty much of a miserable son of a bitch himself. Got too close to some of the wrong people, and we saw how that almost played out." Nodded in Doc's direction. The others made sounds both appreciative and sympathetic.

"*But he was a cop.*" Soft-spoken as he tended to be, people forgot how Stush could project his baritone when he wanted. "At a cop's wake, you set aside any bad history, even if it was with the guest of honor. He wore the bag like the rest of us, and that's why only we're here. No friends. No family. Cops. Because we know how easy it could've been for any one of us to be laid out over at Rusiewicz's right now. Wakes aren't to mourn death. They're to celebrate the life of the cop we lost. They're to celebrate all us cops. And," Stush scanned every face in the room, "it's to celebrate that it wasn't us. Now, I want to see some serious fucking drinking, and all this food ate, or there's going to be some shitty schedules handed out next week. Benny! You're Irish. How's that toast go?"

Doc even broke out the brogue. "Stay hydrated, ye bastards!"

A few hours later, Doc on a stool in the corner, watching about half of those who'd begun the evening. Working on his fifth—or sixth—beer, not worried because he'd taken over four hours to drink them. They were ice cold, and free, and goddamn it, he'd had a shitty week. Six beers—or seven or eight, whatever the final count—wouldn't make tomorrow any easier, but they helped tonight slip away just fine.

Teresa Shimp dragged a stool next to his, facing the room on a parallel sight line. "I thought you'd be more in the center of things."

Doc gestured with his can of Rolling Rock. "These are the

people that drive me to drink." Took a long pull.

Teresa mock punched his arm. "I haven't been here long, but I know better than that. You love these people. You love everything about this town. Don't you?"

"I didn't love Jack." Doc looked over, saw at least a couple of beers in Teresa's eyes. "But that's a different story."

"So what is it? Are you one of those quiet drunks?"

Doc kept his eyes straight ahead. "Yeah, some." A short sip. "And—no point holding it back—Jack Harriger was such a shitty cop he's fucking us from beyond the grave."

Teresa's mouth hung open in his peripheral vision. "What do you mean?"

"All he had to do was wait. Hell, he'd been *ordered* to wait. Maintain a position where he could observe and tell us what to expect. There would've been at least a half-dozen cops there inside of five minutes. This Malick, everything we know about him, he's a jagov, not a hard case. Remember what that guy said about Doug Stirnweiss? How he had hard bark on him? Malick's a birch tree. He sees six cops—seven, including Jack—he puts down his gun and rolls into a fetal position."

A sip of beer. "But, no. Jack has to be a fucking hero. Hand this guy over to us when we get there, show how he's Dirty Harry and Raylan Givens rolled into one. We'll never know how that went down." Finished his beer, crushed the can. "So now, someday, here or someplace else, cops are going to close on this guy and he figures, what the hell, he has nothing to lose. He's already killed one cop, everyone else is free. Gets nicked in a traffic stop? That cop's life's in danger. All because Jack Harriger couldn't help showing his dick."

He glanced to his right, caught her looking at him. She didn't say anything, sipped from a can of Coors Light and turned her attention to the center of the room. They watched the party without speaking for a few minutes. Sean Sisler told an animated story to half a dozen cops. Hand gestures, body language, facial expressions. Funny voices, from the reactions. Had an idea the story might involve a domestic he and Sisler answered over the winter.

"You know him pretty well, don't you?" Teresa gestured with her Coors. "Sisler?"

"If you're looking for dish, I should warn you. That man saved my life a few months ago. Far as I'm concerned, he walks on water and shits rainbows."

"No dishing." Teresa wet her lips with beer. A bird would die of thirst at the rate she drank. "I was wondering...I, uh...do you know..." another sip, then the words tumbled out like a Band-Aid being ripped off. "Isheseeinganyone?"

Doc ducked his head. Stifled the laugh, couldn't help the smile. "I don't have a name to give you, but I can safely say Officer Sisler is unavailable."

"Figures," Teresa said into the can.

"Not that you asked..." Doc more expansive with beer in him, willing to have conversations average people never thought twice about. "You're better off. It's not a good idea to get involved with another cop, especially one in the same outfit. Going to get awkward sooner or later."

"I guess. It's just—the civilians I meet, they're either intimidated when they find out I'm a cop, or that's all they want to talk about."

Fate saved Doc from this conversation in the form of Kathy Burrows, bouncing up fresh-cheeked and smiling. "Hi, guys. I was afraid I was going to miss everything."

"Where were you?" Doc said.

"Working. I had the four-to-twelve."

Doc checked his watch. "Oh, shit. Twelve-thirty? I better get home. I have to work at eight."

Kathy exaggerated a pout. "Stay for one more beer with me. Please? I hustled right over to hang with the cool kids." Indicated Doc and Shimp both. "One beer?"

"Okay, rook. Bring me a Rolling Rock. Teresa?"

"I'm good."

"I heard on the way in they might be out of Rolling Rock," Kathy said.

"Then bring me anything but lite. It's not like I'm going to be able to tell the difference after how much I've had already."

Kathy bounded off to the bar. "You know her better than I do," Doc said to Teresa. "How's Tigger there working out?"

Teresa did a spit take, wiped foam off her chin. "You call her that around anyone else?"

"Just thought of it this second."

"It's funny. I've thought of it myself a few times, never said it out loud."

"Maybe I'm drunker than you get. Especially at the furious pace you set."

Teresa smacked his arm. Kathy came back, handed Doc a wet Rolling Rock. "They found a six-pack in back and stuck it in some ice. The bartender said it should be pretty cold." Doris Schilling tended bar at the Legion on her nights off from Fat Jimmy's. She could pull a can from a fresh case, look a serious drinker in the eye, tell him it's good and cold, and get no argument. Kathy wouldn't have had a chance.

"It'll be fine," Doc said.

They bullshitted around for fifteen minutes, cop bonding, the two women tag-teaming Doc, even got him to laugh a few times. The colder-than-expected beer didn't hurt. About to ask if they wanted another—he'd volunteer the rookie to deliver—when Kathy diverted the conversation. "I feel bad we didn't catch this guy that shot the deputy."

"It happens," Doc said. "No one likes it, but there's nothing you can do about it sometimes." Considered giving the "it's Jack's fault" speech again, didn't have it in him. "Someone will get him. His getting away was dumb luck."

"I go by that house the Sarge asked us to watch on Dutchman Run every chance I get. Not too regular, and I come at it from different angles so no one expects me. I even shine the light around the woods once in a while—you know, pretend I'm spotting deer—and let it pass over the house like it was accidental, but the shades are always down and I can't see anything."

"You can quit spending so much time there," Doc said. "I'll talk to Eye Chart in the morning."

"What's that road like in the middle of the night?" Teresa said. "We drove there in daylight and there were spots where the sun barely got through."

"It is kind of bucolic out there. I like it in the daytime. It's peaceful. I drive through there, or one of those other back roads when I need a few minutes to relax and don't want to go ten-seven."

Doc said, "Teresa, when we were there the other day, were the shades up or down?"

Teresa thought. "Up. Remember? She wasn't home the first time and we walked all around the house looking in."

"What about when we came back and she was home?"

More thought. "Still up. She had food on the kitchen countertops and I wondered what she was going to make."

Doc, to Kathy: "You've had nights since, right?"

"Four-to-twelve."

"Even seen them up?"

"No. They've been down every time I went by."

Doc raised his voice, called Sisler over. "That house on Dutchman Run. You been going by there at all?"

"Whenever I can. Why?"

"The window shades. Up or down?"

Sisler's turn to think. "Down. I've never been able to see in."

"And you started making a point of it since the day after Jack died."

"Yeah, soon as Eye Chart told us it was a priority."

Doc's cell already in hand, hitting Stush's number on speed dial. "These are your last beers. We have work to do."

48

June 21, the longest day of the year. Sunrise at five-fifty. Most of the cops in Penns River in position half an hour earlier. Doc and Stush up all night building the plan, Sisler in the woods since three with eyes on the house. Judge Molchan, upset over being awakened, refused the request for a no-knock warrant; what they had from the first day would have to do.

Doc keyed his mike. "Sisler. Anything?"

Sisler kept his voice low. "No one in or out. No lights."

"Can you see both doors?"

"Not quite, but he'd have to pick a perfect angle to get out the back and not be seen. Of course, it's darker than shit back there, even now. I can't guarantee anything."

"Close enough," Doc said. "Let's roll." Hit the switches for siren and lights, pressed the pedal to the floor. Every police vehicle Penns River owned did the same, the rest of the town as uncovered as a stripper's nipple. Units would draw back if a call came in. Shock and awe were the objective.

Doc pounded on the front door. "Jessica Malick! Penns River police! Open the door or we're coming through." Knew he had cops in back, willing to give her a minute.

She made it with fifteen seconds to spare. Opened the door a crack, said, "What the f—" before Doc pushed it open, broke the chain, and he and half a dozen other cops went through her like a turnstile.

"Hey! What the hell are yinz up to? You can't come barging in my house like this"

"Someone cuff that bitch and show her the warrant," Doc said over his shoulder. "Then take her back to the shop and book her. Aiding and Abetting and whatever else I can think of before I get back." Nodded to Shimp, turned a corner. "Clear!"

Cops charged through the house. Footfalls and voices audible from everywhere at once.

"Clear!"

"Clear!"

"Clear!"

"Dougherty! You better get down here." Nancy Snyder in the basement.

Doc and Shimp hustled down the stairs. Snyder in an extra bedroom in the corner of the house. "Bed's been slept in." Pressed a hand against the sheets. "Might even still be warm. And I found this." Pointed to a revolver on the dresser. "Three rounds missing."

"Where's Jack's gun?" Doc said. "The Sig?"

"Not here."

"Fuck." Doc ran a hand through his hair. "We tipped him." Hollered for Sisler, who rushed down the stairs.

"Yeah?"

"Where was your blind spot?"

Sisler turned to orient himself. "I could see all of the front and right side of the house. I guess that'd be the south. Most of the back. I couldn't see both doors, so I made sure I could see the front and the driveway, in case a car came."

"How much of the back could you see?"

"Not the door itself, but about half the little deck behind."

"Who's out there?"

"Ulizio and Goodfoot, I think. Lester for sure."

"Get him in here." Doc turned to Nancy Snyder. "Take this room apart." Went upstairs, saw Lester Goodfoot in the kitchen. Sent the first uniform he saw for a map. Katherine Burrows hot-footed to her car, running on adrenaline, about to start what would be the third of a triple shift. Doc considered sending her home, thought he owed it to her to be in on the payoff.

"What do you need?" Lester Goodfoot.

"Who had the back? You and U?"

"Yeah."

"Did you see or hear anything could've been someone leaving out the back and into the woods?"

Goodfoot's face sank. "We were looking for the best spots to triangulate and heard something in the brush about five minutes before you went in. We froze and listened, but it stopped. Figured we spooked a deer and went on."

Doc stood at the back sliding door, looking across the deck into the woods. "This guy has to be the luckiest sumbitch in the world. Catches Jack unawares, sneaks through us, and now it looks like he picked the one spot on the whole back porch to get out." His eye caught something in the grass beyond the deck. "What is that, Lester? You see it?" Pointed.

Goodfoot nodded, crossed the deck and down the steps to the spot. "Cigarette." Held it up. "Still smoldering."

Doc laughed at his bad luck. "Perfect. Picks the one spot on the deck where he can smoke a cigarette and not be seen by Sisler, hears something that spooked him, and hops over the railing at the one spot you and Ulizio can't see him. This fucking guy's the Rain Man of criminals."

Burrows back with the map. Doc spread it on the kitchen table, called for Mike Zywiciel. Pointed to their location. "We're here, along Dutchman Run. I want patrols on 366, 780, and..." leaned closer to the map, "Myers Drive. Make a box with these four roads as the perimeter. Units in sight of each other as much as they can, working in pairs when possible. No one gets in, and no one gets out without a detailed search of their car. He's on bad terrain, so he can't go too fast. Seal him in and we'll get help to drive him where we want him to go." Zywiciel nodded, hollered for his officers to form up on him.

Doc dialed Stush back at the cop shop. "Yeah, something spooked him and he's in the woods. Eye Chart's forming a perimeter on the surrounding roads. Can you call Chet Wagenbach to get his dogs out here toot sweet? State police helicopter, too. And I guess you'd better notify Washington Township and Plum Borough to block any roads out of town. Allegheny Township, for that matter, in case he gets a car and slips through us. Armed and dangerous, wanted as a suspect in a cop killing. The usual disclaimers."

A pause while Stush's writing caught up with his to-do list. "What about the college, Benny?"

"What about it?"

"It's right there, where Myers ends at 780. They have student apartments across the street."

"Oh, fuck, me." Doc read his watch. "Call Security there. It's too early for students, but they'll start showing up soon. Faculty and staff's probably already on the way in. See if they have some kind of Code Red status like the public schools. Lock the place down." Needed a second to make the decision he'd hoped to avoid. "I guess you'd better alert the media, too. Tell the commuters to stay away today." Also take the chance of inviting every asshole with a hunting rifle and time on his hands to join the fun.

Two hours away from picking up Aunt Jess's car when they came. Two fucking hours. Steve Malick couldn't sleep, going over how he'd get out of town after she picked up the car. Too wound up to stick to the plan they'd agreed to, "stealing" the car overnight. No way he could wait another whole day. Thought of walking to Bender's now, hiding until her ride dropped her off, then pulling her out and taking off before she knew what hit her. Might make it even easier for her to claim the car had been stolen. Not that Steve cared much anymore. Only a car to her. A lifeboat in icy water to him.

He'd gotten used to the morning noises around the little house in the past couple of days, knew right away someone was in the brush around back. Had the Sig—took it to the bathroom with him since he'd gone underground—vaulted the deck railing and took off parallel to Dutchman Run Road. Veered away when he saw what looked like light bars on the shadows of cars. The only direction and landmark he cared about were away from Dutchman Run Road and the house.

Tripped over a root and almost fell. Readjusted the gun at the small of his back, started picking his way through paths of least resistance. How would they come for him? Helicopter? Good luck seeing him through these trees. Their only chance would be to spot him crossing a road, and he could pick a spot shrouded by branches if he needed to.

They'd probably pick a perimeter to close off, then squeeze him. Malick didn't know where the local roads ran or how far away they were, especially not on foot. He knew how to get to his aunt's house, very little farther out. Still, the more he made them open the net, the better his chances of slipping through.

The immediate problem was time. Hard to get through this underbrush and uneven terrain with any speed as the leaf-diffused early morning lit the ground at random. Knew the sun rose in the east—southeast, he thought—worried he might be running in circles. Sat and rested his back against a tree to let the sun get a little higher while he got his heart rate under control and considered options.

It would be at least an hour before the dogs could get there. Stush back at the station, working the phone to notify neighboring jurisdictions, trying now to squeeze some urgency out of the state police to scramble the helicopter.

Not much for the detectives to do but keep their eyes open until Wagenbach arrived. Snyder had brought up the sheets Malick was presumed to have slept in for the dogs to get a good scent, then left with the other uniforms to patrol the perimeter. Grabek drank coffee and took a position near a window from which he could see all the cars. The other detectives fidgeted until Stush sent a topographic map and Doc tried to pick likely paths Malick might take over the hilly terrain. Wished he could be with the uniforms, driving the perimeter. At least they had something to do.

Hard work moving through the woods, frustrating until Malick realized it would be just as hard for the police. A few hundred yards in he came across a long, narrow cut in the trees, might have been a road or railroad at some time. Easier and quicker walking there, sticking close to the edge to make him harder to see from above.

Guessed north-something as his general direction, used the energy no longer needed to push his way through underbrush to think. Route 780 lay north of his aunt's, and 780 ran past Penn State's Penns River campus. Kids and cars coming and going all day, and the Sig Sauer in his belt would serve as the master key. He didn't know if his cover ran all the way to 780, had nothing better to try.

Saw the clearing from a hundred yards away, the cut he was in straight as a string. He realized how big it was the closer he got, three hundred yards across, at least half a mile long to the road, open as a goddamned farm. If he jogged at an angle, he could meet up with the woods again maybe fifty yards away, keep from having to double back and around a peninsula of cleared ground. Twenty yards into the open, he heard the helicopter and almost broke his ankle stopping and diving back into the brush.

Doc smiled when he heard the turbine-powered chopper scream overhead. Chet's dog's fifteen miles away, he still had to gather them, his gear, and drive back roads. The helicopter at Washington County Airport coming hell-bent for leather, a hundred miles an hour as the crow flew. Let's see how Mr. Malick likes outrunning that number.

Still smiling when a door slammed outside and Chet Wagenbach yelled to ask where the hell all the goddamned police were. Doc explained the situation, let the dogs have their way with the bed sheets, and followed Chet at a distance of about fifty feet, Shimp and Neuschwander twice that far to either side. Chet kept the dogs as organized as he could, a fresher scent to work with than they were used to.

Malick stayed close to the clearing as he skirted it in the interest of time. Had to wait for the helicopter to scan elsewhere before he crossed a track cut for power lines, then back into deep cover. Safer, but slower. No longer sure of his direction, no idea where the police might be. Hands and face torn by jagger bushes, burrs on his socks and jeans, so thirsty his tongue hurt. Thought of the long-sleeve flannel shirt at Aunt Jess's, the brush tearing up his bare arms. Had to hit a road sooner or later, either 780 or that one ran between the campus and those apartments where he'd partied with the college kids a few times. Assuming he hadn't walked in a circle.

Chet's dogs never had it so good. A fresh trail, a good scent to track; like bloodhound Christmas. Noses down and asses up and yelping and tripping over each other in their eagerness. Impressed Doc with how much ground they covered. Spring had been late and wet, vegetation so thick the third week of June there were places he couldn't see more than thirty feet in front of him. Thought of Malick holding Jack's Sig, waiting in good concealment for a cop to turn the wrong corner. The dogs didn't care. They pushed hard through the brush, milling around at a spot where Chet said Malick must have stopped and walked around, then plunging onward again, their baying rising and ebbing with the strength of the scent.

Came to a narrow, clear-cut path and the dogs took off like

there were pork chops at the end. Doc called Stush on the walkie-talkie, told him they were doing great. The plan now to drive Malick like a deer, either to one of the patrol units on the roads or into an open space where the helicopter could run him to ground. He hoped he'd be there when it went down, all the trouble this prick had caused.

Sean Sisler and Katherine Burrows drove back and forth on Myers Road, running more or less parallel to Dutchman Run, a mile east. Sisler knew their chances were slim to none of catching Malick. Even if he came this way, they and another unit had a mile to traverse on each circuit. Few straight sight lines left too many holes for Malick to slip through if he had the sense God gave a woodchuck. Sisler smiled as he drove past the remains of a woodchuck that had lacked the good sense to do even that. Maybe there was hope after all.

"Aren't you tired?" Burrows asked from the shotgun seat. "What time did you start the stakeout?"

"Surveillance." Burrows not sure how to take that. "A stakeout is when you sit on an upholstered seat in a car, out of the elements. Surveillance is when you climb halfway up a tree in the middle of the night to sit in the crotch of a branch regardless of conditions."

Burrows confused for real now. "Did it rain this morning?"

"No. It was beautiful. But it could have." Looked over at her and winked. "Three."

"Three what?"

"You asked what time I started the stakeout."

"Surveillance."

"There you go, rook."

Spending three hours in a tree had pushed Sisler's allergies past the point of runny nose into cement head. He hadn't slept in almost twenty-seven hours. "You look exhausted," Burrows said.

"Been worse, but I'll definitely sleep tonight." A quick peek to the other seat showed the adrenaline of being in on the beginning had worn off for Burrows. Assuming she'd slept the night before—coming off shift at midnight—she might be coming close to twenty-four hours herself. "You all right?"

She nodded. "Stush let me nap in an empty cell while they put the plan together. I filled my Thermos with coffee before we left."

Sisler returned his attention to the road, eyes smiling. "Do you know how hard you're going to crash when the caffeine and adrenaline wear off?"

"Almost as hard as I'm going to pee. Which had better be soon."

"Urgent?"

She smiled and blushed at the same time. "I'm having a biological emergency here."

"Penn State's up around this bend. Call us in as 10-7 and see if they can patch you into a campus cop can show you a restroom where I can keep an eye on the road."

Finally. A road. Didn't look substantial enough to be 780 or 366, sure as hell not Dutchman Run. Had to be the one ran past the college. Malick crept to the edge of the tree line for a better look, saw a house with an elevated pool on the left that looked familiar. Unless he missed his guess, if he stayed behind this house and one more, went parallel to the road a few hundred yards, he'd be at the apartments across the street from Penn State Penns River.

For a fleeting second, he thought of breaking into the house and waiting for the family to come home. Tie them up and steal a car. Not so tired complications didn't come to mind right away. No idea what to do if kids were home. Even worse, if neighbor kids were there and expected back at a certain time. Adding a multiple kidnapping charge to his bill didn't appeal to him, forgetting for a moment the two murders already on his tab made pretty much anything else he did free. Besides, he'd been waiting for three days now; he needed to move.

The apartments and the college were the way to go. Steal a car from someone in the apartments' lot. No one there, stick the gun in the back of his belt and walk onto campus like he lived across the street. His age not an issue, not with the number of young adults taking classes part-time. Hundreds of cars in the lots of a commuter campus. People coming and going all the time.

Made it to the back of the apartments' parking lot. Watched a police car turn around on 780—he knew where he was now— drive back the way it had come. Let it get out of sight, nestled his gun at the small of his back, slicked down his hair as best he could, and stepped onto the parking lot.

It felt off right away: not enough empty spaces. No idea of the time—his watch and cell phone next to the bed at Aunt Jess's—people should be going to school or work or something by now. Stopped to reconnoiter. No cars on the road since the cop went by. None in or out of the campus across the way. No traffic noise on 780. Maneuvered to where he could see the campus. Ghost town. Fuck. Cops must have locked it down.

Two choices: talk his way into the building to buy time, or walk back the way he'd come half a mile and cross the road there, stay in the woods. For how long, though? His current getaway destination was Mexico, seventeen hundred miles away, more or less, but he had to have a car. Pushing ahead to—what?—might not be the way to go. Two houses almost within sight. People were either home or would be back. Find a place where he could see, and make his move at the first sign of someone who could give him the keys to an available vehicle. That meant waiting again, the last thing he wanted to do, but his options were limited.

Then he heard the dogs.

* * *

More fun trailing the dogs than Doc had expected. Beautiful day, not too humid, steady cooling breeze. Good hiking weather. Chet said the dogs' increased excitement meant a stronger scent trail, the distance closing. Still no visible trace of Malick except for the random bent branch or flattened scrub, Chet with no idea how far he might be, except to say not as far as before. Watching the dogs have what looked to be the time of their lives, Doc guessed they knew the distance to Malick within a foot, kept it to themselves.

No need for radio silence with the dogs' constant baying. Doc reported anything that looked like an identifiable milestone. Stush at his desk, Google Earth on the monitor, topographic map on his desk, calling out potential intersection points with the perimeter roads so Mike Zywiciel could adjust his troops' deployment. Malick had angled almost due east, toward the college, but also closer to a corner of the four-road perimeter, where he could be penned in. Whether by choice, accident, or because the dogs were driving him, Doc didn't know. Didn't much care. Every available cop in town within a mile or two, all of them ready for Malick this time.

Malick lingered at the edge of the tree line, working out how to talk his way into the apartment building. Didn't dare backtrack to the houses or the easier road crossing with dogs on his tail. Get inside somehow, cops not expecting that, be a while before they started doing a unit-to-unit search. If they ever did. Antsy, had to convince himself time would be on his side if he could buy some. Stay low, under the radar, and sooner or later they'd figure he'd slipped through and give up the local search. Then he could move.

His first bit of luck all day walked out of the building with two trash bags over his shoulder. The door slammed shut behind him; Malick presumed it locked. That meant the kid had a key, and a good chance of a car key on the same ring.

He wanted to catch the kid at the door, keys in hand, stay out of sight until after the trash drop-off. Crept into the parking lot, keeping cars between them, until he found the optimal location where he'd be out of sight and could intercept in a couple of quick steps. Leaned against the car's windows to catch his breath, gun in his right hand. The student flipped the trash into the dumpster and Malick gathered his legs under him when the window he'd rested his right hand on exploded and he hit the ground hard.

"Call his name," Sisler said. "Let him know that was no miss. Tell him to throw away the gun."

Sisler had got out of the car to stretch his legs while Burrows followed a campus cop to the restroom. Stush had sent word Malick seemed to be on his way to the college, so Sisler worked the field glasses across the road as far as to where the trees blocked his view. Spent most of his time on the building across Myers Road, where the apartments held the greatest concentration of civilians in the area.

Still had the freakish twenty-ten vision that had made him a top-flight sniper. Cocky about it, felt with these binoculars he could read a newspaper over the shoulder of someone in the parking lot, two hundred yards away. Assuming anyone that age still read newspapers.

He'd seen the kid with the trash bags over his shoulders and cursed under his breath. Focused on the woods around the parking lot, willing the kid to go back inside. If the dumbass got in a car, Sisler would leave Burrows alone for the time it would take to rip the oblivious asshole a new one. Heard her call to him about the great burden off her mind, when a man whose face Sisler couldn't see came out of the woods and low-walked behind parked cars, keeping them between him and the trash man, his back to the campus.

Sisler dropped the binoculars on the driver's seat, reached in and retrieved the AR-15 without moving his eyes. "Get in the car and get the bullhorn ready," he said between his teeth. Then he shot out the window a foot from Malick's right hand.

Burrows toggled the microphone switch. "Steven Malick." Tried to keep her voice from cracking. "Penns River police. That shot was intentional. Stay on the ground and throw away the gun."

Malick had no idea where the shot came from. Somewhere in the direction of Penn State, but where? He'd seen no one, and still didn't, not with his cheek leaving marks in the pavement. A female voice said something about the shot, and to stay down and get rid of the gun. Malick backed away on his belly, trying to get the next row of cars between him and the shooter, heard the bullet go by before it flattened a tire no more than a foot from his head.

"Put the mike where I can talk." The sight picture on Malick now, prone in the parking lot. Sisler grunted and Kathy pressed Transmit. "Those were courtesy shots, Malick. Show me empty hands or the next one's in your eye." Moved his finger inside the trigger guard.

Doc knew something had changed when he saw a clearing, maybe a building, and Chet pulled the dogs up hard and pointed. Doc ran to the front, saw Malick on his stomach in a puddle of broken glass, next to a car settling onto a flat tire. Took a quick look to each side for Shimp and Neuschwander. Gestured he'd go up the middle and they should pincer. Weapon drawn, one foot on the lot, saw Malick push his gun away along the asphalt. Doc hadn't said a word, knew better than to look a gift horse in the mouth.

TEN-SEVEN

"Steven Malick! Penns River police. Spread your hands on the ground palms up. I have an excuse to send a round up your ass. Don't give me a reason."

49

Mike Mannarino ate ice cream in Kittanning. Every chance he got. Stopped five minutes after Jordan's opened, had a large chocolate, the cone so big he had to eat most of it before he could drive the car again. Didn't matter he hadn't eaten lunch. Mike never made the trip to his camp in East Brady without a cone or a sundae. Sometimes one of each, coming and going.

Not pressed for time, but none to waste. Stretch Dolewicz due at the cabin by two, bringing the beer. Mike had a tray of his wife's pasta salad and half a dozen sweet sausages ready for the grill, peppers and onions wrapped in aluminum foil. Stretch always on time, Mike wanted to have the boat ready to go, charcoal in the grill when they got there. Put everyone at ease.

East Brady Road, north of Cowansville, farms separated by wooded areas. Rolling Pennsylvania countryside, bands of corn curving along the hills. Relaxing day, warm and a little humid. Mike hoped some time in the sun would loosen up his shoulder, still stiff from the shotgun pellets. Stretch could use a break, too, walking with a cane last time Mike saw him, might need another operation on his hip.

No traffic, lunchtime on a weekday. Mike kept the car five miles over the limit. Easy to think, and thinking needed to be done. New York knew about him and the feds. Not specifics, not the mechanics, but they knew who. And why, the Russians fucking him even now.

He got the word from Buffalo. Tino DeFelice had a cop on the task force, a Jew—it figured—who'd reported back information could only have come from Mike. Something Tino fed him, no less. Mike with a pretty good idea what, the bit about Sal Lucatorre meeting with his captains in Sal's doctor's office when he went in to see about his gout. Right out of the Junior Soprano playbook. Mike felt half stupid passing it along, but Keaton pushed him, anything might be helpful, even if we can only see who comes and goes. Feds acting like those guys that used to watch who stood where for the May Day parade at the Kremlin, see who was in, who was out. Chickenshit. And that's what did him.

Way Mike saw it, he had three options. He could split and see how bad they felt like following him. Had the cash stashed away to live, not like a king, but at least as good as some upper middle-class white-collar asshole, a member of the Five Percent. Not in this country, of course. Mexico, maybe. Costa Rica even better. Shirley would hate it, and the kids would lose everything. Mike could go himself, leave enough to take care of the family—lifestyle changes would be in order for them, too—dismissed it after a few minutes. They could get along without him. He'd miss them too much.

There was always the program. Even Keaton admitted Mike lived on borrowed time if New York suspected anything. Give everyone new identities, Mike get a straight job, still dip into the stash from time to time to keep things tolerable. Not have to learn a new language, and Uncle would move him if anything went bad. Had the same problem as running away: Shirley and the kids would hate it, and he couldn't trust Vincent to keep a low profile, the little prick getting to be a real ball-breaker. Mike didn't like the idea of being the feds' poodle, either. Saw a difference between feeding Keaton gossip and testifying in court under oath. What he'd been doing was getting even with someone who'd done him dirt. Guys who testified were rats, plain and simple. Mike still thought of himself as half a virgin.

Driving through the state game lands, he tried out the idea of convincing Sal and Tino that Buddy had been the rat all along. Mike heard things, he had no reason not to trust Buddy, and Buddy spilled to Keaton. He might even be able to get Keaton to help with that story. Mike's hands carved the air as he drove, imagining the scene where he gets in Sal and Tino's faces, you dumb cocksuckers, you almost killed the wrong guys. You owe me, now.

Across the river from East Brady, turning north on Seybertown Road. Defaming Buddy's name might work—might—meant shitting on memories that went back even farther than Mike and Stretch. Buddy took over for Mike as Tommy Vig's muscle when Mike got his button, and Mike was with Buddy the night he made his bones, clipping Swede Forsberg for blowing what was supposed to be a simple pickup at the racetrack. Fouling Buddy's name even worse in some ways than flipping on New York, Buddy never anything but a stand-up guy.

Pulled the car onto the gravelly driveway outside the cabin, where the river started its bend going up to Bald Eagle Island. A nice place, not some shitty trailer. Two bedrooms and running water, indoor toilet with a septic system. Trees came to within twenty feet of the rear screen porch, front door no more than fifty feet from the dock where the boat bobbed in the current. Mike opened the car door, sat watching the breeze rustling leaves, random birds. The fourth option, the one he didn't want to face, was to do nothing. Enjoy the life he had left until they came for him, as they would, sure as tomatoes ripen in a paper bag.

Mike shook it off. Reached back for the sausages, peppers, and pasta. Stretch would be up in a couple of hours. The only decision to make now was whether to call it a holiday, no work talk at all, relax and catch up with his last best friend. Or pick Stretch's brain for what to do, find a way to get his help without letting him know about the extracurricular activities. Tricky business. Stretch had always been the smartest of the three, the one most likely to find a way out, also most likely to figure out what had been going on.

Unlocked the door and bumped it open with his hip, hands full of food. Kicked it shut and saw Stretch sitting in the recliner, cane hooked to an arm of the chair. Then he saw the nephew, Ted, holding a shotgun.

50

"PR-Four. What's your location?"

Ben Dougherty keyed the mike. "Base, PR-Four. I am at... two-ninety-six Boundary Way and available. What's up, Janine?"

The uniform fit him better than he'd expected, his first time wearing the bag in at least three years. A thousand cops in town, some from hundreds of miles away. Ohio, New York state, West Virginia, Maryland. Even a couple from Virginia and New Jersey. Some had volunteered to ride patrol so Penns River cops could attend Jack Harriger's funeral. Doc talked Stush into letting him work a shift in uniform. Knuckleheads who might be tempted to try something on what they'd consider the same as substitute teachers might think twice if word got out Officer Doc had saddled up. He also didn't trust the message his non-verbal communication might send at the funeral. Jack's family would be there.

"Report of suspicious activity on the corner of Main Street and Third. Can you respond?"

"I'm rolling. Give me five, six minutes."

"Copy. Thanks, Doc."

His patrol instincts rusty, it took a few minutes to decide how to get as close as possible before being seen. Drove past Sixth Avenue on Fourth Street, through on Fifth Avenue all the way to Second Street to double back through the alley. Parked short of Third Street with a decent vantage point of the corner of Main two blocks away, where the marked car didn't stick out like Elton John at a Mormon tabernacle.

The "suspicious activity" appeared to be three kids training to be vagrants. Talking and spitting the only activity he saw. Broadened his field of examination, spotted another kid on the corner halfway between him and the first three. Used the field glasses, saw one across Main, one more a block up.

Doc waited, car windows open to welcome another spectacular day. Tried to remember the last time Penns River had such spring-like weather so deep into June—warm, sunny days with cool nights for sleeping; low humidity—when a slender maybe skinny woman walked up to the group of three and had a brief conversation. She appeared to shake hands with one of the kids. Another faced the stray across Main Street, pointed to the woman, held up two fingers. The solo kid pulled a brick from a low wall that separated a convenience store from the street and took something out.

Ah. *That* kind of suspicious activity.

Not much he could do by himself except test their security. Pulled the car onto Third, heard a reedy voice yell, "Five-O!" and everyone he'd been watching scattered like roaches in the light. He followed the largest knot until it dispersed, curious to see their favored route, the apartment building up the block the same one he'd found Wilver Faison scoping. He'd pay special attention to this corner after he ditched the uniform.

Wilver Faison, Pookie Haynesworth, and JaJuan Leonard watched the hoppers scatter as the police car rolled through. Wilver had done his homework, used his cred with Ike the Barber and a source up the chain for an introduction to people who talked to him because his rep as reliable had got around. Learned Rasheed Mason got his drugs and protection from Mike Mannarino, who would not protect Mason in Penns River and was in no position to do much about it right now, anyway, after that Oakmont business. Mason had been talking out his ass. Time to put those words back where they came from.

Wilver ducked his head when he saw Officer Doc in the police car. Waited for the unit to move out of sight, said, "Let's roll," and pulled a twenty-four-inch aluminum bat from the footwell of his car. Mason didn't see Wilver and his boys coming until their footfalls gave them away, coming hard across the street. Mason stepped on an untied Timberland lace trying to run and Wilver's boys were on him. Wilver said, "Not the head," and he, Pookie, and JaJuan beat the dealer until he lay limp on the sidewalk.

Wilver let Pookie and JaJuan get across the street, turned back to Mason, lying there with unfocused eyes half-open. Said, "Who the general purpose bitch now, motherfucker? I ain't seeing you again, you feel me?"

In the car, driving to their pre-established alibi, Pookie and JaJuan still running off the high. "We for real now, right, Wilver? We motherfucking gangsters now, yo." From JaJuan, who'd been a gnat's eyelash from being cut loose.

Yeah, we gangsters now, Wilver thought. *All the way.*

Doc also took the second call at Third and Main, the one to scrape Rasheed Mason off the sidewalk. Interesting timing, a beat down coming so soon after he cleared the corner. No one knew anything, no one saw anything. He'd come back as Detective Doc tomorrow, see who might be more forthcoming if discretion were available.

Saw the EMTs off, called for one of the foreign officers to sit on the ER at Allegheny Valley Hospital in case Mason became available—and willing—to talk before PR cops resumed their regular rounds. Thought it the perfect job for an out-of-towner, freeing Doc to stick to streets he knew, not that it had done Rasheed Mason much good. Doc had an idea the crew he'd run off belonged to Mason; the call had been a set-up. Someone would answer for that, too. Not that Doc cared much about a drug dealer catching a beating—though the implications for Penns River if turf wars were about to break out weren't good—couldn't let word get out someone set him up to be an accomplice.

"All units, please clear the air." Janine Schoepf's voice. "PR-Two, come in, please."

The final radio call had become as much a part of police funerals as the wake and bagpipes playing "Amazing Grace." A thousand cops at St. Mary's Cemetery, across the bypass from the country club. He wondered how they squeezed everyone in there, small as St. Mary's was, and what a cluster fuck it must be to situate all the vehicles.

"PR-Two, come in, please."

Drove past what remained of Resurrection Mall, the north wing burned out. The south half still looked to be under construction, though no workman had set foot there since the fire, except to stabilize the remains. Dan Hecker bought the property and had yet to decide what to do with it. A riverfront park for the city—plus a couple of other improvements—were promised before the zoning committee voted to award easements favorable to Hecker. Existing businesses between Res Mall and the river—fabricating plants taking advantage of the cheap rents in old mill buildings—were not conducive to parkland. No hint yet of Hecker purchasing them.

"PR-Two, come in, please."

On Esther Avenue, past Barb Smith's old house, where Russian gangsters Harriger had cozied up to tried to kidnap Doc. Thought of the bullet holes in the brick of his parents' house. None of it Harriger's fault—not even Doc thought that—though the Deputy's haste to take advantage of Stush's heart attack led him to accept on faith those responsible, despite reputations available to anyone with an internet connection. All to curry favor with the mayor, which meant getting on his knees for Hecker.

But he'd been a cop, and that was supposed to mean something. Harriger the first to die in the line of duty since Doc came back to Penns River and here he was, torn between his respect for tradition and the uniform and his disdain for Jack.

"All units, PR-Two is ten-seven. Out of service. Gone but not forgotten."

Doc drove past the Sunoco on Freeport Street, eyes straight ahead. He wouldn't soon forget Jack Harriger.

ACKNOWLEDGMENTS

Everyone connected with Down & Out Books: Eric Campbell, Lance Wright, and all my fellow authors. I'd heard stories about how a publisher's cadre of writers was like a family, but never expected it would be such an apt description as it is here.

Eric Beetner, who seems to read my mind with his cover designs, then makes them better.

Kate Hofmeister, all of whose editorial changes were for the better.

The Writers of Chantilly, who helped me workshop the difficult parts of this book. If a scene seems particularly strong, it's probably one of those they worked on.

The Beloved Spouse, who listens to the first and last drafts and whose advice has yet to steer me wrong.

All the readers and fellow writers whose kind words and encouragement buck me up when the inevitable bleak periods come. I'm not the first person to say this, nor will I be the last, but the crime fiction community is as fine a group of people as one is likely to meet. I am always privileged, sometimes flattered, and occasionally humbled to be a member.

DANA KING'S Penns River series of police procedurals includes *Worst Enemies, Grind Joint*, and *Resurrection Mall*. His Nick Forte series has two Shamus Award nominations, for *A Small Sacrifice* and *The Man in the Window*. Down & Out Books released the newest book in the series, *Bad Samaritan*, in January 2018. His short fiction has appeared in *Spinetingler, New Mystery Reader, A Twist of Noir, Mysterical-E*, and *Powder Burn Flash* as well as the anthology *Blood, Guts, and Whiskey*, edited by Todd Robinson. He lives in quiet near seclusion with The Beloved Spouse.

DanaKingAuthor.com

BOOKS

On the following pages are a few
more great titles from the
Down & Out Books publishing family.

For a complete list of books and to
sign up for our newsletter,
go to DownAndOutBooks.com.

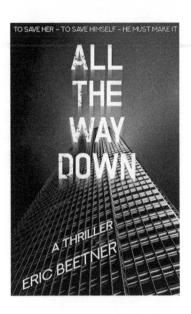

All the Way Down
Eric Beetner

Down & Out Books
January 2019
978-1-64396-010-4

In order to save the Mayor's daughter from a ruthless drug kingpin, crooked cop Dale must infiltrate a fortress built from an abandoned office tower and fight floor by floor against an increasingly difficult and dangerous set of obstacles.

To save her, and to save himself, he must make it all the way down.

Hell Chose Me
Angel Luis Colón

Down & Out Books
February 2019
978-1-948235-60-0

Bryan Walsh is a killer for hire. He is haunted by those who have fallen by his hand. He will stop at nothing to avenge his brother's death.

When a lifetime of bad karma finally lands on Bryan's doorstep and leaves his brother dead, he must survive long enough to find the killers and get his revenge, but he may not be able to handle the steps he'll need to take against his enemies.

As he becomes more unstable and his past crashes into his present, Bryan must decide if vengeance is worth becoming the monster he always denied or if he could find a another path; one that could lead to something like redemption.

Repetition Kills You
Stories by Tom Leins

All Due Respect, an imprint of
Down & Out Books
978-1-948235-28-0

Repetition Kills You comprises 26 short stories, presented in alphabetical order, from 'Actress on a Mattress' to 'Zero Sum'. The content is brutal and provocative: small-town pornography, gun-running, mutilation and violent, blood-streaked stories of revenge. The cast list includes sex offenders, serial killers, bare-knuckle fighters, carnies and corrupt cops. And a private eye with a dark past—and very little future.

Welcome to Paignton Noir.

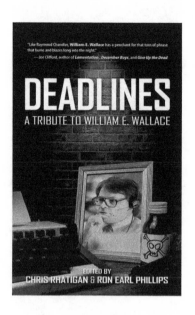

Deadlines
A Tribute to William E. Wallace
Edited by Chris Rhatigan and Ron Earl Phillips

A Joint Publication of Shotgun Honey and
All Due Respect, imprints of Down & Out Books
978-1-946502-48-3

Deadlines is a tribute anthology dedicated to the memory of
writer and crime fiction enthusiast, William E. Wallace. All
proceeds of this publication will be donated to the Comic Book
Legal Defense Fund in the name of William E. Wallace.

Contributors: Preston Lang, Jen Conley, Joe Clifford, Will Vi-
haro, Paul D. Brazill, Patricia Abbott, Rob Pierce, Sean Craven,
Eric Beetner, Sarah M. Chen, Nick Kolakowski, S.W. Lauden,
Scott Adlerberg, Gary Phillips, Renee Asher Pickup, Eryk
Pruitt, Todd Morr, Travis Richardson, Anonymous-9, Sean
Lynch, Alec Cizak, Greg Barth, C. Mack Lewis.

CPSIA information can be obtained
at www.ICGtesting.com
Printed in the USA
LVHW091715280821
696355LV00001B/26